THE WANDERING MAN

A Charlie Doherty Novel Five

TERRENCE MCCAULEY

WOLFPACK
PUBLISHING
— EST 2013 —

The Wandering Man
Print Edition
© Copyright 2022 (As Revised) Terrence McCauley

Wolfpack Publishing
5130 S. Fort Apache Rd. 215-380
Las Vegas, NV 89148

wolfpackpublishing.com

Paperback ISBN 978-1-63977-085-4

THE WANDERING MAN

Chapter 1

1927

I FLICKED my dead cigarette out the car window and lit another. I hated chain-smoking. I only did it when I was angry.

And you could say I was pretty angry at that particular moment.

Why? Because I was wasting my time playing fetch.

Who'd thrown the bone? Andrew J. Carmichael, Himself. The Chief of the New York Police Department.

The bone he wanted me to bring back? John Spann, Detective, Missing Person's Bureau. I enjoyed the irony of that.

And where had I dug up this bone? Right where the chief had told me he'd be. At a stationery store on 45th Street and Madison Avenue. I could see through the window that he was currently arguing with a clerk.

What was Spann arguing about with the clerk? Beats me. And that was the heart of the problem.

Because I was Detective Charles Doherty. Officially I

was assigned to the Office of the Chief of Police. Unofficially, I was Charlie Doherty, Carmichael's best friend from childhood. His shadow. His errand boy and confidant. His black hand. His hatchet man. Once a week, I even served as the bag man between him and the boys down at Tammany Hall.

The main part of my job was to know what the chief wanted, usually before he knew it himself.

This time was different. Spann was different, too. He might've been a cop, but he wasn't one of us. He wasn't a Tammany man. That made Carmichael's order for me to get him even stranger. In our world, if you weren't Tammany, you were nobody.

What made John Spann so special? I had no idea. That more than bothered me. It made me curious.

In fact, there was nothing special about any of this. The stationery store was no different from the others sprinkled around that stretch of Madison Avenue.

And Detective John Spann was just as forgettable as the stationery store he was in now. He was tall and quiet. A loner who had lots of acquaintances, but no true friends. He had a wife and two little girls in Queens. He'd drawn glowing fitness reports from every superior he'd served under.

We weren't exactly pals, either. He thought I was a two-bit political hack. I thought he was a naïve do-gooder out to save the world.

None of that explained why Carmichael wanted to see him so badly. Only time would tell. Until then, all I had to do was wait.

'Yours is not to reason why, Detective Doherty,' the chief had told me in front of two deputy chiefs. Fitzgerald and Ross were their names. They were Tammany men, too. 'Just bring Spann back here as soon as he heads back to his car. Not a moment before. Make it PDQ.'

PDQ was chief-speak for Pretty Damned Quick.

'Here' was police headquarters, which was also known as 'the Castle' because the place had been built to resemble one. By Tammany contractors, of course. No one stacked one brick on top of another in Manhattan without the Hall getting a piece.

Carmichael's bark still rang in my ears as I watched Spann continue to argue with the clerk. Why any self-respecting cop would bother arguing with some scrawny geek about paper was beyond me.

I quickly burned through my cigarette, tossed it and lit another.

Why Spann? Why didn't I know the answer to that question?

It wasn't a matter of pride. I did the things the chief needed doing. I was the one who cracked the whip or soothed the wound depending on what Carmichael told me to do. It was a job I loved.

Having a sergeant tell his captain I was waiting in his office was enough to give said captain heartburn. Coming home to find me on your doorstep was the worst way to end a long day on the job. A wife covering the mouthpiece of the phone and whispering, 'It's Charlie Doherty' to her husband was enough to ruin any meal. You get the idea.

A man develops a certain kind of reputation with a job like that. A reputation I had come to enjoy.

My visits were always official, even if they weren't always legal. I never just dropped in to chew the fat about the wife and kids. I didn't peddle gossip with the brass and I never split a bottle of bootleg gin with the boys after work, even though we were all in on 'the joke'. The joke being that the Big Apple didn't shine because it

3

was clean. It shined because it was covered in a thick coat of grease.

The same grease that kept the political machinery that really ran this town running. That machine was Tammany Hall, and we were just cogs that helped the big wheel turn.

I kept a familiar distance from everyone else in the department because I was Carmichael's eyes and ears. I was his memory. I saw everything and heard everything about every senior officer in the department. I spoke to the men they had stepped on as they climbed the department ladder. I collected dirt by listening to the men under their command. I knew every bone of every skeleton in their respective closets better than anyone. I kept records for the chief's sake and my own. Mrs. Doherty hadn't raised any fools.

Everything I knew was for the chief's good, not mine. I only told him something when he asked. I didn't rat out men for fun. I never used what I knew to wind him up and send him off in a direction for my benefit, either. What's more, Carmichael knew that. It gave my words weight with him.

Keeping other cops in line either by threat or implication was a lousy part of the job, but if I didn't do it, Carmichael would get someone who would. Someone who might use that information for their own betterment, not the chief's.

In some kind of odd way, I figured I was protecting the chief by doing his dirty work for him. At least that's what I told the face I shaved in the mirror each morning. And I hadn't cut myself yet.

Which explains why I was sitting in my car, stewing in my own juices on a September afternoon. I didn't know why the chief wanted to see Spann so quickly. I had never even heard Carmichael mention Spann's name until that exact moment.

The fact that he had given the order in front of Fitzgerald and Ross made me even more curious.

Spann wasn't even a Tammany man, and in a department where all of us kissed the Tiger's paw, that meant Spann was practically a civilian. He might've had a badge, but he wasn't one of us.

So why had Carmichael barked at me to bring him a nobody from Missing Persons? He could've sent a uniform to find Spann and bring him back to the Castle. Why me? And what did a couple of hacks like Fitzgerald and Ross have to do with it?

I didn't know. And I wouldn't know until I brought him back to the Castle. I might not know even then, but I'd make it my business to ask Carmichael about it later. For my sake and the chief's.

I flicked another dead cigarette out the window and willed myself to keep from lighting up another. I stifled a yawn as I watched Spann continue to argue with the clerk inside the stationery store.

Although I couldn't hear what they were saying, I could tell they were arguing because Spann was pretty worked up. He kept pointing down at something on the counter, but the clerk's expression didn't change. Working on Madison Avenue, I figured he was used to dealing with difficult customers. It was clear he wasn't giving Spann the answers he wanted.

As for what a Missing Persons cop could be looking for in a stationery store was anyone's guess. I just hoped he gave up soon because I was getting awfully tired of sitting in that damned car, killing time.

I checked my wristwatch and saw it at five o'clock on

the nose. Rush hour in old New York was officially underway.

I forgot about Spann for a moment and took in the growing herd of workers beginning to spill out of every office building in sight. It was early September, and the chill of autumn was drawing closer with each passing hour.

And while my Giants were making a run at the pennant, the Yankees looked unstoppable. Ruth sure could make that ball fly. The Babe was a hero to every kid who had ever held a stick and pretended it was a bat.

That always made me laugh. If they only knew Georgie Boy as well as I did, they might choose their idols more carefully.

I watched the crosswalk behind me get jammed with people and vehicles as the city that never slept began to pack it in for the night. Office workers going home for the day. Men waited for the trolley or hailed a cab or headed for the trains that would take them home. Dinner and hugs from the wife and kids beckoned. Secretaries had kids or cats to feed.

With any luck, they'd get everything done in time to go to bed for a good night's rest just so they could get up in the morning and start it all over again. I pitied the poor bastards. They were hamsters on a wheel. Success always just a bit out of reach no matter how fast they ran.

With Prohibition still the law of the land, I figured more than a few of them were headed for their local blind pig for a couple of illegal drinks. Who could blame them? It took a lot to live in a town like this, and this town took a lot out of you in the bargain. Living here took money and talent, and it took a lot of guts to stand up to what this city threw at you day after day, year after year.

The summers broiled you and the winters froze you. The traffic drove you crazy and the noise never stopped. Somebody was always rushing somewhere and, if you were lucky, you were one of them. If you weren't, you were left behind.

The city never gave an inch, so neither could you. If you did, you were finished. Forgotten.

And what did they get for all of this trouble when it was time to kick back and call it a career?

Nothing except the satisfaction of knowing the toughest city on earth hadn't beaten you. You'd gotten yours and lived to tell the tale. Not that anyone would care to listen. Because the people who'd never lived here wouldn't understand and the people who understood didn't want to talk about it. It was like Marine Boot Camp had been for me during the war. The victory was whatever you could make of it for yourself. Otherwise, no one really gave a damn.

I stifled another yawn and checked the stationery store again in time to see Spann take back whatever he had put on the counter and quickly stuff it into his inside coat pocket.

"Happy days," I said to myself as I got out of my Ford. I wanted to get Spann's attention before he left the store and headed off in another direction. I tried to cross Madison Avenue to reach him, but traffic lurched forward in uneven lines, blocking my way.

I saw Spann as soon as he hit the street and, as luck would have it, he was waiting to cross over to my side of Madison.

"Spann!" I called out to him over the blare of horns. By luck or fate, he actually heard me over the traffic.

"Doherty?" He looked about as surprised to see me as I was at being there. "What are you doing here?"

"The boss wants you back to the Castle," I yelled back. "PDQ."

Most cops looked worried when I told them the chief wanted to see them, but Spann looked like he'd been expecting it.

That was strange. I'd never even seen Spann at the Castle, much less in Carmichael's office. Maybe he was just the unflappable type?

He waved to acknowledge me just before I saw him lurch forward off the curb, as if someone had shoved him hard from behind.

But as I watched him fall, I saw three red holes appear on his shirt just as the echo of three gunshots filled the air.

I'd seen enough men die to know Spann was dead before he hit the pavement.

I watched the panic unfold across Madison Avenue. Men and women around where Spann had fallen ducked and crouched as the last echo of the gunshots died away. The stream of people heading in both directions on the sidewalk bumped into those who had stopped in their tracks. Curses mingled with the screams.

I saw a group of people just to the north of where Spann had fallen begin to move the way tall grass bends as someone runs through it.

I knew the only kind of man who runs through a crowd right after someone gets shot is usually the one who did the shooting.

I couldn't see the killer, but I saw where he was going. New screams told me he was probably waving his gun around to clear a path as he tried to get uptown.

Knowing Spann was already dead, I went after the

shooter. With three holes through the middle of him, I knew he needed a priest instead of a doctor.

I ran through the crooked maze of cars that jammed the width of Madison Avenue as the shooter kept running north. I lost ground to him as cars jockeyed for every inch they could get despite the snarled traffic.

I hit a few sideview mirrors as I followed the shooter's path. I was tracking him by the number of heads I saw bobbing out of the way and the number of screams I heard. I ignored the horns and curses hurled my way as I bolted between two cars and hit the sidewalk at a dead run.

I ducked when I heard another gunshot ring out. Everyone around me ducked, too, or ran toward me and I caught a glimpse of a man now running west.

I pushed the frenzied people out of my way and dodged others as I ran after the killer. But at five-seven and barely a buck fifty soaking wet, I wasn't exactly a fullback. I had to pick my spots through the crowd as I tried to get a clean look at Spann's murderer.

I broke into a clearing mid-block and got my first look at the shooter. Average size and build. Gray overcoat and gray pants. A rumpled gray fedora was pulled down low on his head and the collar of his coat was pulled up, hiding his face.

But now that I had good footing under me, I quickly closed the distance between us. I didn't bother announcing myself or yelling for him to stop. He wouldn't stop and might even take a hostage if he knew I was chasing him.

I pulled my .38 from my hip holster just as the shooter was forced to slow down for a knot of pedestrians at the corner of Fifth Avenue. It was more than a block from the shooting, and in Manhattan, that was a world away. They had no idea a cop had just been killed over on Madison.

A woman saw me running with my gun in my hand and began to scream.

The element of surprise gone, I pointed at the killer in gray and yelled, "Police! Grab him! He's getting away!"

I thought that might make the shooter panic and take off in another direction.

I was wrong.

Instead, he skidded to a halt as he turned toward me; his face still hidden by the hat and the upturned collar. All I could see were his eyes. Eyes that were wide and wild and jet black.

Eyes I had seen years before. In combat, just before someone cut loose with a chain gun on a charging enemy or that look they got right before they went over a trench and hit the wire.

The look of commitment to death.

Time slowed as instinct and training took over. I dove forward as he raised his gun and fired in my direction.

The bullet went high over me as I hit the pavement hard but landed on my elbows. My .38 was in the perfect firing position and the gunman was in my sights.

On the periphery, I saw frightened New Yorkers scatter like pigeons. Some were about to fill in the space between me and the killer. Innocent people were all around him.

My target turned and started to barrel through the group of confused people jammed together at the corner.

I fired before anyone got in my way.

I squinted through the gun smoke and saw the bastard stumble forward before I lost all sight of him in the crowd. I knew I'd hit him in the rear right side above the belt line. Either in the kidney or in the back. The gray raincoat billowing out behind him made it tough to know where I hit him.

All I knew was that I hadn't missed.

My shot sent everyone running in all directions. I almost got knocked over as I got to my feet and ran toward where I had seen the shooter fall.

But when I finally reached the exact spot where I'd seen the man stumble, there was no sign of him. Nothing on the pavement. Not even his hat or a drop of blood.

I pushed people out of the way as I looked around for him. I even grabbed a few people coming from the opposite direction and asked them if they had seen a man running away. They all looked at me like I was crazy and pulled away from me.

I looked around for anyone who was standing around, who might have seen what had happened. But they were all gone. Lost in the anonymity of rush hour foot traffic. No one wanted to get involved. They just wanted to get the hell out of there. I couldn't exactly blame them. Curiosity killed more than just cats in Manhattan.

A young patrolman came out of the crowd from the south, aiming his gun at me.

"Drop the gun and don't move," the kid yelled with all of the authority a twenty-year-old could muster.

"I'm a cop, damn it." I showed him my gun as I fished my badge out of my pocket. "Detective Charlie Doherty. And you'd better get some men to block off this area fast. A cop has been shot over on Madison and the shooter is headed west."

The kid holstered his weapon and fumbled with his call box key as he ran to the nearest box to call it in.

I holstered my .38 as I stepped out into the street and kept looking for some sight of the gunman. I scanned the crowd for bobbing heads. I strained my ears to hear distant screams. I knew a man could go a long way with a bullet in him, but he had to be somewhere close by. He simply didn't have enough time to get very far.

All I saw was people going about their business. My shooting the man in gray had already been forgotten on a busy Manhattan sidewalk. The streets had no memory.

None of these people would know or care that Detective John Spann had been murdered just one block over. All they'd care about is the inconvenience of a street blocked off by the police as they tried to get home after a long day at the office.

For this was New York, and everyone had troubles of their own.

And one of my mine was out there right now with my bullet in his back.

Chapter 2

THE SCENE back in front of the stationery store was a mess of cops and reporters and curious civilians. Patrol cars had blocked off the street to traffic, making a bad situation even worse. Everyone was trying to get a look at the reason for the commotion.

Many of them looked disappointed that all they could see was a police slicker covering most of Spann's body.

The uniforms were doing a good job of keeping the area clear. They ignored the gripes of people annoyed about having to make a detour.

A cop getting shot in the line of duty always drew a lot of attention from the department heads and Spann's death was no exception. There was more top brass standing around Spann's body than you'd find in a French marching band. All of them were looking down at Spann's covered corpse which had fallen between a truck and a sedan.

All of them were good Tammany men like Carmichael and me. It was tough to get promoted in the department without a nod from the Tammany Tiger. And, like me, I doubted any of them knew Spann all that well.

But seeing a man die had a way of changing how you remembered him. I knew it did for me. Whatever he'd been in life, he was dead now. I didn't know who'd killed him or why. That didn't matter, either. He was a cop, and someone had gunned him down. I took some measure of pride that the biggest police force in the world would be gunning for him as soon as my description of the shooter was circulated. I wouldn't give a plug nickel for his chances to make it to morning. The department was far from perfect, but if there was one thing we knew how to do, it was how to avenge each other.

My pride was replaced by anger as I saw the shutter-bugs pushing against the line of cops protecting the scene to get a shot of Spann's body. Pictures of dead cops made for good copy and sold plenty of papers.

I checked my watch and realized the chief was due any minute, so I headed over to the spot over on Lexington where I was supposed to meet him. I'd gotten to a phone in a drug store right after it happened and called it in to the chief's office directly. Rosie, his secretary, had told me where to meet him so I could tell him everything I knew before he got to the scene. Carmichael hated surprises, especially at crime scenes.

I'd been standing on the street for a few minutes when I saw Carmichael's Chrysler Imperial glide to a stop in front of me. The chief opened the back door before I could open it for him.

One glance at Andrew Joseph Carmichael told you this was a man in charge of things. Even the members of one of those lost Amazon tribes you read about would know he was someone important. Carmichael was tall and broad shouldered. Lean at the waist and square-jawed. He stood six feet-five inches tall in his stocking feet and weighed a solid two-hundred pounds. He was silver-haired and had active blue eyes that could enchant a pretty lady or freeze a veteran detective where he stood. Boys looked up to him, cops admired him, and husbands hated him because he had a reputation for not allowing a wedding ring to get in his way of a conquest, including his own.

The press adored him because he knew how to play the game. He always made for good copy. He was the image of how everyone expected a police chief should look.

I watched Carmichael lean in the passenger side window and tell Dooley, his driver, "Wait here twenty minutes, then drive over to the scene and get me. Understood?"

Dooley acknowledged he understood as Carmichael began walking toward Madison at a brisk pace. Being almost a foot shorter than him, his legs were longer than mine. I had to struggle to keep up.

"This is a hell of a mess, Charlie," Carmichael said. "I wasn't counting on Spann ending up dead when I sent you to bring him in." He spared a quick glance my way. "You're sure you're not hurt?"

"I had to hit the deck when the shooter turned and fired at me, but I'm fine."

"Heard you put a bullet in the bastard." He slapped me on the back as we continued moving along. There was no trace of his earlier impatience. "Glad to hear it. Can't afford to lose my best man, especially not now."

I had plenty of questions to ask him before we got to the scene, but he didn't give me the chance to ask them.

"Tell me more about the shooter. You're sure you didn't get a good look at him?"

"All I saw was the back of him as I chased him west across town. Average height and build. Shabby gray clothes. Never saw his face, just his eyes. Can't give much of a description on him except his eyes were black."

Carmichael frowned. "I arranged to have Booker and Adams work the shooting. Tell them everything you saw and hold nothing back. They're good men."

I knew who they were. They were Tammany Men, just like us. That made them good men in the chief's book.

"Whatever you say, boss," I told him. "But I wish you'd tell me what made you need to see Spann in the first place. Might keep me from saying the wrong thing."

"There'll be time for that later," Carmichael told me. "The coroner here yet?"

"No, but I heard they're sending Kronauer. Should be here any minute."

Kronauer was technically the assistant coroner and although he wasn't a Tammany man, his duties didn't require him to be. The chief coroner was a Tammany figurehead who spent his days at the Union Club and signing whatever the boys down at the Hall told him to sign. Kronauer, on the other hand, lived for the job and was excellent at what he did.

I didn't want to push him, but I had to ask, "You want me to tell Brooks and Adams that you sent me to pick up Spann?"

"Of course." He looked around to see if anyone was within earshot of us. There was no one except civilians annoyed by the detour in their daily routine. "Tell them everything you know and have them check with me if they have any questions. After you're done with them,

meet me back at my office before you write your report."
He held up a finger to drive his point home. "That's very
important, Charlie. We need to talk *before* you write your
report."

I didn't know why that was so important, but I didn't
ask. Carmichael was clearly in no mood for questions.

The chief drew in a deep breath and slowly let it out.
"Spann's dead. Christ, what a mess."

I wanted to ask him what he meant by that. I wanted
to ask him why he'd asked me to bring him back to the
office in the first place. I wanted to ask a lot of things,
but I knew there'd be a time and place for all that. This
was not it.

As if he could read my mind, he said, "I can hear
those gears turning in your head, Charlie. Don't trouble
yourself with questions now. There are some matters we
need to discuss. Heavy matters that concern you now. I'll
clear up everything when I can, but for now, just do what
I tell you."

"Yes, sir," I said as we reached the spot where Spann
had fallen. "You can count on me."

He patted me on the back as he moved toward the
department heads who had stepped out from the crowd
to greet him. "I always have."

I hung back and let the men go to work. The chief
preferred me to keep a low profile in public as my role as
his black hand wasn't exactly official. Formality meant
scrutiny and neither of us wanted that. Neither did the
boys at the Hall.

I spotted Keith Booker and Ron Adams walking the
perimeter of the crime scene. Adams was scribbling
something in a beat-up notebook with a stubby pencil
while Booker told him what he saw.

I had never seen the value of taking notes. I always

had a way of remembering things I saw and wrote them down later in my report. Not that I wrote many reports about the things I did each day.

Detective Keith Booker was well past fifty and wore an old dark raincoat. His stained fedora that looked as if it hadn't been blocked since the day he'd bought it. He looked like a man who had spent the best years of his life watching the worst this city could do to itself. Every case seemed to have left a new line on his fleshy face. The bootleg whiskey I knew he enjoyed had raised a roadmap of blue veins on his nose. He was about a year away from retirement and looked like it couldn't come fast enough.

By this time next year, Booker would probably be a driver for one of the Tammany sachems. That was how guys like Booker and I usually wound up. If we didn't end up like Spann first.

Ron Adams, on the other hand, was one of those skinny, energetic types that made everyone around them nervous. Just like me, he'd been in the war. Unlike me, he never missed a chance to tell you about it. But he was a good kid on the whole, and his old man ran his own ward on the Lower East Side, so most of us put up with him. Bothering a ward heeler was simply more trouble than it was worth.

Booker spotted me and beckoned me to join him at a clear spot on the sidewalk.

"Evening, Charlie," Booker said as we shook hands. "Sorry about the circumstances. You know Adams here, don't you?"

"Nice to see you again, marine." Adams always found a way to work a man's branch of service into a conversation. "Only wish it was under better circumstances." He used his stubby pencil to gesture toward the corpse. "Spann was a good man."

"Did you guys know him?"

"Get a load of this Leatherneck, Booker," Adams joked. "We're here to ask him questions and here he is, already pumping us for information. Guess that's why the chief likes you so much, Charlie."

I shrugged it off. "That and my charming personality. Now answer the question."

Booker said, "I worked Missing Persons with Spann a few years back. Quiet guy. Real quiet. Not a snob, but never spoke much about anything personal. He didn't have it easy. Lost his son a while back and never got over it."

I looked down at his covered corpse and had a newfound respect for the man. I only knew about his family. I hadn't known he'd lost a son. I had two girls of my own and didn't know if I could survive losing them.

"He was a bit of an oddball," Booker continued, "but a good detective. Took the best notes of any cop I'd ever worked with. Wrote great reports, too. Read like dime novels. Saved us a lot of time explaining things to the captain, I can tell you that."

"What about you?" Adams asked me. "How well did you know Spann?"

"Can't say I knew him at all. He didn't run in the same circles we do."

That should have been enough to remind Adams that Spann didn't run with the Tiger like the rest of us. I could tell they both got it, but that didn't keep Adams from asking his next question. "Mind telling us why you were waiting for him outside a stationery store on Madison Avenue?"

"I was following orders."

"From who?" Adams asked.

I'd heard Adams could be pretty dense, but I hadn't seen it for myself until then. The disappointed look on Booker's face told me he agreed with me.

But Carmichael had told me to cooperate, so I did. "Chief's orders. He told me I could find him at this stationery store and that I should bring him to the Castle as soon as possible. I was in the process of doing that when Spann got shot."

Adams wrote that down. "If the chief was in a hurry to see him, why didn't you go into the store and get him?"

"Because he was working. He was talking to a clerk in the store when I got here, and the chief had already told me to not interrupt him."

Adams wrote that down, too. "What were they talking about? Spann and the clerk, I mean."

I almost didn't understand the question and I was glad Booker seemed to be as frustrated with his partner as I was. "How the hell should I know? I was in my car across the street waiting for Spann to come out, remember?"

Adams tapped the brim of his hat with his stubby pencil. "You see, that's what's eating at me. If the chief told me to get someone and bring him to his office, that's just what I'd do. I'd have gone in the store, pulled him out of there and brought him with me. I wouldn't have waited around in my car. Why did you?"

Booker cleared his throat. "I think Charlie already answered that question, Ron. We just want to hear what happened while it's fresh. There'll be plenty of time to ask more questions later if we have to."

But Adams persisted. "Charlie's a big boy, Booker.

He can answer for himself. You say he was talking with the clerk. How did he act? Calm? Upset? Even?"

I didn't know where Adams was going with all of this, but I'd make it a point to remember it later. "He looked agitated, but the clerk kept his calm. When Spann left the store, I got out of my car to flag him down. He waved to me, was about to cross the street toward me and that's when he got shot."

While Adams wrote that down, Booker asked me, "How many times was he shot?"

"Three times in the back."

"You're sure about the number?" Adams asked.

"It was easy. All I had to do was count the number of holes in his shirt." I traced a circle on the left side of my shirt to show him where I saw the exit wounds. "Tight pattern around the heart. The shooter was standing at point blank range, but he still knew where to hit him. That tells me he might have done this kind of thing before."

Adams looked up from his notebook. "You see anyone hanging around the street before he came out."

"No," I admitted. "It was rush hour and the street was crowded. I saw the guy for a second right before I shot him, but I hadn't seen him before that."

Adams kept scribbling in his notebook as Booker asked me, "What did he look like?"

"Medium height and build. Dressed in all gray. Gray hat and raincoat and pants. All the same shade, too. His hat was pulled down low and the collar of his coat was pulled up, so I couldn't see his face. All I could see was that he had black eyes."

Adams looked up from his notebook. "That's it? That's all you saw? An average guy in a gray outfit with black eyes?"

My annoyance made me remember something else. "He had gray hair, too. I saw some of it poking out from under his hat. It was straight, kind of like straw."

Adams shook his head as he wrote that down, too.

"The street was crowded," I told him. "People were running in every direction, ducking bullets. I caught up to him and he turned and fired at me. I hit the deck, had a clean shot at him and fired." I motioned to my right kidney. "Hit him right back here. I got up and went after him, but he disappeared into the crowd before I got there."

"Good for you, Charlie," Booker said. "What happened then?"

"He stumbled into the people in front of him but didn't go down. I checked the area right after I hit him, but he was gone."

Adams looked up from his notebook. "Maybe you missed him?"

I shook my head. "Not a chance, junior. Not at that distance. Besides, I'd fired into a crowd. If I'd missed him, someone else would've gone down. They didn't."

The two detectives traded looks. Adams spoke first. "Were there any witnesses to this shootout between you and him?"

I knew that tone and I didn't like it. "Dozens, but they all took off. If you don't believe me, ask the patrolman who stopped me. He's the same guy who called it in."

"We already have his statement," Adams told me. "He said he only heard the shots and didn't see anything except you waving your gun around on a crowded street. You're lucky he didn't shoot you, Charlie."

I was no genius, but it didn't take one to see Adams was being vague. I didn't know why, but I knew I didn't like it. "We're all over twenty-one here, Adams. Something's on your mind. Save yourself the headache and spit it out."

"Don't take it like that, Charlie." Booker moved between us to smooth it out. The older, wiser cop putting it into perspective for us relative youngsters. "We're just trying to cover all of the angles is all. Not everyone has the chief at their side. We've got a job to do, too, remember?"

I didn't need to remember it because I'd never forgotten it. I also didn't like Adams's implications. "He shot at me and missed. The shot went wide and didn't hit anyone behind me. That slug landed some place and, if I was you, I'd get busy trying to find it. Might help you get a line on the shooter."

From behind Booker, Adams asked, "What kind of gun was it?"

"I don't know," I told him. "I was too busy diving out of its way. It was a pistol, though. Didn't sound like a .45."

Booker pulled out a handkerchief from his coat pocket. He held it in his hand as he opened it up for me to see.

It was a slug. From a .38 by the looks of it.

My stomach dropped for a moment, thinking it was one of mine and I had missed the shooter after all.

I held my cool. "Where'd you find it?"

Adams said, "In the headlight of a car parked next to where you say you took your dive. Lines up exactly with what you just said, too."

I began to breathe again. "Then why all the questions? I was beginning to think you boys didn't believe me."

"We believe you," Adams said. "For the most part."

Before I could ask him more, Booker gently took me by the arm and steered me away. "I think we've taken up enough of Detective Doherty's time for now." Booker nodded to where I was parked across the street. "Come on, Charlie. I need some air. Let me walk you back to your car."

I didn't like the idea of going back to my car until I found out what Adams was getting at. But with Chief Carmichael only a few feet away, I didn't want to cause a scene. Not with all the reporters snapping pictures and asking questions. Those bastards always loved a sideshow.

Booker was a bit bigger than me, so he walked in front and cleared a way through the crowd of cops around Spann's body. When we got clear of the group, Booker hung back and let me catch up. We walked in the street to my car together.

"Thanks for not slugging Adams back there just now." Booker dug his cigarettes out of his coat pocket and offered me one. They weren't my brand, but I took one anyway. "He's what you might call eager."

"A pain in the ass is more like it." I held up Booker's cigarette. "Is he going to accuse me of taking a bribe for smoking this?"

"Let him try," Booker laughed as he used a lighter to light my smoke, then his. "You know how it is, Charlie. I'm on my way out and he's on his way up. He's trying to make a name for himself. They stuck me with him to show him the ropes."

I took a long drag on the smoke. "Hinting I'm covering up something about a dead cop won't win him any favors with me." I looked around to make sure no one could hear us. "His old man's a ward boss, for

24

Christ's sake. He ought to know how this works better than I do."

"He knows," Booker assured me. "That's why he took a run at you just now. In fact, he knows the game all too well. Maybe too well."

I didn't like the sound of that. "How so?"

"I wish I knew," Booker admitted. "Adams is a political animal and I think he's putting his chips on more numbers than just his old man. He's got other friends down at the Hall, but I don't know who. Just vague hints about all the new pals he's been making. All the high-class dinners he's been invited to lately. Probably just some new Turks looking to move up in the party." Booker shrugged. "He can never keep his mouth shut for long, so I'll find out who eventually."

That wasn't exactly what I'd call good news, but it explained a lot. Tammany Hall was no different than any other political organization. The men at the bottom were always looking for an express elevator to the top. They knew how to do things better than the old guard. I'd read somewhere that the Chinese character for 'chaos' was made up of the characters that meant 'danger' and 'opportunity'. I didn't know any Chinamen, but that sounded just about right.

The schemes of men like Adams never amounted to much. The grand sachems who ran things now had been young once, too. And when they found themselves in charge, they did things exactly the same way the old guard did it. Why? Because it worked.

"So young Adams has hitched his wagon to a shooting star." I took a drag on my cigarette. "Together, they're going to shake things up. The sky's the limit."

"Pretty much." Booker said. "My guess is he has his eye on your spot. If he can make you look bad in front of the right people, maybe his new pal at the Hall can pull some strings. Make a compromise. Put Adams in your chair instead of you." Another shrug. "Like I said, it's nothing new. Forget it."

"Let him try." I flicked my ash before it got on my coat. "He'll be walking pretty funny with Carmichael's boot in his ass."

Booker flicked his own ash, too. "You know how these things go. Adams's pal will probably step on the wrong toes at some soiree and find himself out in the cold again. But until that happens, be careful of him. Give him whatever he wants and answer all of his questions. If you let him rile you, he'll use it against you and now's not the right time."

"Thanks for the advice."

"Just self-preservation is all." Booker gestured with his cigarette toward the group around Spann's body. "A dead cop puts the whole department on edge. People do a lot of stupid things at times like this. I'd hate like hell for you to get caught up in it more than you already are."

I appreciated the concern, but I wasn't worried. I was pretty sure that Carmichael would protect me if it came to that. And even if he didn't, I had dirt on enough people in this town to bury the Woolworth Building twice over.

We had reached my car when I said, "Sorry I didn't get more of a description on the shooter, but it all happened so damned fast. I didn't even know who I was chasing until it was almost over."

"You gave us more than we had before we talked to you," Booker said. "The get up sounds like a disguise, so I doubt it'll help us, but it's something. And at least he's got your bullet in his back. He'll need help getting it out. We'll get him. Don't worry."

A thought hit me. "You're also going to want to talk to the clerk from the stationery store. It looked like things got pretty heated between him and Spann in there. He'll probably be able to tell you why."

Booker said, "Adams already has him on one of his lists in that notebook of his. I'll keep you posted if we find anything." He held out his hand. "That's a promise from me to you. Adams doesn't need to know."

I shook his hand before I got in my car. "Tammany takes care of its own, right, Booker?"

He smiled at the old slogan as he began to walk back toward the crime scene. "When it's convenient, Charlie. When it's convenient."

Chapter 3

CHIEF CARMICHAEL'S office was a large, wood-paneled affair meant to intimidate anyone fortunate or unfortunate enough to be invited inside, depending on the circumstances. It was the Holy of Holies of the department, the inner sanctum of the NYPD.

An ornate wooden desk with hand-carved images of the city's past dominated the room. A scene of Indians and Dutch trading beads for Manhattan Island was the one that stood out the most. I'd never gotten around to finding out where the desk had come from, but I'd heard it rivaled the one in the Oval Office.

One wall of the office was dedicated to all the medals, commendations and awards Carmichael had earned before and since becoming chief. The wall was just large enough to fit them all.

A long leather couch was against the wall opposite his desk while an ornate round table with uncomfortable chairs sat near the window looking out onto Centre Street. There was no view to speak of, so he kept the wooden blinds closed most of the time.

While I preferred the couch, I spent most of my time at the table while Carmichael met with people in his office. He usually only met with two men at a time. He liked his meetings to be as small as possible. He believed the larger the group, the greater the temptation someone might feel to perform to the crowd. The chief found intimate settings were best for getting his point across.

I'd been on that couch leafing through the evening edition of *The Herald* when the chief finally got back to the Castle.

I'd hoped to talk to him about Spann and my run in with Booker and Adams, but I quickly saw he wasn't alone. Deputy Chief of Department Edward Fitzgerald trailed close behind him. Technically, he was responsible for running the department, but like me, he spent his days doing whatever Carmichael told him to do.

Deputy Chief Stuart Ross walked in after Fitzgerald. He was in charge of the detectives. All of us were Tammany men to our bones. We wouldn't have been in the office if we weren't.

The same question that had been bothering me rose to the surface again. *Why was Spann so special?*

Since I was as much a fixture in the chief's office as his desk lamp, neither of the deputy chiefs paid me much mind as they filed in behind Carmichael. The deputy chiefs grumbled a hello my way as they took seats in the leather chairs opposite the chief's desk.

Carmichael didn't sit down. He stood behind his chair and rested his hands on it instead. His face was dark and appropriately grim.

"This is a damned shame, boys," he said to no one in particular. "A damnable shame. To lose a man like Spann like this is a tragedy. And in such a needless way, too."

"Another casualty of reckless driving," Fitzgerald said, louder than he needed to.

I perked up when I heard that and set my paper aside before I dropped it. Reckless driving hadn't put three holes in Spann's chest.

Ross added, "It's that damned poison the speakeasies are serving up these days. It's turning people's minds into pudding. Making them shells of their former selves. They're a danger to society, especially when they get behind the wheel."

"A good crackdown is what we need," Fitzgerald added. "I'll have the boys put a renewed emphasis on enforcing speed limits and traffic laws. Maybe raid a couple of the gin mills, too. Remind those characters they need to be responsible for the kind of swill they serve in their dives."

Carmichael looked over at me for the first time since he'd returned to his office. "What's that look for, Detective?"

That was the second time that day he had referred to me as 'detective'. I was beginning to think it was my real first name. "Nothing. Just trying to figure what this is all about."

"We're talking about Detective John Spann's cause of death, of course," Carmichael replied. "It's as clear a case of vehicular homicide as any of us have ever seen. Why even Kronauer agreed, didn't he, boys?"

Fitzgerald and Ross said he had.

I'd been around the department long enough to know a gag when I heard one. I knew not all of them were meant to be funny. Usually, I was in on it.

But the way these three were talking made me wonder if I wasn't off my nut.

I asked, "What did Kronauer say about the three holes Spann had—"

Carmichael cut me off. "As you were the first officer on the scene, Detective, I need you to write up a report on everything you saw. Immediately."

This was getting stranger by the minute. "Mind telling me what that was? I wouldn't want to complicate things by accidentally telling the truth."

Carmichael nodded to Fitzgerald, who turned in his chair to face me. "Your report will reflect that Chief Carmichael sent you to bring Detective Spann back to his office so that he could congratulate him personally on a commendation he had been selected to receive."

As far as I knew, it might even be true. "Ok. Then what happened?"

Fitzgerald looked like he was annoyed that he had to remind me. "That you beckoned him to cross the street when you saw him leaving the stationery store, and when he did, he was hit by a careless driver. You chased the vehicle on foot but unfortunately lost it as it sped away."

I looked at both deputy chiefs. Neither of them met my gaze. Finally, I looked at Carmichael, who managed to seem like he actually believed all this.

"It sped away," I repeated. "In midtown traffic. At rush hour."

"That's how it happened, Detective," Carmichael said. "All you have to do is put it in your report and sign it. Bring it to me as soon as possible."

I'd gone from not believing my ears to being insulted. "And what about the son of a bitch who shot—"

Carmichael pounded his chair. "The only thing that sped like a bullet on Madison Avenue earlier this evening, Detective Doherty, was the gray sedan that cut down a gifted detective in the prime of life. Make sure your report reflects the facts as we have reviewed them and submit it directly to me with your signature. I'll expect it within the hour." He looked away. "Now leave us as we have much to discuss."

I could feel my mouth move, but no sound came out.

Ross turned in his chair and said, "Don't worry, Charlie. No one's blaming you for what happened. That man you chased through the crowd was probably a man rushing to catch a train or get home to his family."

Fitzgerald piped up, "We all know what it's like out there, Charlie. Everything happens at once. No time to make sense of it all. One thing leads to another so quickly that it's easy to get carried away. What you heard was obviously a truck backfiring. We're just lucky no one got hurt."

Deputy Chief Ross added, "Your gun must have discharged by accident when you hit the ground in pursuit of the man you thought had pushed Spann into traffic."

"And, like we said, no one was hurt," Fitzgerald repeated. "That's the most important thing. The chief here and I were talking, and we don't see any reason why any more should be said about it. Just put it in your report and it'll be forgotten."

"No harm done," Ross said, "so we can give Detective John Spann the hero's funeral he so richly deserves. Without distraction or complication."

I felt like a drowning man looking for someone to throw him a line. I looked at Carmichael, who had folded his arms and looked away.

Whatever all of this was about, the message was clear. I was on my own.

I knew there was no upside to me fighting whatever story they had cooked up, but I needed to know I hadn't completely lost my mind. "Will there at least be an autopsy?"

Fitzgerald and Ross hesitated, but Carmichael jumped in to answer for them. "Of course, there'll be an autopsy. Dr. Kronauer will do it personally. And afterwards, there'll even be a report, that the head coroner will review and sign off on. You know Hugh Lang, don't you? Just named the Head Coroner this week. Good man Hugh."

"He's one of us," Fitzgerald pointed out.

"A good man," Ross agreed.

They might not have been subtle about it, but even I got the hint. There was more to Spann's death than anyone wanted to admit, even in here. It was being handled so keep your mouth shut.

I somehow found the strength to stand and got to my feet. "Sounds like I've got a report to write."

"Within the hour, Detective," Carmichael reminded me. "And keep it between us. Don't mention a word of this to anyone. The newspapers will have a complete account of what happened in their evening and morning editions."

Fitzgerald even managed a smile. "Charlie knows that, Andy. After all, he's one of us."

"A good man," Ross agreed, "who knows his duty when he sees it. Why, men like him are the backbone of the department. I've always said so."

I got the hell out of there before I got sick. Besides, I had a story to write.

————

I WENT DOWN the back stairs so no one would see me leaving the chief's office. I exited through the door that led to the alley Carmichael used to go into his car without anyone seeing him. He didn't like the rank and file keeping tabs on him.

I walked around the block to try to clear my head before I went in through the front door. After the nonsense the chief and his boys had peddled for truth, I needed a good dose of reality before I began writing my report. And the streets of Manhattan were just about as real as a man could hope to get.

There was a reason why Carmichael and the others wanted to gloss over Spann's death. I didn't know why, and I knew they wouldn't tell me until they were good and ready, if ever.

But a cop killer was out there with my bullet in him. No amount of double-talk or false reports could change that. I'd get to the bottom of it eventually and sooner than the three wise men up in the chief's office wanted.

Not for Carmichael's sake. Not even for mine. But for Spann.

I rounded the block like a respectable citizen and headed back toward headquarters. The official address of the place was 240 Centre Street, but that was only as far as the maps and the post office was concerned. To cop and criminal and civilian alike, it was simply called the Castle.

It was a sprawling, overbuilt affair whose façade was grander than some of the more opulent buildings I'd seen in Paris after the war. It had been built with Tammany labor, so no expense had been spared. Why spend one million when you could spend three? It had marble columns and arches and a great big dome on top of it that looked too big for the building beneath it.

The place had more rooms, hallways and odd corners than any one man could ever know. I doubted some of the janitors who'd worked there their entire lives had even seen all of it.

The building was intimidating enough above ground, but only a privileged few had ever been in the darkest recesses of the building. And, like most buildings, the basement was where the bad things happened, to cop and criminal alike. They called it the Dungeon and for good reason. I did my best to avoid going down there whenever I could, but something told me this case would have me heading down there before this was over.

I returned the usual nods and waves to the cops who acknowledged me as they entered and exited the building. They didn't do it because they liked me. They did it because they knew I worked for the chief. They hoped a nod and a kind word from me at the right moment could help them out of a fix somewhere down the road. After all, it didn't hurt to be polite to the chief's Black Hand, now did it?

They could've saved themselves the effort and just ignored me. I only helped the cops Carmichael told me to help. I'd let every man in the building swing if Carmichael told me to do it, no matter how many forced smiles and waves they threw my way.

I walked up the wide marble staircase to the Detective's Bureau, which was one floor below Valhalla, the floor where all the department brass worked, including the chief.

Since I spent all of my time in the chief's office, I hardly ever used the desk they kept for me there. But on that particular evening I'd be putting it to good use.

I ignored the strange looks I drew from the rest of the detectives in the bureau as I sat at my desk and began to bang out my report. The night shift was well underway by then, so the place was quieter than normal.

I didn't blame them for looking at me like a lion in a zoo. I hadn't spent more than an hour there since getting my detective shield six months before.

Half of my mind was busy keeping my own questions at bay as I fed the paper into the typewriter and began tapping out the fiction Carmichael and his friends had dictated to me.

Why the lie about Spann getting hit by a car?

Why had Adams made it sound like I was wrong?

What's really going on?

A cop had just been murdered in broad daylight on Madison Avenue. We shouldn't be mincing words. We shouldn't be turning a blind eye to what had happened. Every cop on the payroll should be turning the city upside down looking for the bastard who'd killed Spann.

But we weren't. We weren't even admitting he'd been shot. We were saying it was a car accident. A hit and run job.

Why? Why? Why? It played like a goddamned tom-tom in my head over the sound of the keys striking paper.

I had just about gotten into the rhythm of it all when Lieutenant Todd 'Mac' McNally, technically my boss, sauntered over to my desk. I knew the third-degree was coming. He was Tammany, too. He was in on the joke, so I was more annoyed than worried.

When I'd gotten my detective's shield, Carmichael had told McNally to not ask any questions about me and Mac had been more than happy to comply. He even gave me glowing fitness reports whenever the need arose.

Mac was one of those guys who had looked forty since the academy and hadn't aged a day since. He was as bald as a bean, so he never had to worry about his hair turning gray to betray his age. His trim mustache had been black for all the years I'd known him, though I knew he was in his late thirties, same as me. And I saw a new gray hair pop up in my crop top every time I looked in a mirror. It was tough to see, given how close I kept my hair cut, but I knew they were there.

"Bless my soul, boys, it's a miracle!" McNally said loud enough for the benefit of the rest of the squad. "The great Detective Charles Doherty has descended from Valhalla to grace us mere mortals with his presence." He bent dramatically at the waist. "To what do we owe this great honor, your Grace?"

The boys of the squad laughed and went back to whatever they were doing.

"Knock it off, Mac," I said as I hunted and pecked for the letter 'H' on the typewriter. "I'm having enough trouble finding the letters on this damned thing without you needling me."

"Could it be," he whispered, "that you're actually writing a report?" He took a seat in the chair next to my desk. "I think I may need to sit down for my heart simply can't take it."

"You missed your calling," I told him as I found the 'h' and hit it. "Vaudeville's loss."

"No kidding, Charlie," Mac said. "I never expect to see you down here. What gives?"

I was too busy hunting the letter 'B' to look up. Whoever laid out typewriter keys like this should be kicked in the nuts. "You heard about Spann?"

Mac dropped the act. "I heard. Hit and run job. Bad luck. John was a good egg. Smart, too. He deserved better." His cop instinct kicked in. "What's that got to do with you?"

I felt like an idiot carrying on Carmichael's lie, but I did it anyway. "I was in the area and saw him fall, which

37

is why I'm writing up a report. I wanted to get it all down on paper while it was still fresh."

Then one of my few detective instincts kicked in. I sensed a lead. "Sounds like you knew Spann pretty well."

"Sure did," Mac told me. "Or at least as well as anyone could know Spann. Worked with him at Missing Persons for a while before I got the bump up here. Booker, too. I heard he and Adams caught the case."

I had almost forgotten about my run-in with Adams. "They did. I talked to them up at the scene."

"Damned shame him going like that," Mac said. "Spann, I mean. He had a tough life."

"I didn't know him very well," I admitted. But Booker had mentioned something about Spann's tough life, too. "How tough?"

Mac's eyes narrowed. "You mean you never heard? I thought you were plugged into everything that happened in the department."

I was beginning to get annoyed and didn't bother hiding it. "If I knew, I wouldn't be asking you, now would I?"

Mac sat back in his chair and surrendered. "Don't get testy, Charlie. I just figured you'd remember what happened. How he lost a son about ten years ago. One minute, he was playing with some neighbor kids in the yard and the next he was gone." He snapped his fingers. "Just like that."

I thought I knew everything worth knowing about most of the men in the department, but I hadn't known this. It made me remember my own girls again. Anne and Mary. The thought of them going missing turned my stomach. "How'd it happen?"

"Happened out at Spann's place on Staten Island. He was on patrol here in Manhattan when the kid went missing and when he came home, he found his wife frantic. Neighbors and cops swarmed the area looking for the boy day and night. Had over two hundred cops covering every square inch of the neighborhood looking for him for a week. Uniforms and detectives alike."

I might not have remembered at first, but I remembered hearing something about it now. "You say this happened about ten years ago? Back in '17?"

"That's the number," Mac said.

"That explains why I missed it. I was getting ready to ship over to France around then."

Mac immediately looked embarrassed that he'd forgotten I'd been in the war. He'd gotten out of it. Color blindness or some damned thing. One of his cousins had been a Tammany bigwig at the time, so he got lucky. "Yeah, I guess that's why. But if you have any questions about what happened back then, you should ask the chief."

"Carmichael? Why?"

"Because he was in charge of the search for the kid back then," Mac told me. "He wasn't stationed in Staten Island, of course, but he got tapped to run the search. Did a hell of a job, too. I remember being impressed with how organized he was."

Mac gave it some thought. "Come to think of it, that case really put Carmichael on the map. He was one the fast track for brass anyway, but his hard work on the Spann case made him a lock for it."

Normally, my main concern was anything that involved the chief, but just then, I was more concerned with Spann. "They ever find the boy?"

Mac shook his head. "Not a stitch of clothing or a broken twig or a drop of blood anywhere. And believe me, we looked. It was like someone swooped down out of the sky and carried poor little Tommy away."

That didn't sound right to me. I might not have been much of a detective, but I had put in my time on the street. I knew how things worked. People didn't just disappear, not even kids. "Staten Island's remote, but it's not the Sahara. Someone must've seen something."

"From what I remember," Mac explained, "there weren't many witnesses. The kids the Spann boy was playing with saw him walking away with a man, but they were young and didn't see much. I remember they said he looked dirty and old, whatever that means."

I could see Mac digging deeper into his memory. "There was also a neighbor who was getting up to go to work for the night shift that afternoon. He thought he saw a man walking with a boy toward a nearby wooded area. But since he was half asleep and didn't have his glasses on, he couldn't be certain."

Mac threw up his hands. "That's all I remember, really. That and I got a bad case of poison ivy. Carmichael was a real hard ass about it, too. Wouldn't let me see a doctor. Told me to walk it off and offer it up to God."

"That sounds like Carmichael."

"The press ran with the story all summer. A missing cop's kid sells plenty of papers. They even pegged the kidnapper with a catchy title. Called him 'The Wandering Man'."

Mac shook his head. "Damned jackals. They never helped us a bit, except to point out that we didn't have a single lead. Made us look like fools. Probably would've stayed in the papers longer if the war hadn't started grabbing all the headlines."

Mac must've heard what he'd said and regretted it.

"I'm sorry, Charlie. I didn't mean to sound cold about it. I know it wasn't easy over there for you boys."

I let it drift. Unless you were actually there, no one could ever know what it had been like. "No harm done."

Besides, I still had questions and wanted to keep pumping while the well was flowing. "I can't imagine the hell Spann went through."

"Poor guy was never the same after that and who could blame him? Don't think he ever let it go. He got real quiet after that. Haunted. Hardly talked to anyone if he didn't have to, but I don't think he ever stopped working the case, even after all these years. I'm pretty sure he kept on looking for leads and following up on them in his spare time."

Given all that I was learning about Spann, that didn't surprise me. I'd probably do the same thing. But then he told me this:

"Spann's wife got the worst of it. She never stopped blaming herself for Tommy going missing. Always said she should've paid more attention to him and what he was doing. Poor woman wound up killing herself on the first anniversary of the kidnapping. Spann was all alone in the world with nothing but the hunt for the man who took his life away to comfort him."

I sagged in my chair. The poor bastard. Not only did Spann lose his boy, but his wife, too. All because some monster dipped into his life and ruined it forever.

Mac's curt laugh snapped me out of my thoughts. "Ain't this a kick in the head? I'm usually the one who gets his men to tell him things and here I am reporting to you." He dropped his voice to a whisper. "You know, I'm still your boss, Charlie. At least on paper."

"Your secret is safe with me." I went back to my

typing. "I'll snap off a salute if it'll make you feel any better."

He nudged me as he got to his feet. "Just put in a good word for me with the gods upstairs if you can." He cleared his throat and played to the rest of the squad. "Now get back to work, Doherty. That's an order."

The men laughed again and so did Mac.

But before he headed back to his office, one more question struck me.

I called out to him. "Do you remember what section of Staten Island he was in? Spann, I mean."

Mac shook his bald head. "Ten years is a long time, my friend. And it's always been part of Jersey as far as I'm concerned. But use that golden key of yours to open up the files downstairs. It's all there, believe me."

I watched him walk between the desks back to his office and shut the door behind him. He'd given me a gift and hadn't even realized it.

I forgot about my report for a moment and mulled it over. Spann had spent the last decade hunting the man who'd taken his child. And tonight, someone had shot him dead outside a stationery store on Madison Avenue for no good reason.

Or did they?

And Carmichael had been involved in the Spann investigation up to his neck. *Interesting.*

I decided it was time for me to get some answers. I wasn't sure if I'd get any, but I had to try.

I tapped out a quick ending the report just as The Three Wise Men had told me to write it, pulled it from the typewriter and signed it.

I set my pen aside and looked at the report for a long time. It wasn't the first false report I had ever written, and I doubted it would be the last. But something about this one bothered me. Why cover up a cop's murder? Had Spann been up to something or was it Carmichael? And why were Fitzgerald and Ross in on it with him instead of me?

The information Mac had given me by way of conversation had been more than helpful. It had opened my eyes to a lot I didn't know was there.

What little I knew about Spann hadn't come from the chief, but from Booker and Mac. Men who had worked with him and knew his past.

I might be waiting a long time if I pinned my hopes on Carmichael giving me the truth. He'd made me part of his lie the moment he ordered me to write a phony report about a cop's murder. And I'd become part of it as soon as I signed it.

I wanted answers and I wanted them quickly. And I knew just the man who might be as confused by all of this as I was. He'd also happened to be the most likely one who'd have some answers to the questions rattling around in my head.

I took my hat and coat off the rack and walked up the main staircase to Valhalla. Sgt. Bohannan was assigned to the guard desk that night and watched the chief's wing of the floor. He waved me through and made a point of not writing down my name in the visitor's log.

The name of everyone who walked up those stairs was supposed to be logged. Where the log went had always been a mystery. My name never appeared in the log. I was the exception. I was officially a nobody and had no complaints.

I walked past the rows of empty desks and headed for Carmichael's assistant Rosie. She was busy on the phone and barely acknowledged me as I placed my report on her desk. The door to the chief's office was closed. Normally, I would've knocked on the door to see if he was there or wanted to talk, but I wasn't interested in what the chief had to say just then.

I said good night to Bohannan as I shrugged into my coat and walked downstairs to the main lobby. The chilled September night air hit me as soon as I stepped outside, and it woke me up a bit. Good thing, too. Because anyone who went to speak with Kronauer should do so with a clear mind.

Chapter 4

THE MORGUE at Bellevue Hospital had never bothered me as much as it should have. Maybe it was because I'd grown used to death as a beat cop long before I saw it in France. Maybe I'd lost a piece of whatever made me human somewhere in the tangle of Belleau Wood.

Or maybe it was because the place never smelled like a death house because Hank Kronauer's cigars always overwhelmed the stench. I sometimes wondered if that was why he smoked the damned things in the first place.

I found him sitting at his desk in the far corner of the lab, writing out a report beneath the dim golden bulb of an ancient desk lamp.

I looked around the autopsy lab and was glad to see no one else was there. No one else alive, anyway. Three steel examining tables had cadavers beneath blankets. I didn't dwell on the fact that they'd once been alive not too long ago.

I didn't want to think that one of them was probably Spann.

Hank Kronauer had been well over three hundred

45

pounds on the first day I'd met him more than a decade before and he hadn't changed since. His beige braces strained to keep his pants up over his massive girth. His fleshy chins wagged as he wrote something down in a ledger, mumbling to himself as he did so.

I stood in the open doorway for a while, watching him work. He looked as peaceful as an old monk transcribing an ancient manuscript in an abbey library. But instead of translating the given word from Hebrew into Latin, he was translating medical terms into the language of the layman about some poor bastard who'd met his end before his time. He might even be writing up the autopsy he had done on Spann.

Anyone who didn't know how Kronauer worked might have thought he was touched in the head for muttering to himself as he wrote. I'd always taken it as a sign of genius. In busier times like the summer, I'd seen him write a perfect report of an autopsy he'd done five days before, completely from memory and without referring to notes.

I'd seen him on the witness stand recalling an autopsy he had done years before, also without notes. His incredible mind was his notebook and written in a language only he could read it.

He had not looked up from his report since I'd walked into the room, yet he said, "Evening, Charlie. What has you out so late? Shouldn't you be home with the family or in a speakeasy somewhere drowning your sorrows?"

He never ceased to amaze me. "One of these days, you're going to teach me that trick."

Kronauer continued writing. "And what trick would that be?"

"How you always know who's in the room without seeing them," I said.

"Everyone has a different silent clue," he said as he kept writing. "With some it's the smell of their hair tonic combined with the type of cigarette they smoke. Some reveal themselves by how they clear their throat or some other nervous tic. In your case, it's footfalls. The sound one's shoes make as they walk down the hall has a certain cadence to it that's almost as good as a thumbprint. Yours has a very distinct pattern. Heavy left foot and a lighter right foot. A rhythm you likely acquired in your days in the Marines, I trust."

He set his pen aside and glanced at me over the black glasses perched at the end of his stubby nose. In that split second, I knew he could describe what I was wearing in complete detail a year from now.

The metal chair creaked under his weight as he folded his hands across his belly. "So, are you going to answer my question about why you're here or will I be forced to venture a guess?"

"I'd bet my pension you already know why I'm here."

"Yes," he frowned. "I'm afraid I do. This Spann business is most odd, isn't it?"

He plucked his smoldering cigar from the ashtray as he stood up and paddled around his desk and toward a body on the examining table closest to where I was standing.

I watched Kronauer whip off the sheet covering the body on the table closest to me. It was done without ceremony, and he allowed the sheet to fall to the floor like a painter unveiling his latest work of art.

John Spann bore Kronauer's mark, the mark of the coroner. The stitched 'Y' cut that began at his chest and ran down the middle of him. A man who had been alive and well only a few hours ago was now reduced to a cold thing on a coroner's slab.

"The decedent suffered from three bullets to the heart." He traced the exit wounds with his little finger without touching the skin. "As you can see, his wounds are visible. I'm afraid yours are not."

He looked up at me. "You're suffering from an acute attack of conscience, Charlie. A chronic inability to grasp the absurd." He gestured toward the corpse. "Well, here's the source of your trouble. The mortal remains of Detective John Spann. Take a close look and tell me what you make of it?"

I was beginning to think Kronauer had lost his mind, too. "You just told me. Three bullets to the heart. I saw it happen."

"Yes, you did," Kronauer said. "You saw him die. What do you see here?"

I took a closer look at the corpse and saw everything I had expected to see. "Three exit wounds in the upper left chest from a handgun. A .38 caliber handgun."

"That based on what you see or other evidence?" Kronauer popped the cigar in the corner of his mouth. "Be specific."

"Both," I told him. "From the wounds I see now and from what I heard at the scene." I pointed at the three holes in his chest. "Anything smaller wouldn't have made that much damage. Anything bigger, like a .45, would've made more."

Kronauer removed the cigar from the corner of his mouth and released a great plume of grayish black smoke. "Anything else?"

I looked closer at the body to see if I had missed anything. Other than some scrapes on his left cheek that looked like he'd received when he hit the pavement, there was nothing else. "No. I'd say that's just about it."

"Precisely." He flicked his cigar away from the examination table, allowing the ash to drop to the floor. "You saw what happened with your own two eyes. You know exactly how he died. He was not struck down by a car. Which brings me back to my original question. Why are you here?"

"Because Carmichael, Fitzgerald and Ross told me to write a report that Spann had died because he'd been hit by a car. And I don't know why they did that."

"They told me to do the same thing. What of it?"

I pointed down at the three holes in Spann's chest. "He didn't get those by being hit by a car, Hank. He was shot."

Kronauer's bushy eyebrows rose. "Of course. I don't need you to tell me he was shot. I'm the one who performed the autopsy, aren't I?"

But that only made me even more confused. "Then why did you write up a report that said otherwise?"

"I didn't," Kronauer told me. "I said they told me to write such a report. That doesn't mean I did it. My report clearly states that Detective Spann died from three shots to the heart from the back at near point-blank range."

I suddenly felt like a fool for doing what Carmichael had ordered me to do. Kronauer had the courage of his convictions. I was just a lacky who'd followed orders. "Then why are they saying it was a traffic accident?"

"They saw the same injuries that you and I saw. They obviously have a reason for drawing another conclusion."

I had come here for answers, but I was getting more confused by the second. "But why? A cop getting shot isn't a shoplifting charge. We need to have every uniform on the payroll hunting this guy right now. Why the stall?"

"I haven't the slightest idea," Kronauer said. "I don't know their motives and I don't know why they cooked up that ridiculous story about him being hit by a car. I don't care, either." He squinted at me through the cigar smoke. "Want to know why I don't care, Charlie?"

He waved his cigar over Spann's corpse as if the cigar was a magic wand. "Because my world is very simple. This corpus is my office. The human body. And a very specific human body at that. A dead one. I can look at a specimen like this and tell you how it died and when it died. I can tell you how it had lived; about conditions only an autopsy can uncover. Heart disease. Liver disease. Kidney function. Cancer. I can even tell you what its last meal was from the contents of the stomach and whether or not it was poisoned."

He picked the sheet up from the floor and placed it over Spann's corpse with one shake of his wrist. It draped the body perfectly. "But none of my training or knowledge or experience will be able to help you determine why three high-ranking members of the New York Police Department have decided to hide the fact that one of their own was gunned down on Madison Avenue. Hit by a speeding car amid stand-still traffic, no less." He grumbled a wet laugh. "The very notion of it is absurd."

All of this made me feel a bit better, but not in the way I'd hoped.

"Then why—"

"Come," he said as he beckoned me to follow him to his desk. "You want to know why I didn't stand up to them when they asked me to write a bogus report."

He shook his head as he shuffled behind his desk. "Because I learned a long time ago to keep opinions to myself when they're not asked for, particularly where chiefs are present. You are Carmichael's eyes and ears. You grew up with the man, for God's sake. What would I possibly have to gain by debating him in public? In front of the entire department, no less. Would it have changed the facts of Spann's death? Would it have made the conclusions we have discussed tonight any different?"

He shook his head. "All it would've done is make them more suspicious of me than they already are because I'm not a Tammany man. Which is fine by me. Coroners never fit in anyway and I have no need to feel the Tiger's warm embrace. Nor its hot breath on my neck at times like this."

He picked up a folder and held it out to me. "It's all right there if you won't take my word for it. My honest findings, just as we've discussed them here tonight."

I waved the file away. "I believe you, Hank. But why take the risk?"

"I'm not taking any risk." He put the file back on his desk. "I've lasted this long in my position without following the herd and I intend to continue to do so. They may be angry at my defiance once they read my report, but they won't punish me for it. They need me, you see, for all of the cases they actually want solved. My superior will be forced to write one on his own to the chief's specifications, which will give me a good laugh. That quack has narrowly escaped being sued for malpractice half a dozen times. If his wife wasn't a cousin of Mayor Walker's, he probably would've been in jail several times over. At least they gave him a position where he can't hurt anyone. Even the dead are beyond the scope of his incompetence."

I sat on the edge of Kronauer's desk. I suddenly felt dizzy. "I wish I had your courage."

"Don't confuse comfort for courage," the coroner told me. "There's only one of me. You're in no position to stand up to them. You have a wife and young family to consider. You'd be a fool to defy them and while you have many faults, you're no fool, Charlie."

I wasn't so sure.

Kronauer pointed at the radio on his desk before flicking his cigar ash in the ashtray. "The newsmen on the radio have been reporting the unfortunate hit and run attack on Detective John Spann earlier this evening. A manhunt is underway, but for the driver. They even have a good description of the car and driver. A man dressed in all gray." He cocked his round head to the side. "Sound familiar?"

I steadied myself on the edge of his desk. "There's no manhunt going on. I just came from the Castle. It's like St. Patrick's Day up there. No one in sight."

Kronauer raised his palms to the sky. "I can't help you there, Charlie. Mine is the realm of the dead. Yours is the realm of politics. Such answers are your concern, not mine. I've done my part. I've written my report. My conscience is clear."

I let out a long breath and dropped my head. "Wish I could say the same."

"Fortunately, I have a remedy for that." He opened the bottom drawer of his desk, took out two glasses and a bottle of Cutty Sark. With his cigar tucked in the fingers of his right hand, he opened the bottle and poured three fingers of the whiskey into each glass. "It's not a permanent cure, mind you, but it'll provide temporary relief from what ails you."

He thumbed the cork back in the bottle and set it on the desk. He pushed one glass toward me and took the other. "Drink up. Doctor's orders."

I looked at the glass for a while. I hated Cutty Sark. It was piss Joe Kennedy passed off as honest booze. It always gave me a headache. But it would probably drown out the tom-toms thudding in my head, so I took it and drank. The burn in my throat took my mind off my other troubles.

I looked up when I felt Kronauer studying me again. "What?"

"Guilt is the most useless emotion in the world, Charlie. You're not a crusader and there's nothing wrong with that. You do as you're told because that's the life you have chosen. There are forces at work here beyond our comprehension, certainly mine. You're hurt that Carmichael has kept you in the dark about his reasons for this charade. My advice is to either get over it or find the answers you seek elsewhere."

Kronauer nodded over at John Spann's slab. "He's beyond caring what they say about him now. And although it's cold comfort, you and I know the truth. Sometimes that simply has to be enough."

I finished my drink and set the glass on the desk as I got up. "You're right about one thing, Hank. I'm going to find out why they're doing this no matter what happens."

Kronauer offered a weary smile as he toasted me with his glass. "Then God go with you, young man, for I'm afraid He's the only one who will."

As I left, the stench from his cigar followed me down the length of the long hallway. It was beginning to turn my stomach.

Maybe because I knew it was tinged with truth.

Chapter 5

EVERYTHING in me wanted another drink. Dreams of stopping by The Longford Lounge or the Stage Left danced in my head.

But I knew I'd end up drinking too much and all I'd get for my trouble was one hell of a hangover. I needed to keep a clear head.

Which was why I found myself sitting at the dinner table with a cold plate of chicken in front of me, a glass of flat near-beer beside it and Theresa jabbering away at me.

Anne and Mary were already in bed by the time I'd gotten home, and I saw no point in waking them. Besides, Theresa hadn't given me the chance. She was on me from the moment I walked in about all she'd done that day and all of the neighborhood gossip she'd heard. She'd kept up the dialogue as I pulled my dinner from the ice box and didn't even notice I hadn't touched a bite. I'd even let my beer grow warm.

My wife didn't care if I was listening. She only needed an audience. Participation was not only unnecessary but discouraged. She was like an engine that kept running, only instead of gasoline, her fuel was gossip and she always had a full tank.

I passively listened to her tell me all about Mrs. Horowitz giving her sass at the butcher shop again, but I was too lost in my own thoughts for it to register.

At least the beat of the tom-tom in my head had changed its tempo. It went from *Why-Why-Why* to *Carmichael-Fitzgerald-Ross-Booker-McNally-Spann-Kidnapping-Lie*. Everything was connected through Carmichael. That wasn't the mystery.

But why was Carmichael lying about Spann getting shot? And why Spann had been gunned down in the first place?

The more I thought about it, the more I was sure it had to be connected to the reason why Carmichael had sent me to get Spann. There was a reason why Carmichael hadn't told me about it. That reason involved Fitzgerald and Ross. So why not pull me aside and tell me about it?

Then, something Theresa said finally caught my attention. "Oh, Rosie from the chief's office called earlier."

The sound of the tom-toms died away. "She did? What did she say?"

"Sure, you heard that, didn't you?" Theresa sneered. "I've been talking my head off for the past hour and you didn't even bat an eye. But one mention of the chief and you snap out of it damned fast."

I looked at the woman scowling at me now from across the dinner table. I tried to be angry with her but couldn't. I could work up a lot of hate for a lot of people, but she'd always been different. What's more, she knew it.

I'd broken one of the cardinal rules of law enforcement when I took up with her. Never fall in love with the women you bust. But Theresa had been the exception, at least for me.

She wasn't as pretty as she had been when we'd first met up. She was prettier now. She'd been skinny back when she'd been working in a house run by Sally Balls. Heroin skinny. Her eyes vacant of anything close to hope. The warpaint she wore had covered up a lot, but not everything.

I'd been able to see beneath all of that and knew she was different from the other working girls. Maybe I saw it because I wanted to believe it.

She wound up becoming my own personal project. I'd sat with her in the days after I pulled her out of that joy house. I was with her through the shakes and the cravings and the night sweats and all the hell that comes with returning from that empty world. I did for her what no one had done for me when I'd come home from the war. I'd fought those battles alone.

But now, you'd never know she'd been in The Life only six short years before. She had beautiful skin with just a hint of a natural Italian tan. Her thick black hair and oval brown eyes gave her an exotic look that always drove me wild.

I thought of her as one of those pictures of Castilian beauties the boys used to carry around with them back in the war. Her crooked smile never failed to stop me dead.

But I hadn't seen that smile in a long time and as I looked at her now, all I saw was fire and resentment from neglect. I couldn't blame her.

I remembered how Andy Carmichael had laughed that night in The Longford Lounge when I told him Theresa was pregnant and I was going to marry her. 'So

Charlie Doherty has finally found love. With a two-bit guinea whore from the Lower East Side, no less.' I remember how he'd raised his glass and gave a toast. 'Never let it be said that an Irishman is afraid to associate with his betters. Here's to everlasting love.'

The bastard had not only been my best man, but he danced at my wedding and charmed the hell out of everyone.

But that had been a long time ago. Now, six years and two girls later, Theresa was glaring at me over a plate of cold chicken and a glass of warm beer.

I'd never lied to her before and now wasn't the time to start. "I wasn't ignoring you, honey. I'm just off. I saw a cop get killed today."

That took some of the fire out of her. She sat a bit further back in her chair. "You mean that cop who got hit by the car? I heard about that on the radio. You were there? Did you know him? Were you friends?"

I knew I had to be careful. Telling Theresa anything was as good as telling the *Times*. She'd been prouder of me making detective than I had been. And not because of anything I had done to earn it, but because of the status it gave her in the neighborhood. And the extra money in the envelope I brought home every week. Being Carmichael's black hand had its privileges.

"I knew him from a distance. We weren't friends, but he was a good detective, and his death is hitting me harder than I thought it would."

I reached for her hand, hoping it would give me comfort and keep the tom-toms quiet for a while longer. She gave me her hand, but only as an afterthought as she continued with her line of questioning.

"Why were you there? What kind of car hit him? Was he married? Did he have kids?"

I closed my eyes and held on to whatever fleeting comfort holding her hand gave me. I tried to remember back to those awful nights when she'd held my hand while she fought off the demons that hunted her. When she held on to me like I was the only thing she had in the world. Maybe because I was.

The questions kept coming fast and furious, often with her providing the answers herself. Give her a phone book and a rubber hose, she would've fit right in down at the Dungeon while Carmichael's bully boys beat a confession out of a suspect.

I jumped into one of the rare silences by asking, "You said Rosie called. What did she say?"

Theresa frowned, clearly annoyed by the interruption. "She said the chief wants you to take tomorrow off, but he wants you at Calvary Cemetery in Queens the next day. Eleven o'clock. He said to be on time, and you should call the office first for instructions."

Then those dark eyes brightened, and for a moment, she was that lost girl I'd fallen in love with all those years ago. "It must be the funeral for this detective you knew. Swan, wasn't it?"

"Spann. Detective John Spann." The cold chicken suddenly lost any appeal it once had. I needed to see my girls.

Theresa was still peppering me with questions as I got up from the table. "I'm going to check in on the kids. I'll see you in bed."

Her questions were quickly replaced by complaints about how I never appreciated her cooking and was a lousy father for working as much as I did.

I didn't bother to remind her she was married to a Tammany man and a bag man at that. That the china we ate from and the dining set and the full kitchen and the entire house was thanks to the work I did when the lights came on while the rest of the city enjoyed home-cooked meals and wholesome conversation. She'd chosen to forget about all that a long time ago. She'd grown to believe the lies that she told her friends. About how her husband was a high-ranking official in the police department and best friends with the chief of police. Why he was even on a first-name basis Mayor Walker.

If holding the mayor's head over a toilet after his latest bender meant we were friends, then Lil' Jimsy and I were blood brothers. But she didn't need to know that, either. She'd never been one to let the truth get in the way of a good story, especially the lies she told herself.

I walked down the hall and turned off the light before I cracked open the door to the girls' room. I didn't need to actually see them, and I didn't want to risk waking them up. I knew they'd be too excited to see me to go back to sleep. I didn't want my anxiety to disturb their peace. I wasn't that selfish. Just knowing they were there was enough.

Anne was asleep in her bed closest to the window. Mary's bed was closest to the door. At five, she was the youngest by a year and was afraid of the man that lived in the back of their closet. I'd only recently gotten her used to the idea that I'd put him in jail, and no one would ever harm her ever again.

I leaned against the doorway for a while and shut my eyes. The sounds of their gentle snores comforted me. The tom-toms all but forgotten.

God, how I wished that was true. I wished there was no one lurking in closets or under beds or in alleyways waiting to harm them. I wished there weren't men like The Wandering Man running loose in my city.

Making that promise to a five-year-old was one thing. Making it to myself was different.

I knew better.

John Spann had known better, too.

What would I do if someone took one of my girls? What had John Spann done when the man popped out of the dark and took his boy?

The slow sound of the tom-toms started up in my head again.

Charmichael-Fitzgerald-Ross-Booker-McNally-Spann-Kidnapping-Lies-Why?

I quietly closed the door to their bedroom, just in case they might hear my thoughts in their dreams.

My nightmares were my own.

Chapter 6

I MADE sure I was out of the house the next morning just after dawn.

I hated missing the girls getting ready for school, but I didn't want them to see me like this. The tom-toms in my head had kept me awake most of the night and I looked it. My skin was blotchy, my eyes were red and even my flap-top looked crooked in the rearview mirror as I drove into the city that morning.

Carmichael may have given me the day off, but I had work to do.

Last night, while I was staring at the ceiling, I remembered something Captain Devlin used to say back in France. 'Any decision is better than none. Anchor yourself and pivot if you have to. And even if it gets you killed, at least you can go to Glory having had a say in the matter.'

That's when I decided to quit waiting for Carmichael or Kronauer or anyone else to give me answers about Spann. I had to find them on my own.

The beat of the tom-tom in my head changed a bit after that. *Carmichael. Fitzgerald. Ross. Spann.* They had been connected long before Spann was killed yesterday. Before Carmichael had ordered me to fetch him. The Spann Kidnapping explained why The Three Wise Men were so secretive. Why they had lied about Spann's cause of death.

The Spann Kidnapping was iceberg cold and long forgotten except by a chosen few. And since they weren't talking, I followed Captain Donavan's advice. I picked a direction and got moving.

If I hit up the file room at the Castle, Carmichael would know. He might get mad. Things were too tense for me to risk his anger now. That meant the best place to find information on the kidnapping was the file room at *The New York Journal.*

I parked in front of the place and walked inside. I didn't need to badge my way past the lobby guard or the receptionist at the newsroom's front desk. They all knew me well enough by now to know who I was.

I found Wendell Bixby where I'd expected him to be. At his desk in the middle of the newsroom, hammering away at his typewriter, working on his next story for the sports pages.

Bixby was in his mid-twenties and about my size, maybe a little smaller. Thinning wisps of brown hair were pushed across the top of his head. It was only a matter of time before he started wearing a wig. Wendell wasn't the type to let Mother Nature have her way. Thick round glasses made his quick eyes look bigger than they already were.

Women found him attractive in a dogged sort of way. Men, particularly ball players, found him harmless. They tended to forget he was around when they shot their mouth off. Their error was the sportswriter's gain.

He was also a Tammany man, just like me and the chief. When the Tiger roared, he listened and fell in line. He covered all sports in New York, but his specialty was building up boxing matches where the Hall had a betting interest. He could make or break a fighter's career with just a few choice taps on his typewriter. He could make you the second coming of John L. Sullivan or the biggest bum who'd ever stepped into the ring. Word had spread through the fight clubs and boxing gyms. Play along and you're a pal. Balk and pay the penalty in print.

Bixby's columns had earned him his share of black eyes and busted jaws from athletes who didn't like what he'd said about them in his column. But I never heard the scribbler complain. He knew the only thing worse than doing a favor for Tammany was to not be asked to do one at all.

Bixby had a warm spot in his heart for me. I'd introduced him to the Babe back in '23. The two hit it off and Bixby had been one of Ruth's drinking buddies ever since. Bixby had pledged undying loyalty to me ever since.

I figured the Spann case was a good chance to cash in on the good will.

The sportswriter jumped when I plopped down in the chair next to his desk.

"Jesus, Charlie! Don't you ever knock?"

He'd always been an excitable boy. "I would if you had your own office."

"Don't remind me." Bixby glared longingly over at the editor's office at the far end of the newsroom. "I'm working on it, brother. You can believe that."

I did. Wendell Bixby had always been an enterprising boy.

I looked at what he was typing. Another baseball column. I liked to go to a game or hear it on the radio now and then but reading about it put me to sleep. I could've used his column last night. "How are the balls and strikes treating you?"

"Lousy," Bixby pouted. "I got a little too loaded with our boy the other night and ran my mouth to this girl he was sweet on."

I winced. George Herman Ruth led a very complicated life, especially for a married man. "That so?"

"It gets worse," Bixby went on. "Seems my lies didn't match up with the lies he'd told her about where he'd been that weekend. She's slammed the lid on the honey pot but tight and the big guy's been giving me the cold shoulder ever since."

I shrugged it off. "You know how he gets. Give him a couple of days to forget about it. As soon as he starts missing you, you'll be back in his good graces in no time."

"I sure hope so, because it's mighty cold out here." He even shivered for effect. "I've been reduced to writing about ball games like every other schnook with a press pass."

Then he looked at me strangely. "Say, what brings you around here anyway? Surely not to hear my tale of woe."

I was glad to get to the point. "I need a favor."

Those busy eyes went shrewd. "This favor come from our friends downtown or from your boss?"

"Neither. For me."

His eyes went wide. "Me? Doing *you* a favor? Boy,

that's rich. Usually, it's the other way around." He sat back in his chair as he threw open his arms. "Just name it, brother, and it's yours. The world is your oyster, so long as oysters don't cost more than five cents since that's about all I've got on me at the moment."

I knew he was lying about that. Bixby didn't gamble or whore around. He drank for free wherever he went, or he didn't drink at all. He banked every penny he made, including the extra scratch he got for doing Tammany's bidding.

He paid for the odd tip from a snitch now and then and, when his editor had him work on a real story, he paid his cop informants well. I saw to it they didn't take advantage of him when he did.

That made Bixby smart in my book. It meant I could trust him. As much as anyone could trust any reporter, anyway. "I need to get into your file room, and I need as much time as I can get. No one can know about it, either."

He blinked at me twice as if he was waiting for something else. "And?"

"That's it," I said. "I just need enough time to look up a couple of things and then I'll get out of your hair." I nodded at the few strands holding on for dear life on the top of his scalp. "Not that there's much to hold me back."

"Up yours," he said, "and what you're asking for is hardly a favor at all. Hell, I think it's even legal. What's the fun in that?" He grabbed his keys off his desk and led me back the way I'd come in.

He kept his voice low as he asked, "Why come to me with this? Anyone around here would've let you into the file room. You know that."

"I want to keep it a secret, remember? I don't want to have to sign in or have someone remember I was here. This never happened no matter who asks. Understand?"

"I've got it," he said as we headed for the file room. "But I'd also like to get a guarantee on the exclusive if all your snooping results in a story."

Bixby never failed to remind me of man's basic greedy tendencies. "You don't even know what I'm looking for."

"Don't want to know either," he said. "Not yet anyway. But if I read about you cracking a big case under someone else's byline, I'll be awfully sore." He held up the keys and jingled them in front of me as a reminder. "Deal?"

"Deal," I agreed. "I'll even throw in a good word with the Babe for you the next time I see him. How's that sound?"

"Just do it soon, will you?" Bixby shivered again. "Like I said, it's awfully cold out here."

———

FOR WHAT I NEEDED, the file room of the *Journal* was better than the New York Public Library. I wasn't just looking for news. I needed a particular angle on the news. The kind of sensational angle the *Journal* always gave its readers. The more sensational the story, the closer the *Journal* got to the truth.

Once Bixby had shown me where the back issues of the paper were kept, I sent him on his way. Even the hint of a story linking a cop's death to his son's disappearance would put Bixby in good with his editor. And it would get me in a lot of trouble with the chief. Things being as they were, I had to be careful.

I found the thick book of editions from 1917 and looked up the stories in the index. There was a whole list of articles dedicated to The Wandering Man.

I hauled the big book open and found the first story on the case. The headline was typical Journal splash:

GHOUL GRABS COP'S KID ON STATEN ISLAND
Police hunt for 'The Wandering Man'

It certainly grabbed the eye. *The Journal* never played it humble.

I spent the next few hours crawling through every sordid detail the paper had printed on the Spann case. The story remained front page news for almost three weeks.

They milked it for all it was worth from every angle. How the father was a patrolman, keeping the home-front safe while our brave boys went off to fight the Hun in France. Pictures of young Tommy Spann as an infant.

Pictures of a slightly older Tommy standing next to his father, John, the policeman.

Pictures of Tommy hugging his mother on the front steps of their simple Staten Island home. The yard from where Tommy had disappeared was in the background. The caption under the picture told me so.

Seeing the joys and pain of the Spann family in newsprint made me sick. I imagined John must have felt the same way. Had he read the papers at the time or had that come later, when the pain scabbed over, and the hate took root? Was one of these articles the one that finally pushed Mrs. Spann to take her own life?

I ran my fingers along the newsprint, looking for any

information on The Wandering Man. *The Journal* had glommed onto the moniker and hadn't let go.

I found a pad on a desk in the file room and began taking notes. There were a lot of details to keep straight. I didn't want to risk jumbling them all. The death of a kid, even one that had happened a decade ago, never sat well with me. I didn't trust my memory to hold all the details, hence the notes.

Unfortunately, I didn't have to write much. The articles were heavy on speculation but short on details.

I saw old pictures of then-Lieutenant Carmichael leading uniforms searching a field. The shutterbugs had always loved Carmichael. He exuded authority and competence. He looked like a younger cop version of General Pershing. He made for great frontpage pics and helped newsies sell papers from street corners all over the city.

I found more pictures of Carmichael speaking to reporters flanked by then- Lieutenants Fitzgerald and Ross. Interesting. The tom-toms in my head started up again, only louder than before. The cadence was the same.

Carmichael-Fitzgerald-Ross-Spann.

I drowned them out by reading quotes from Carmichael about the case. He talked about following up on several promising leads. I read stories about how the two hundred officers had left no stone unturned. An arrest was all but imminent.

History told me it was all just bluster. No one had ever been formally charged with taking little Tommy Spann. It had probably been Carmichael's way of keeping the papers interested. Buying time until they caught a break, or The Wandering Man made a mistake.

I re-read the earlier articles with a more critical eye. I

matched up details and trimmed the fat from the articles. *The Journal* ran accounts from dozens of eyewitnesses who'd claimed they'd seen what happened. It was clear to me they were only parroting what they'd read in the papers or had heard from their friends. Two-bit neighborhood gossip. They should've put Theresa on the case.

My culling of accounts left me with three, maybe four credible witnesses. The two kids Tommy had been playing with were young, but consistent. So was the neighbor who had just woken up to go to the night shift. The fourth account was from a dock worker on Staten Island.

The Journal had even hired a sketch artist to make a composite sketch of The Wandering Man. The drawing filled the front page.

The sketch was a joke. It looked like a cross between The Captain from the Katzenjammer Kids and Edward Earle. People remembered what they saw every day, not what they saw once.

I boiled down their varying accounts to a basic description of the suspect. The Wandering Man was of medium height and build who had a limp. Only the dock worker added anything new. He said he may have seen the man before and he never saw him limp.

Descriptions of clothing and appearance were reasonably similar. Gray clothes. Old clothes. White hair. Gray hair. Rumpled old hat. Gray hat pulled down low on his head. The coat buttoned up tight and the collar up despite the oppressive heat and humidity of August.

It was the same description of the man I'd shot on Fifth Avenue yesterday.

And, like me, none of the credible witnesses saw his face.

A cold sweat broke out across my back. The file

room went into a spin. I braced myself on the cabinet and shut my eyes. I willed myself steady.

The son of a bitch hadn't just taken Tommy Spann. He'd killed his father, too.

And he was still out there. With my bullet in him.

I had shot The Wandering Man. *Was this the reason why Carmichael had wanted to see Spann?* It had to be.

Was he the reason why Fitzgerald and Ross went along with his cockeyed story about a hit-and-run job? It had to be.

Is this 'Wandering Man' business from a decade ago the reason why they've let a cop killer go free? I didn't like where that question led me.

Was Carmichael trying to protect his image? Was he letting a cop killer go free to keep the case that had made him hidden? I didn't dare answer that one.

I used the indexes and leafed ahead through time. I read stories the Journal ran weeks and months later, sifting for any new facts in the case. But as the leads dried up and summer faded into memory, so did the Spann case. I guess parents didn't want to read about missing kids when their own were going back to school.

The Wandering Man surrendered the front page to the War in Europe, scandals and gossip. Business as usual for the old town rag.

It wasn't until I checked the 1918 book that I found anything further about the case. It was an article about how Tommy's mother had killed herself on the one-year anniversary of her son's disappearance. *The Journal* dropped the story entirely after that. No reason had been given for her suicide. No coverage of John Spann's grief. Not enough sensationalism in a man's broken soul.

I closed the book and placed it back on the shelf where I'd found it. I breathed in the stale air of the file room and caught the smell of old paper and dust for my trouble.

I'd walked into the file room hoping for answers. All I found for my trouble was shame. The NYPD had failed the Spann family three times. Once in failing to find the boy's kidnapper. Once in the failed search that caused Mrs. Spann to kill herself. And now in the lie about the death of Detective John Spann.

At least now I had an idea about the reason for the lies. Spann's death was bound to bring up new questions about the missing boy from ten years prior. The department probably didn't have much to offer except a shrug.

If the papers found out the cases might be connected, they could blow it up into a major scandal. And Chief Carmichael couldn't have that, now could he?

After all, the dead were dead and beyond all caring.

The thought turned my stomach.

I suddenly felt dirty, like some kind of goddamned Peeping Tom who'd seen too much of the Spann family's sorrow. But now that I had seen the public aspects of Tommy's kidnapping, I wanted to see the department's side of it.

My next stop should be the central filing room at the Castle. To see the files for myself. To see what Carmichael and his men had really known about The Wandering Man.

Central Filing might be the next logical step, but it wasn't practical. Everyone who went into that room had to sign in and sign out. Even me.

That was because Central Files was the heartbeat of the NYPD. It was the foundation upon which all our cases were based. Personnel files were particularly sensitive. Tammany men and regular rank-and-file, all mixed in. There were a lot of facts in those drawers some very important people wanted to forget.

Since Central Filing wasn't an option, I'd have to get my answers from the source. From Chief Andrew J. Carmichael himself. Right after Spann's funeral tomorrow.

Chapter 7

I HATED FUNERALS. Cop funerals most of all.

If standing in a cemetery surrounded by mortality wasn't bad enough, the sight of the grieving family always got me. Crying kids only made it worse. Throw in the plaintive wail of 'Amazing Grace' on the bagpipes and it made for a lousy way to start the day.

But I wasn't there to mourn Detective John Spann. I wasn't there because Carmichael had ordered me to be there. I was there for answers. And I intended on getting them before the last spade of dirt had been shoveled on top of Spann's coffin that day. The Spann family deserved that much from me.

I'd decided to skip the mass at St. Patrick's Cathedral and got to the cemetery early. I found a shady spot beneath an old elm tree and stayed there for the duration. I was far enough away from the rest of the mourners to be inconspicuous, but close enough to see everything.

And there was a lot to see if you knew how to look.

I spotted Spann's second wife, Dotty, perched on a

white folding chair across from her husband's flag-draped coffin. Even from where I stood, I could see she looked haggard behind her thin black veil. Her two daughters looked to be about the same age as my girls, around five or so. They wept as they hugged their mother tightly. Dotty held them close, bound in grief.

I wondered if she knew about the tragedies of her husband's life. The life he'd had before her. I wondered if she'd been able to give him something close to peace. Judging by how her vacant eyes looked at her husband's coffin, I could see the traces of the love they'd shared. It only made me feel worse.

It made me think of how Theresa might act if that was me in the box beneath a flag-draped coffin. Anne and Mary would be devastated, but their mother would be another story. She'd play the widow act to the hilt. She'd probably faint at least three times before I was properly planted. She might even throw herself on the coffin for added effect. The role of the Grieving Italian Widow would be her chance to shine.

A small part of it might actually be from the grief of losing me. But I knew most of the tears would be from the loss of the extra money I brought home each week. My slice of the Tammany pie. She'd have to make do on whatever death benefit the department decided to pay out. It wouldn't be enough to keep her in the life to which my corruption had made her accustomed. Those late nights she hated came with a benefit and a price.

I figured she'd probably wring out every drop of sympathy she could manage from anyone who'd listen. She'd bore the hell out of everyone within earshot about how her husband had died a hero and how the city owed her a debt it could never repay.

Of course, she'd reluctantly accept the kindness of

the cops who lined up to comfort her. Her reluctance would be part of the act. She was a good-looking woman and wouldn't have any trouble finding my replacement. But she wouldn't look at anyone under the rank of captain. She'd already put her time in as a beat cop's wife. Any man from the lower ranks simply wouldn't do.

I guess everyone had standards, even former working girls from one of Luccania's joy houses on the Lower East Side.

Thoughts about my own death weren't making me feel any better. I decided to cheer myself up by concentrating on the funeral instead.

I'll admit that I felt a surge of pride as I saw the honor guard holding the American and police department flags. The men had been hand-picked by Carmichael. They were sharp and dignified. Their movements crisp and solemn.

Carmichael had always been a stickler for ceremony. I guess we had our Catholic upbringing to thank for that. Say what you will about us papists, but we know how to put on a show.

I guess part of my pride came from the fact that I had bled for both flags in my time. For the Stars and Stripes in the muck of France and for the department flag on the hard concrete of New York City.

I hadn't always been a cynical bastard. I'd believed in things once, just like Spann. Maybe I still did. Maybe that's why the mystery around Spann's death had hit me deep. Bone deep.

The history I'd spent the previous day uncovering had given me a clearer picture of what I had seen. Two days ago, I thought Spann was a simp. Aloof. Too good for us common corrupt types. Today, I wished I'd known him better. I felt like I already did, though it was too late to do either of us any good. I guess the old saying was true. You've got to die to be a good guy.

I looked on as all the department brass stood at attention in all their polished finery. Badges and buttons gleamed in the morning sun. The jagged skyline of the city we served stood in the background and completed the scene. The men upfront were all mirror images of Carmichael. Tall, square-jawed, silver-haired types who were broad shouldered and lean-waisted. This was Carmichael's NYPD.

But none of them outshined the chief. He stood like a granite statue beside Dotty Spann and her girls. Tall, tough and handsome. The very picture of official power.

We'd made eye contact above the heads of the rest of the mourners, so he knew where I was. When the time was right, he'd give me the nod to start moving to the back of the cemetery and wait for him there. His secretary Rosie had called me at the house earlier that morning and told me where to meet him.

Cardinal Patrick Hayes, Archbishop of New York, had celebrated the funeral mass at St. Patrick's and had come to the cemetery to conduct the final blessing. I wasn't sure if Spann was Catholic, but his personnel sheet defined his religion as 'Christian'. In Chief Carmichael's department, that made you Catholic by default.

Mayor James Walker was among the front row of mourners, clad in a dapper black suit and looking appropriately somber. Only a practiced eye like mine could see he was slightly hungover. My sources had told me he'd spent the previous evening in The Longford Lounge with a couple of show girls on his arm. Champagne and blarney flowed. Never let it be said that the Night Mayor of New York didn't know how to grieve like a champ.

I wish I could've been impressed by all the pomp and ceremony. By all the famous faces in the crowd. But I wasn't blinded by the brass and vestments. I saw the rotting wood beneath the veneer of dignity.

All I saw was a group of well-dressed, high-ranking gamblers and drunks, whore mongers and coke addicts. I saw a deputy chief who had a secret family with a black woman in Harlem. I saw a captain who'd been raising his best friend's child for the past ten years, though he didn't know it. The real father, also a captain and his best friend, was also fair haired and blue eyed, so the kid passed as legit. Mom had a type, which had made the ruse work.

I saw a lieutenant who had an expensive heroin habit that was quickly getting out of hand. I'd be delivering a reprimand from Carmichael soon. I saw a borough commander who was growing too fond of a particular opium den off Canal. I had already given him a subtle warning. My next would be more pointed.

Not even His Eminence was without sin. Cardinal Hayes had funneled money to the Irish Republican Army. It drew the ire of some powerful politicians on both sides of the pond. Men powerful enough to make the Tammany Tiger hide her fangs. Carmichael and I had personally stopped two plots against the cardinal's life. Said plotters were currently at the bottom of the Gowanus Canal. His Eminence might have denounced corruption from the pulpit on Sunday, but he still enjoyed our protection. After all, New York City was our city. It wouldn't look good if we allowed our English cousins to kill an Irish archbishop in our backyard.

I didn't begrudge any of these men their vices. I certainly didn't judge them. Why should I? Their weaknesses were my leverage. Their shortcomings were my advantage. My stock in trade. They helped Carmichael keep them in line.

A good number of the brass saw me beneath the tree and were quick to look away. Fitzgerald and Ross among them. I didn't mind. I hadn't expected those two to throw me a salute. They were the co-authors of the fiction of Spann's death. I'd like to think they felt guilty about it, but I knew the men. I knew better.

I fought the urge to light a cigarette as I watched Cardinal Hayes, in full regalia, crack open his prayer book and begin to pray over Spann's casket.

The cardinal had just finished his final blessing when the bagpipes stirred and began to play 'Amazing Grace'. I made eye contact with Carmichael, hoping he'd get me out of there before the hymn played. That one always got me. He nodded and I ducked behind the tree to head to our meeting place.

The mournful sound of the pipes trailed me as I took a slow stroll through the tombstones. I walked past the parked cars that lined the roadway. Black-suited drivers huddled together in groups as they gossiped about their charges and snuck smokes.

None of them paid much attention to me as I walked toward the bottom of the hill where Carmichael had signaled for me to go. One of my greatest strengths was how forgettable I could be. At least I still had that much going for me.

I pulled out the gold cigarette case Theresa had given me the day I had made detective. Well, the day Carmichael told me I was going to be a detective, anyway. It was a smooth case with my initials engraved on the cover in block letters. 'CVD' for Charles Vincent Doherty. I opened it and read the inscription inside the cover.

To Charlie:
Nothing but blue skies from now on.
Love, Theresa

Blue skies, all right. For her, not for us.

I selected a Lucky from the case, tapped it on the inscription and snapped the case shut, putting it back in my breast pocket.

This was why I hated cemeteries. They made me think too much about the past. About what might happen in the future. That was dangerous for a man in my line of work. A waste of time, too. My future wasn't defined by me. It was defined by circumstances beyond my control.

It was set by Carmichael's whims. At least that's how it had always been until a couple of days ago. Spann's death and the coverup that followed had set all that on its ear.

I didn't like it. I didn't like the change that loomed over me like the sullen sound of the pipes that followed me among the graves.

I had some hard questions to put to the chief. Questions he wouldn't like. Not even from an old friend like me. If I played it wrong, I'd be out in the cold right next to poor old Bixby. But Spann was worth the risk. So was my sanity.

I was already on my fourth cigarette when I saw the chief's black Chrysler Imperial glide around the road of the cemetery and come my way.

I don't know how he had managed to get away so quickly from the crowd at the grave, but he had.

I dropped my cigarette and crushed it into the grass beneath my shoe as I walked along the roadway to greet him.

I opened Carmichael's door for him when Dooley, his driver, brought the Imperial to a complete stop. "Morning, chief."

"If only it were, Charlie," he sighed as he unfolded himself and stepped out from the back seat. "If only it were."

Carmichael pulled his white gloves tighter and spoke to his driver through the open window. "Take a slow spin around the circuit and come back here when you're done. We'll be off back to the Castle when you do."

Dooley knew the drill and pulled away without another word.

That left me and the chief alone to stroll among the dead on a fine September morning.

He clasped his gloved hands behind his back as we began to walk. "'Tis a terrible thing, burying a man in the prime of his life, Charlie. Especially as good a man as John Spann. Yes, sir. As good a man as we have on the force. A true credit to us all."

That fake brogue he always trotted out for special occasions used to make me cringe. I knew the closest he'd ever gotten to Ireland was a picture postcard his grandmother had pasted to the kitchen wall when he was a kid. His parents had been born in Queens, not that I held that against them.

At least they'd had the good sense to move up to Washington Heights when Andy was still in diapers.

Fortunately, he only trotted out the lilt for fundraisers and funerals and St. Patrick's Day when people expected a bit of the blarney. He usually dropped it by lunch when he went back to his usual gruff Manhattan deadpan.

I fought off my growing nerves about my questions by lighting another cigarette. I took a healthy drag and watched the breeze carry the smoke away. "I wish I knew

Spann better, sir. He seems like he was a good man. Sounds like he had a tough life."

The chief let my reference go and frowned at my cigarette instead. "I'd expect you to have a bit more respect for the dead, Charlie."

I looked around the tombstones. Most were simple grave markers. Some were headstones. Some were statues of weeping angels with sagging wings. "I don't think they'll complain, chief."

Carmichael stifled a laugh as we kept walking. "That's one of the many reasons why I've always liked you, Charlie. You've got a gift for seeing things exactly as they are, not as you'd like them to be."

"Don't know if I'd call it a gift. Sometimes I think life would be a whole lot easier if I didn't know so damned much."

I felt sweat break out under my hat as I decided now was as good a time to hint at what was bothering me. "Ignorance has its upside. Knowing things can be a burden sometimes."

We walked in agonizing silence for a bit. I wondered if I'd been just cute enough to have cut my own throat.

Carmichael said, "I guess that depends on the kind of knowledge we carry. Sometimes it's to our benefit. Sometimes it's to our detriment. It's only a burden if we allow it to be. It comes with the badge, though they don't teach us that in training."

He brought a gloved hand to his mouth and cleared his throat. I knew something big was coming. "I can see you're carrying a particularly heavy burden yourself this morning. Would it have anything to do with your visit to the *Journal* yesterday?"

I tossed my cigarette away before I dropped it. I

TERRENCE MCCAULEY

should've known he'd find out eventually. "Who told you?"

Carmichael grinned. "I'm the one man in the whole damned department who has secrets from you, Charlie, though probably not as many as I'd like to think. I plan on keeping it that way."

His grin faded. "But I suppose I've kept you in the dark long enough and that isn't fair to you. One of the lobby guards at the *Journal* is an old partner of mine. He gives me daily reports of everyone who comes in and out of the building. It helps to know such things. Yesterday, your name came up."

I fought the urge to panic. I'd come here looking for answers, so I had no right to get cold feet now that I was about to get them. I knew if I came off as sorry, I'd be done for.

"After Spann got killed," I explained, "someone mentioned you'd worked his son's kidnapping case. You've been acting different, and I didn't want to pester you with questions, so I did some digging on my own. That's all."

"Of course." The chief closed his eyes in the comfort of knowledge. "McNally. I should've known. You ran into him when you went down to the bureau to write your report." He frowned. "That dumb bastard always talked too much. Always eager to show everyone how smart he is."

I didn't want to get Mac in trouble. "We were just talking about Spann being hit by a car and he told me the guy had a tough life. It just came up in conversation."

Carmichael side-eyed me. "And you *did* confirm it was a hit-and-run job, didn't you?"

I was almost insulted. "Of course, I did. You must've

seen my report by now. I wrote it up just the way you wanted. You know I'd never tell anyone anything different." I appealed to his ego. "Hell, you'd probably know if I had."

"I would if you'd told McNally," Carmichael said. "So would everyone in the department." I felt some of the tension go out of him. "You were curious but cautious and discreet. And loyal." He gave me a hard pat on the back. "There's no hard feelings, Charlie. I mean it. You're used to knowing why I do things and this time I kept you in the dark. I also didn't treat you very well while I did it." He cleared his throat again. "I'm sorry about that."

I stopped dead in my tracks.

It took Carmichael a couple of steps to notice. When he did, he turned around. "What the hell is the matter with you?"

"You apologized."

"So?"

"You never apologize."

He drew himself up to his full height. "That's because I'm never wrong." Then he grabbed my arm and shoved me ahead of him. "Get moving, you idiot. We've got important business to discuss."

I took off my hat and wiped the sweat from my brow with the back of my hand.

Carmichael laughed. "Jesus, Charlie. Were you really that nervous?"

I stuck my hat back on my head. "I read some pretty awful stuff at the *Journal*. Pile on you changing Spann's cause of death and how short you've been with me lately and I didn't know what to think."

He clasped his hands behind him again as we kept

walking. "I had my reasons. And probably not the reasons you think."

"I can't think of a reason," I admitted. "That's why I was worried."

"Well quit worrying because you've got one hell of a job in front of you. And we don't have a moment to lose."

I knew Andy wasn't one to exaggerate. If he said it was serious, then it was. "What do you need me to do?"

"Right now, I just need you to listen. The Spann boy's kidnapping was horrible in more ways than one. If you had gone into our files, you wouldn't have found much more than what the stories the *Journal* printed, or the other papers for that matter. It's still the damnedest case of my career and it's haunted me all these years."

I knew that meant something. Carmichael's Tammany connections aside, I knew he'd come up the hard way.

The chief continued. "Little Tommy just up and vanished, Charlie. We only had a vague description of the bastard who'd grabbed him and there was no sign of the kid anywhere. No blood. No torn clothing. Not even evidence of a struggle. Nothing to tell us what happened to him after he was lured away from his yard. We checked all the boroughs, too and came up with nothing."

I didn't know much about kidnappings, but I knew enough to say, "That's not unheard of, boss. I know how you work. If you didn't find anything, there was nothing to find." I wasn't kissing his ass. It was the truth.

Carmichael kept talking. "I stuck with that case for more than a year before my bosses finally threatened to write me up if I didn't hand it over to Missing Persons. But Spann never gave up and who could blame him?

He searched everywhere. He followed up with departments in other parts of the country. He built files. Tracked news articles. Suspects. He became obsessed, even more so after his wife killed herself. His grief turned him into one hell of a detective. He got his shield all on his own merit. Not an easy thing to do in this system of ours."

I hadn't known that. Spann had always been a detective since I'd known of him. "That poor bastard."

"I bet you don't think too highly of Fitzgerald and Ross after they backed up that nonsense about Spann's death being a hit-and-run job," Carmichael said. "Don't be too hard on them. The three of us never stopped helping Spann with his case over the years. We gave him access to any files that might help him. We sent out interdepartmental notices for him. We put him in touch with people from other states who might be able to help him. Other countries, too."

This was the first I was hearing of any of this. It made me wonder what else Carmichael might be holding back from me. Because what I didn't know could hurt us both. But that was a worry for another time. "But why lie about Spann's shooting in the first place? That's the part I don't get. Was it because his killer matched the description of The Wandering Man?"

"No." Carmichael let out a deep breath and looked down at the ground as we continued to walk. "You know I trust you, Charlie. I trust you with my career. My life. The lives of my family. No one knows me as well as you do, and no one ever will." He nudged me with his shoulder. "You even know more about me than Helen does."

"I sure hope so," I said, "or else you two wouldn't still be married."

He lowered his voice. "True, and believe it or not,

what I'm about to tell you is worse than anything you could ever tell her about me."

That opened my eyes, because I knew a hell of a lot that Helen Carmichael should never know. "Okay."

"It's something that only Fitzgerald and Ross know because it's dangerous. To me. To the department. To the Hall. Even to the city."

Like I said, Carmichael didn't exaggerate so I knew if he said it was bad, it must be worse than that. "I'm ready."

"I know you are." Carmichael lifted his head again and kept walking. "Spann's pursuit of the man who took his child was as thorough as it was extensive. He'd spent the last ten years running down every lead he could. I lost track of the number of times he ran into a brick wall. But then, two months ago, he found something."

"What?"

"He found something in an old batch of files. The case of a young Negro boy in Harlem who went missing two years ago. Lester Washington. The lad was about sixteen or seventeen at the time and eager for summer work. Like Tommy, Lester had just disappeared one day without a trace. Spann sat down with them. He said the Washingtons are a close family, and it wasn't like Lester to disappear like that. He didn't drink, didn't smoke and did very well in school. They'd spent two years wondering what could've happened to him. That is until the day they received a letter."

I knew I should've let Carmichael keep talking at his own pace, but my curiosity got the better of me. "A letter? What did it say?"

But Carmichael wouldn't be rushed. "Spann was intrigued by the case and met with the family. They let him read the note. It was unsigned and typewritten. It came on nice stationery, so they assumed it must be some kind of official notice. But when they opened the letter, they saw it described in detail how the author had taken and killed Lester."

I almost stopped walking. "What?"

Carmichael went on. "The man who wrote the letter said he knew Lester was looking for work outside the city. That's how he had convinced the young man to follow him with the promise of work on his farm upstate. It went on to tell him that their son was dead. I'm afraid it went into some pretty gory descriptions of how he had killed their son."

Answers and questions blurred in my mind. Details flew in from all different directions and began to fall in place.

I didn't like the picture it was showing. "Those poor parents," was all I could think to say.

"It gets much worse," Carmichael continued. "The letter was signed 'The Wandering Man'."

If I hadn't spent the previous day at the *Journal*, the name would've meant nothing to me. But today it meant everything.

And it opened the cellar door to a world of ugly possibilities. "Did Spann think it was real? Maybe the guy was just glomming on to an old case he'd read about years before?"

"That's what Spann thought at first," Carmichael said. "He never let his personal feelings about his son's case get in the way of his objectivity. He was thorough and decided the letter was real before he brought it to my attention. I agreed he was on to something and told him to keep digging."

"Then what?"

"He revisited files of other missing cases of other

boys around the same age who had gone missing at the same time. Boys who were white. Boys who matched Lester Washington's description. Many of the cases solving white children had been closed. But the number of the Negro boys from Harlem who still had open cases was nothing short of horrifying."

"How horrifying?"

"Fifty."

Bile rose in my throat.

Carmichael didn't notice. "Spann started contacting the parents of the missing boys to see if any of them had received letters. Of the parents he had been able to reach, about twenty of them had received similar letters over the past decade. Some more than one. Each of them as cruel and explicit as the letter the Washington family had received."

The bile in my mouth receded and I was finally able to talk. "Did the families report it?"

"Most of them had." Carmichael's jaw clenched. "But there didn't seem to be much interest from some of our detectives. They didn't see a string of missing Negro boys as being much of a problem. Or worth their efforts."

A rash of kidnappings and our men had done nothing about it. I wish I could've said I was surprised, but I wasn't.

Carmichael went on. "I looked into it personally as part of my ongoing Harlem plan. I even went after men who'd since retired from the force. Some swear they'd never heard from the families, though the files proved they were lying. A few had the decency to admit they didn't care about some missing black kids and wrote it off as boys being boys."

I noticed Carmichael had balled his gloved hands

into fists until the bones cracked. "You know how I hate that kind of attitude, Charlie."

I did and I knew why, too. As if I'd forgotten, Carmichael reminded me.

"Harriet raised me as if I was her own son. She was more of a mother to me than my own mother ever was."

Harriet had been the nanny Carmichael's parents had hired to raise him. They couldn't really afford one, even though his old man was a ward boss for the Hall in the Heights, but appearances had been everything to Carmichael's family. "I was there, Andy. I remember. She was good to me, too."

Carmichael wasn't talking to me anymore. He was looking straight-ahead and into the past. "It could've gone either way for you and me for a while. It was always going to be about the law, but which side of it we'd be on. God, how that woman gave me hell whenever I stepped out of line. Old Joe, too. My parents were too busy ingratiating themselves with the Hall to pay any attention to me."

I knew. I'd been there for all of it. "Your parents did it for you, Andy. You know that. Look at where it got you. The top job."

Carmichael scowled. "What good is being the chief of police if you can't control your own people? What good is it if your own men ignore a monster preying on young boys. I don't care if they're in Harlem or on Park Avenue, they deserved justice."

I thought quick and came up with a way to calm him down. He was no good to anyone when his temper got rolling. "You said these letters have been coming to folks for ten years. You've only been chief for six months. What could you have done about it?"

But he was still hung up on Harriet. She had always

been a sore spot with him. He'd been heart-broken when she moved back to Georgia after her husband died. I knew he sent her money once a month and kept a picture of her on his desk back at the Castle.

"I could've paid more attention even before I was chief," he said. "And now that I'm chief, it's my problem now. I'm responsible."

Carmichael had always been popular among the rank-and-file, but the only knock against him with the men was his 'Harlem policy'. They said he was 'too soft on the darkies'.

Carmichael made a monthly pilgrimage uptown to Queen Madame Saint-Claire. She ran the numbers racket and, as such, ran Harlem. He had approached the Queen and bent the knee. He pledged allegiance, cooperation and protection as long as she kept uptown crime to a dull roar. He even offered to take less of a cut of the action than his predecessors. She'd complied and Harlem had been quiet ever since.

As part of the deal, Carmichael issued a decree to the underworld and his own men alike. Beatings and shakedowns in Harlem were *verboten*. Peace was better for all legitimate and illegitimate concerns. Blood was bad for business. Any beef was to be hashed out with words, not weapons.

Meyer Lansky and Archie Doyle and Bumpy Johnson got the same message as the boys in blue. Any violation of said decree meant Carmichael's wrath. *Don't test me. I will burn you down.*

The boys at the Hall didn't like the ripples the edict had caused but wrote it off as a new chief putting his stamp on things. In a few months, things would go back to normal.

But in the six months since Carmichael had taken

office, Harlem had been Eden. No blood had been spilled. Felony arrests went up. Bums and junkies were kept inside. Working girls stayed off the streets and plied their trade indoors. Regular people began to feel safe in their own neighborhood from cop and crook alike.

All of them thought Carmichael was to thank for it. Little did they know that the maternal love of an Irish cop for his black nanny had been the reason for it all.

I was glad when Carmichael returned to the present. "When Spann told me about the letters two months ago, I pulled him off everything else and gave him a special assignment. Build a case, find leads and stop this lunatic before he has the chance to kill anyone else. He briefed me on his progress twice a week, usually when I knew you wouldn't be around."

"Thanks for the trust," I said, immediately regretting it.

"I didn't know if we had anything, Charlie," the chief admitted. "The letters didn't give us any new suspects. But Spann believed the letters were still important. He figured out the envelopes and stationery were all from exactly the same stock of paper. He thought if we could trace where the paper had come from, we might be able to find who'd sent it."

I hadn't thought of that. At least it explained why Spann was in the stationery store when Carmichael had sent me to get him. "What about postmarks?"

"All mailed from Grand Central Terminal," he said. "Could've been anyone. But the stationery angle intrigued Spann. He was late for one of our meetings when I sent you to bring him back. Fitzgerald, Ross and I decided it was time to bring you in on this since Spann hadn't turned up anything new in a couple of weeks."

"Considering he got shot coming out of the

stationery store," I said, "it looks like he was closer to the truth than you thought."

"Which makes it all the more important for you to find The Wanderer as quickly as possible."

The chief had just dumped a lot of things on me, but I still had a job to do. That job being to protect the chief. I asked him the first question that came to mind. "Will the Harlem families keep quiet?"

"For a while," Carmichael said. "Spann kept in weekly contact with them and made sure none of them knew there were any other victims except their son. As long as none of them decides to talk to the press for some reason, we should be fine for a week or two."

I moved that hot pot to the back burner and picked up a new one. "Does Spann's widow know what happened?"

"No. We insisted on a closed casket due to the injuries he suffered from being run over. She was in no state to argue or ask many questions. I don't expect her to. I'll handle her personally if it comes to that."

"What about the undertaker?" I asked. "He saw the body. Can he be trusted?"

"He's into Archie Doyle for quite a bit of money. I made sure he was aware that I can make that go away or increase his debt should the need arise."

That took care of my initial concerns, but not all of them.

"What about Fitzgerald and Ross? Will they hold their water?"

"They have as much to lose as I do so they'll keep quiet for now. But if this finds its way into the press, it'll be every man for themselves, but that's to be expected."

Not even I could begrudge them self-preservation. The urban jungle was still a jungle. Loyalty only got you so far for so long. Like Booker had reminded me, Tammany took care of its own, but only when it was convenient.

Now that I knew the stakes, I was all in. "Tell me what I need to do, and it's done."

We resumed our walk. "I need you to pick up where Spann left off. I think you're right about his death meaning he was closer to capturing this maniac than he thought. That's why I need you to retrace his steps and go on from there."

He held out a gloved hand with an old skeleton key. "Ross took this off Spann's corpse before Kronauer arrived."

I took it and quickly pocketed it. "What does it open?"

"The door at the half level just below the back staircase to my office," Carmichael said. "You've passed it a million times and probably never noticed it. An old door that looks like it hasn't been opened in a hundred years."

I knew exactly what he was talking about. It was so forgettable that I'd never thought what might be behind it. "What'll I find?"

"Spann was working the case from there. It's an old storage space the maintenance men use from time to time. I ordered them to clear it out and confiscated all keys. You have one. I have the other. I've left some other evidence Ross took from Spann's body for you to review. You'll find the letters Spann was able to get back from some of the families who still had copies."

I pocketed the key. "I'll get right on it as soon as I get back."

"I'll expect your first report tomorrow morning at nine o'clock sharp," Carmichael told me. "I'm afraid it'll mean you'll have to work all night, but it has to be done.

I want your report in person and verbal. Nothing is to be written down from here on in."

Speaking of written down, I remembered something. "Kronauer's report will need to be handled. I read it and it's nothing like the one I wrote up."

"It's already being handled," Carmichael assured me. "And Kronauer won't be punished. He was only doing his job. He knows the game."

So did I. What's more, I knew myself. I knew what I could and couldn't do. This mess was shaping up to be something that was beyond me.

Carmichael seemed to be able to read my mind. "What's troubling you, Charlie?"

I'd learned my lesson about holding back from him, so I came right out with it. "Spann and I are different kinds of detectives, Andy. I've never built a murder case before. Nothing that ever had to stand up in court. You know that."

"I know," Carmichael said as we kept walking. "That's why I'm only asking you to pick up where Spann left off. I'm not asking you to build a case, Charlie. I have no intention of bringing this to trial."

He stopped walking and looked down at me. He wasn't Andy anymore. He was Chief Carmichael again. "You heard that right. I'm ordering you to find this man, run him down and put a bullet in his brain. I want him left in an alley or dumped in the river without any means of identification. When The Wanderer is dead, our troubles will be over."

The key in my pocket suddenly felt a lot heavier. I heard the words plain enough. It was their meaning that bothered me. "Andy, I—"

Carmichael cut me off. "You're a cop sworn to protect the people of this city. You've also got the added burden of protecting me and the Hall. All of that's in danger if this crazy son of a bitch ever sees the inside of a booking room much less the inside of a courtroom. A trial will raise questions none of us are prepared to answer. It'll start a firestorm that will burn down everything we hold dear, including the two of us."

I wasn't so sure. "With all the dirt we've got on them, they wouldn't dare."

"That's why we're dangerous," Carmichael said. "With what we've got on them, they couldn't afford to let us live. We might talk to save our own skins and cut a deal. That makes us a liability. And we know how our friends deal with liabilities."

He bent at the waist and spoke directly into my ear. "This thing ends with someone catching a bullet in the head, Charlie. If it's not The Wandering Man, it'll be us."

Like I said, Carmichael wasn't one to exaggerate. I knew every word he'd just said was true. "Okay, Andy. Okay."

And just like that, I'd agreed to murder someone. I never thought it could be that simple.

Carmichael stood upright again. He even looked relieved. "Besides, it's not like killing is new to you. I know your service record, both from the department and while you were in the war. You racked up quite an impressive number of kills in France. Around forty, wasn't it?"

It was fifty-three. Numbers had never been his strength. "That was war."

Carmichael looked down at me. The brim of his cap shadowed his eyes. "So is this. And it's one we have to win."

We stood together in silence as his Imperial rolled

along the roadway. We were silent because there really wasn't anything more to be said.

I'd been given my orders. Find The Wandering Man and kill him. It didn't get any plainer than that.

Dooley brought the car to a stop beside us. This time, I didn't offer to open the back door for Carmichael, and he didn't look for me to do so.

He climbed into the backseat and shut the door behind him. Through the open window, he said. "Don't forget. Nine o'clock tomorrow morning. Not a moment later. I'll be looking forward to hearing what you have to say."

He told Dooley to take him back to the Castle, and the car sped away down the path that had been cut through the grassy graves.

I took my time heading back to my car. I had come to the cemetery intent on getting answers. I was leaving it with more than I had bargained for.

A lunatic had been roaming the streets and killing black kids for a decade. Now it was up to me to find him and kill him.

I looked to my left and saw a stone angel kneeling atop a headstone. Its wings were open, its hands were raised to the heavens, smiling at the approaching glory.

"What are you so happy about?" I asked the statue before lighting a new cigarette as I headed back to my car.

I had a long walk ahead of me. And an even longer night to come.

Chapter 8

On my way back to my car, I looked around when I heard a *clack*.

I knew that sound. It hadn't come from a bird or a cricket. It hadn't come from someone stepping on a branch or a twig, either.

The second *clack* confirmed it. It was a bug, alright, but not the insect kind. A shutter bug. Probably a photographer from one of the tabloids hiding among the tombstones taking my picture.

I figured he must be a stringer. None of the pros would've been dumb enough to follow us. Crossing Carmichael didn't exactly lead to a long career for the press boys.

I didn't know how long he'd been there or worse, what he might have heard. They were questions I needed answered, even before I began to hunt The Wandering Man. If this reporter caught even the slightest whiff of what we'd just talked about, my investigation could be over before it even started.

I stopped walking and blew a plume of smoke high

into the air. I wanted to give the kid some time to compose himself lest he made like a rabbit and run away.

"I know you're out there," I said loud enough for him to hear, "so you might as well come out. Let's talk. If you ask nicely, I might even give you an item for your column."

Another clack was followed by a weak voice. "I don't have a column."

That was my hook. "A quote from me will go a long way to helping you get one. Come on out. It's a long walk back to my car and I'm lonesome. We can share the air on the way."

I watched a tall gawk lugging a camera step out from behind a tree. I pegged him at maybe twenty-five. He'd managed to tuck a thick mess of curly black hair under a green hunters cap. The fur-lined ear flaps were pulled down, but at least he hadn't tied them under his chin.

He had cut the fingers off his gloves to allow himself to manipulate the camera shutter easier. He was painfully thin, and his Adam's apple looked like it was straining against his throat.

He was over six feet tall and walked toward me with all of the confidence of a newborn fawn. "I know who you are." His voice quivered, but he'd done his best to make it sound like a threat. "You're Charlie Doherty. Carmichael's black hand."

"Guilty as charged." I tried a smile. "Sounds like you graduated top of your class in Stringer School. But you're not old enough to call me Charlie. Let's stick to Detective Doherty and work our way up from there."

I extended my hand to my new friend. "This is the part where you tell me your name."

The gesture put him at ease, and he shifted his

camera from his right hand to his left so we could shake. "I'm Leon Street. I'm a stringer with—"

I forgot about the handshake and nailed him with a right cross to the gut. I snatched his camera before he dropped it and let him sink to his knees on his own steam. I left my slapper tucked in the back of my pants. No reason to use it on a newbie so soon into our budding friendship.

"That's for being a creep," I told him. "Any other reporters follow you out here or are you the only bright boy in the group?"

"No," Leon gasped. "They thought I was crazy to follow you."

"Now you know why." I opened his camera and ripped out the film. "No one takes pictures of the chief without his approval. Got it?"

"No," Leon grunted. "You're the one who's got it. That film had some nice shots of the widow and the coffin. Now I'm out a pay day thanks to you."

"We'll talk about that when you get up. Just do it fast, will you? I'm getting a pain in my neck looking down at you."

I rolled his name around in my mind as he got to his feet. Leon Street. The chief liked to keep files on all the boys who covered him regularly. Their editors and publishers, too. I kept it updated with all sorts of nasty tidbits I picked up along the way. It came in handy when we needed leverage to kill a negative article.

But none of the dirt I had would be strong enough to keep The Wandering Man off the front pages. It would take an act of God to keep any editor worth his salt from running a hot item like that and I couldn't really blame them.

I waited until he got to his feet to ask my next question. "Who are you stringing for?"

"The *Mirror*." He rubbed his sore belly. "But not after this. They wanted me to get pictures of the Spann funeral. Had a bunch of good ones, too, until you came along and ruined it."

"Serves you right for trusting a stranger." I stuffed the film in my pocket as I handed back his camera. "Sorry for belting you like that, but the chief doesn't like people trailing him without him knowing about it." I shrugged it off. "You know people get all sorts of squirrely notions once they become famous."

Street cradled his camera against his belly. "You're the one who hit me and caused me a day's pay, not the chief."

"I get paid to protect him," I told him. "But you coming out here against the advice of your fellow scribes shows me something."

"Shows me something, too," Street moaned. "Shows me that I'm nuts."

I needed to get him to tell me what he'd overheard, and I needed to know quickly. The fastest way to a reporter's heart was a story. "How about we start over? How about I give you something better than a bunch of lousy pictures?"

"Yeah?" The kid looked like he was afraid I might hit him again, but he was curious. "Like what?"

"Like an exclusive interview with Chief Carmichael himself. That'll soothe things over with your editor, won't it?"

His belly seemed to ache a little less with the promise of an exclusive dangling in front of him. "He sent me out here to get pictures, not write a column. And the chief's already left. How can I interview him now?"

I found a card in my coat pocket and turned it over to the back. I pulled out a pen from my jacket pocket and began writing. "I saw Krajnak standing with the rest of you over at the grave." I finished writing my note and handed the card to him. "Hand him this and tell him to give you some of the shots he took. Those, combined with the interview should make you employee of the month."

The kid looked at the card like I'd just given him the keys to the city. "Thanks, but my editor's going to ask why he'd talk to me instead of one of the other fellas he knows better?"

"Tell him you caught him on his way to the car. Tell him your youthful enthusiasm won him over. Tell him anything you want. He'll call the chief's office for confirmation, and we'll confirm it." I poked him in the chest with a finger, which caused him to flinch. "I'll tell you what to say and it'll be as good as the chief telling you himself. You got a pen and paper? I'll give you the whole thing right now, assuming you can walk, talk and write at the same time."

We began walking and Leon Street had no trouble keeping pace with me as he dug out a notebook from his back pocket.

"I'll even write the headline for you. 'Carmichael Mourns Detective. Bright light of NYPD will be missed.'"

The more I thought about it, the more I bought into it myself. There'd be plenty of pictures of a stoic Carmichael at the funeral. Street's story would show something the chief had been lacking lately. A soul. People would see another side of him. A side they might like. And a little humanity right now could go a long way for the chief in our current predicament.

Leon Street managed to avoid dropping his camera as he produced a pen and pencil. "Okay. Go ahead. I'm ready."

But I wasn't ready to be generous just yet. "How long were you trailing us anyhow?"

"Since you left the service," Street told me. "I hung back to keep you from seeing me. I didn't know what would happen, so you can imagine my surprise when the chief showed up. I dodged his driver, but never got closer than that tree back there." He frowned. "I didn't even get many clear pictures of the two of you, so it was a wasted effort."

I'd been lied to enough to know the truth when I heard it. Leon Street was truth personified. He'd been too far away to hear anything we had said. It looked like I'd finally caught a break that day.

"Hope your pencil's sharp because I've got a lot to tell you. And I'll expect to read most of it in the *Mirror* tonight over dinner."

"Don't worry," the kid told me. "It's sharp enough."

"Good. See, now we can be pals."

Leon Street winced as he held his arms close to his ribs. "You treat all your friends this way?"

He had a point. "At least I didn't break your camera."

Chapter 9

AFTER I SHOOED Leon Street away, my drive back to the Castle was a blur.

My run-in with the kid gnawed at me. I'd allowed us to be ambushed by a cub reporter. A lousy stringer at that. It was blind luck on his part, but I should've known he was there. I'd missed him. I'd been distracted by the Spann case. I'd let the basics of my job slide. That was dangerous. We couldn't afford such slip-ups now.

All I could do was thank God he hadn't been close enough to hear anything. The interview I'd fed him seemed to more than satisfy. I made sure Carmichael came off as a commander who had just lost a good man. The city needed more good men like Detective John Spann. He would serve as the model for the kind of detective the department – and the city – would have in Andrew Carmichael's police force.

It was harmless enough. There was nothing new in it and I doubted the chief would object. What's more, Street had been grateful. I knew he had bought it. I only hoped his editor would be just as gullible.

I made a mental note to remember to tell the chief about my run in with Street. I didn't want him reading the interview in the evening edition without knowing about it beforehand. We had more important things to worry about. I know I did.

Because the head of the biggest police department in the country had just ordered me to assassinate a man.

And it wasn't just some crook who'd robbed the wrong guy out or some punk who'd thrown a cop a beating. This was a professional monster who had easily hidden from us for more than a decade.

A man who was better at committing his crimes than we were at catching him. A man who not even Spann, with all his skill and motive had been able to catch. A man who had even bested Carmichael when he'd searched for him ten years before.

I didn't stand a chance against a man like that.

The chief's pep-talk in the cemetery aside, I wasn't fooling myself. I was a bagman. An errand boy. I dug up dirt and kept files. I kept the troops in line through terror and guile. I might've put a bullet in The Wandering Man, but I'd gotten lucky. I couldn't match wits with a guy that cunning.

My only solace was that if my bullet didn't kill him, he'd be laid up for a couple of days to recover. Back wounds were tricky. If I'd hit or nicked his kidney, he'd need a hospital if he wasn't already dead. Hospitals reported gunshot wounds to the police. I'd put out a call to all precincts to let me know if any reports came across their desk. It wasn't much, but it was a start.

Even working through the night wouldn't give me much time to catch up to where Spann had left off, but it was all the time I had.

The idea of killing The Wandering Man didn't

bother me as much as I'd let on to Carmichael. I'd lost any notion of divine sparks of life and the Sixth Commandment back in France. All that stuff about love for one's fellow man went out the window when they started firing machine guns and mortars at me.

No, killing this lunatic didn't bother me.

The fact that he'd killed Spann did.

Because it not only meant Spann was close to catching him. The Wanderer *knew* Spann was close to catching him. *How?*

He'd known where he'd be and when to kill him. *How?*

I didn't know how, but it meant The Wanderer was on to us now. I hoped the answer would be waiting for me in the old storeroom Spann had been using as an office.

I hoped Spann had been a good enough detective to help solve his own murder.

I threw the Ford into a reserved spot in front of the Castle and headed inside. It was just after noon by then and the place was a hive of activity. Cops and secretaries going out to lunch. Some coming back from an early lunch. All of them had big waves and bright smiles for Good Ol' Charlie as we passed each other. Banking that good will for a rainy day.

I walked up the main marble staircase like I always did but was careful to cut over a floor below Valhalla. I kept my head down and moved fast. I didn't want to risk running into McNally again. He might have even more questions for me that I didn't want to risk answering.

I made it through unnoticed and took a left up a corridor to the back stairs. I found the key in my pocket and stood in front of the storeroom door for a while. I ran my thumb over the ridges of the key, knowing that as soon as I opened that door, my entire life would change.

I hadn't felt like that the day I'd been sworn in as a cop or as a marine. I hadn't felt it when I'd taken that first step on French soil or when I'd reached New York Harbor after the war, either. I'd been a kid back then.

This was different. More deliberate. I felt like I was trespassing because I was. Chief's orders or no, I was opening a door into a man's private hell. A hunt he'd carried on every day of his life for the past ten years.

A hell that was about to become all mine.

According to the chief, it's already yours, dummy. Might as well get on with it.

I slid the key in the lock and turned it. The lock opened easily but the old door had been painted over so many times that it had swollen in its frame. It took me a couple of tries to force it in before it gave way.

I was greeted by a damp darkness and a cloud of dust that filled my lungs, sending me into a coughing fit. The light from the stairway was the only light to see by. I used my heel to keep the door open while I fumbled for a light switch. I found a pull chain dangling on my right and gave it a tug.

A weak yellow light came to life, and I let the door slam shut on its own. I was alone with Spann's ghosts.

I pulled a handkerchief from my back pocket and wiped away the tears brought on by my coughing fit. The air in the room was close and humid. The smell of stale rat shit and poison made my eyes water all over again. I looked around for a window to open, but all I found were brick walls.

The space was less of a room and more of a walled off portion of the stairwell. Thick waterpipes and valves converged at all angles, emerging from the walls and disappearing into the floors. The weak yellow bulb cast a gloomy light on everything, not that there was much to see.

A small steel desk had found its way in there along with a chipped wooden chair on wheels. The seat looked like it'd had a leather pad once that had been long since worn away.

The light was still swinging and throwing nasty shadows. I managed to grab hold of the chain and pull it steady before I got seasick.

The steadier light allowed me to see what was on the desk. Files and notepads piled high. The floor around the desk was lined with boxes with tops that barely covered thousands of overflowing papers of all shapes, sizes and colors. Brown papers and yellow papers and some that were green. I didn't know if they had always been that color or had turned that way from age.

Each box was labeled. Each box was a case. A life lost to The Wandering Man's whims. Every box was a step Spann had taken in his hunt for the man who had taken his son and other sons throughout the city. A step he had taken to find his own murderer, though he hadn't known it at the time.

I knew any one of these boxes might hold a clue about who had killed Spann and all those young men. A clue I knew I'd miss because this was a lot of information to get through before nine the next morning.

I looked at the piles of paper on the desk and the dozens of boxes all around it. I'd already become used to the stale air and let out a long breath. "Well, it ain't much but it's all yours, Charlie boy. Best dig in."

I sat in the chair and wheeled it closer to the desk. I saw Spann had scrounged up a couple of desk lamps and turned them on. Lucky for me, they worked.

They illuminated the last professional acts of Detective John Spann, NYPD.

A crumpled paper with blood on the edges sat atop the pile. I figured that must be the paper Carmichael had told me that Ross took off Spann's body.

I opened it up and found it was folded around an envelope. The paper was thick stock and even to my untrained fingers, it felt different.

I turned the envelope over and saw it was addressed to The Washington Family at an address in East Harlem. One-hundred-and-twenty-seventh Street to be exact.

There was no return address on the upper left part of the envelope because someone had cut it out and pasted a small piece of paper in its place. Strange, but I'd come back to that. The post mark was from Grand Central. No leads there.

I went back to the pasted envelope where the return address could be. I ran my thumb over it and found it was exactly the same stock as the envelope and letter.

Interesting.

I held the envelope up to the desk lamp and looked through it. The paste was clear. No fingerprints evident.

I lifted the flap and looked inside the envelope. The Wanderer had pasted another piece of paper on the inside, too. Same stock.

Interesting and strange.

I found a fresh pad of paper on the desk and a pen and began writing notes of my own.

No prints on the paste.

Why cut out the return address?

Why cover both sides?

The answer hit me as soon as I finished writing.

'Stationery' I wrote and underlined it twice. Our boy was using stationery with the return address already

printed on the envelope. He didn't want us tracing him, so he cut it out. Smart.

It also explained why Spann was at a stationery store before he died. He was trying to trace the origins of the paper. Who made it? Who might order this type of stock? Judging by what I'd seen of his questioning of the store clerk, he hadn't gotten very far.

I set the envelope aside and opened the letter. I didn't blame the Washington Family for thinking it was official. It was properly formatted and neatly typed.

But once I got past the form, the true horror of the contents hit me hard. The mistakes in the letter are The Wanderer's, not mine.

The Washington Residence
231 East 127th Street
New York City

Dear Mr. and Mrs. Washington (XX):

I write this letter in relation to the disappearance of your young son, Lester. I not only had the extreme pleasure of knowing him during his brief life. I had the honor of taking said life from him.

Your son was a most industrious young man. Hard working and eager for opportunity. He sold his papers on the corner with pride. He had a sharp mind and an easy smile. Perhaps that was what attracted me to him in the first place. Ambition can make even the dullest flower bloom fullest; don't you think?

Not that your Lester was dull, mind. Quite the opposite. If anything, it was his good humor and willingness to work that allowed me to take his life so easily.

I'm sure by now you've heard from his friends and numerous acquaintances that he had the promise of good work and was on his way for an interview for the same. He was in such good spirit that day. It was an oppressively hot day in August. Do you remember? I know I do. I shall never forget it, for I even mentioned the heat to him, but he was too kind to complain. He said the heat never bothered him. Nor hard work, either.

He obviously hoped I would find that encouraging, which I did, but for reasons beyond his comprehension at the time. But I knew right then and there his earnestness would make him easy prey. I knew he would make a fine addition to my Menagerie of Misfortunates as I have come to call them fondly. I assure you I have a most impressive collection and he made a prized addition indeed.

Stop reading here if you don't want to know how he died, but I pray you'll continue. It's a beautiful story in its own way.

He inquired about where my farm was located and I told him it was just north of here, less than an hour's ride by train. In the event you show this letter to the police, you can tell them to not bother looking for one. There may be farms up there, but none of them are mine. I fashion myself a farmer, but not of crops. I am a farmer of souls. The younger, the better.

Lester fretted about taking such a journey without telling his parents where he was going. He was such a conscientious boy, wasn't he? I assured him that he would be up and back long before supper and you would hardly miss him.

He was hesitant at first, but I won him over with the promise of the grand story he would be able to share over your humble dinner table. I told him how proud you would be at the news that he had found himself a job. A good one, too. Better than selling newspapers on a street corner all day. Honest work and a better wage that would help his family. How could such a boy refuse such an offer?

I assure you that I can be quite pervasive when I choose.

We took a train north. To where, I'll never tell as it may lead to my capture, but you may rest assured it is a quiet, secluded place.

We were the only people at the station and when the train pulled away, I'd like to think we were the only people around for miles. I know we were the only people near the station. I made sure of that.

I remember how happy he was. He said he'd spent all of his life in the city except for that time you all took him to Coney Island when he was younger. I'd like to think he was smiling then, but I can't tell you that. You see, by then, I had allowed him to walk ahead of me.

I didn't want him to see the knife in my hand. A knife, as fortune would have it, that had just been sharpened that very mourning by a street vendor near the same corner where your son sold his newspapers.

I should recommend that vendor to you for I assure you he did a most excellent job. But to do so might lead you to me and we couldn't have that, now could we? What would be the fun in that?

I waited until we were a good bit away from the station when I decided the time was right to strike. There was a fair distance between us then as Lester took in all the nature around him.

I was able to run up behind him with a good amount of speed and tackle him into an overgrown drainage ditch off the side of the road. Before he knew what was happening, I drew the knife across his throat with the practiced hand of a concert violinist. I assure you my stroke was as deep and thorough as it was deadly.

That's not to say your son gave up easily. Far from it. He was a strapping lad and keeping him subdued was no easy task. But he was dying after all and I had renewed strength from the thrill of the hunt pumping through my vains.

I stayed atop him until his struggle was over. You may take comfort in the fact that he did not die alone. I was there until the very end. It was a peaceful way to die, Mr. and Mrs. Washington. Better than many of us get.

I waited until I was sure he had passed before I took my trophy. I won't bore you with the details of what it is, but as I said before, it made a fine addition to my Menagerie of Misfortunates.

I know you may question my motives for sending you this letter. And, as Lester's parents, you're entirely entitled to do so. But I thought enough time had passed to let you know that your son is, indeed, dead and that his passing meant a lot to me.

I understand you may be too old by now to have another Lester, but I know you have other children.

Take comfort in the fact that I have not come for them.

My journeys take me elsewhere.

With sincerest condolences and fondest memories,
   The Wandering Man

I let the note slip from my fingers. I didn't want to touch it. I didn't even want to be in the same building with it, much less have it right in front of me.

I couldn't look away from it, either.

I thought I'd seen evil before. In the trenches and in Belleau Wood and the streets of New York. I was wrong. I'd never known true evil until I'd read that letter.

I knew anyone could kill for any number of reasons. War. A temporary loss of control. Jealousy. Fear. I'd known men who killed just because they felt like it.

But that note changed things. The words. The intent of sending it to the parents, knowing the pain it would cause them. The words on the page. The stark horror of a man's polluted mind neatly typewritten on fine stationery mailed to the family of the young man he'd killed.

It was the care and forethought that made the letter even more disgusting. That doesn't really capture what I felt when I read it, but it's as close to a description as I can get.

As the shock of the words and deed began to sink into my mind, I thought less about what the letter said and focused on what the letter was.

It was a confession. It had come from the killer. It was evidence.

Quit acting like a father and start acting like a cop.

I took my pad and my pen and began adding to my notes. I treated the letter like a crime scene.

Stationery – fancy, expensive, thick stock.

I read the words for themselves, not their meaning. Misspellings – 'vains' instead of 'veins'. Other mistakes. I wrote them all down.

The language itself seemed fake, like someone trying too hard to sound smart. I couldn't write a letter like that if I'd tried.

The type itself was another clue. I picked up the letter again and held it under the light. The line on the 'e's was faded and almost looked like 'c's. The ink was a bit faded, too, but that was probably due to the ribbon. That could be changed out easily enough and probably already had been since the letter had been typed.

But that line in the 'e's wasn't from any ribbon. It was a problem with the key itself. Could be from wear and tear.

I made another note: Typewriter – old?

Even the postage stamp gave me a clue. Mailed from Grand Central on purpose. The writer wanted to blend in. He didn't want to be remembered. Did he think he'd be remembered? Why?

I set the letter and envelope aside and began digging

into the rest of the pile on Spann's desk. Whatever was here was current. It had led him to that stationery store.

I checked my watch. Two o'clock on the button. My first report to Carmichael was at nine the following morning. It may have seemed like a lot of time, but I knew it wasn't. I didn't have a second to lose.

Chapter 10

AT NINE O'CLOCK THE next morning, I took my notepad and files with me up the back stairs to the chief's office. My back and legs were stiff. My knees were sore from sitting so long. My shoulders ached from spending the night hunched over file after file.

I staggered up the stairs like I'd just finished a bender. In a way, I had, but one that had nothing to do with booze.

I was punch drunk on the horror I had been drowning in for the past nineteen hours.

I found Rosie typing away at her desk to the left of the great man's door.

"He's in there with Fitzgerald and Ross," she told me without looking up. "But he said you should go right in. They're expecting you. Just make sure you shut the door behind you."

I followed Rosie's orders and found Fitzgerald and Ross sitting in the two leather chairs in front of the chief's desk.

"Come in, Charlie," Carmichael greeted me after

glancing at the fancy clock on his desk. "You look like hell."

I hadn't changed my clothes or shaven since the previous morning. I hadn't even stopped to use the bathroom in all that time. The urge had never crossed my mind. "Thanks. I feel even worse."

Fitzgerald turned to offer me a weak smile. "Sorry about the run around, Charlie, but like the chief told you, it was necessary at the time."

"Necessary until we knew you were all in," Ross added. "And we're real glad you're on our side."

Fitzgerald concurred. "Real glad indeed."

My head was already swimming from a night spent slogging through the mind of a killer. These two sounding like a bad comedy routine didn't make me feel any better.

Carmichael said, "I can see by the look on your face that you've got plenty to tell us. Pull over a chair and tell us what you think. Speak freely. Don't hold back."

I guess that was my cue to be on the level in front of Fitzgerald and Ross. I didn't like the idea, seeing as how those two would run for the hills if The Wandering Man case blew up. But Carmichael was chief for a reason, so I didn't question him.

I pulled over one of the uncomfortable chairs from the table and sat down beside Ross. I thought about referring to the notes I'd brought with me, but the idea of re-reading what I had written made my skin crawl. As tired as I was, I decided to go from memory for as long as I could.

"I looked at all the letters Spann had managed to get from the families who'd kept them. All of them were sent on the same kind of stationery. The paper feels thick, so I think that means it's expensive, but I'm no expert.

Spann had made a list of stationery stores in his notebook, but he'd crossed them all off except for the last one he visited. The store on Madison Avenue."

Fitzgerald said, "He'd spent his last couple of days visiting those stores. The last report he gave us said he hadn't found anything useful at the first batch he'd visited."

Ross asked, "Did you find anything in his notes to indicate he'd found anything as a result of those visits on his last day?"

"Nothing," I admitted. "It looks like his search boiled down to the store on Madison. And judging by how I saw him act, he didn't seem to get anywhere with the store clerk there, either."

"Damn it," Carmichael swore. "I'd been afraid of that."

I was glad I had an idea that might make him feel better. "I think the stores themselves are a clue. I think that's how the killer figured out where he was going to be."

The chief's eyes narrowed. "Explain."

I gave it a try. "Spann had spent two whole days visiting stationery stores, but not every store in the city. He only picked a few. Nothing I've seen in his notes yet explain what made those stores so special. Since he was too good a cop to miss a tail if he picked one up, I think the killer found out about his search somehow and sat waiting at the store on Madison to see if he'd show up."

Judging by how the three chiefs traded glances, I could see that I had just plowed new ground.

"How did he know what Spann looked like?" Ross asked.

I'd already thought of that. "His picture was all over the papers when Tommy had been taken. Spann hadn't changed that much, so he probably knew him from that."

"Good thinking." Carmichael pointed at Fitzgerald. "Get on the phone to the owner of that last store and tell him we want a list of every customer he's had for the past ten years. I want it as soon as possible. Whatever it takes."

Fitzgerald nodded curtly. "Consider it done."

When he didn't get up from the chair, Carmichael slammed his hand on the desk. "What the hell are you waiting for? Get off your ass. I said now, goddamn it!"

The deputy chief popped out of his chair and practically ran from the office. I'll admit I got a kick out of it. I'd never seen Fitzgerald move that fast.

Carmichael pointed to the empty chair. "Move up, Charlie."

My backside was grateful for the accommodation. The chair in the storage room was only slightly better than standing.

"Ten years of records is a lot," I told him as I sat down. "I'll need help going through all of them if you want me to keep up Spann's pace."

Carmichael looked at Ross. "Make sure Fitzgerald gets a couple of detectives to sort through the list. Make sure they're our boys, understand? I don't care if you have to spread the work over a couple of shifts. This is a top priority."

"I'll see to it." Ross moved to the edge of his seat. He clearly didn't know if Carmichael wanted to do it now and was ready to run in case he got yelled at.

I kept myself from smiling. Typical Carmichael. Keep everyone off balance, even in a crisis.

The chief asked me, "What else did you find, Charlie?"

"I saw from Spann's notes that he already told you about the return address on the envelopes being removed. That detail might help us narrow down suspects as I keep digging. But I noticed something in the letters themselves that I don't know if he pointed out."

"He'd used the letters to build an idea of where the killings took place," Ross said. "The details didn't match up neatly, which might've been The Wanderer's intention. What did you find?"

"The line in the letter 'e' fades more and more throughout the letters," I told them. "In the later letters, they almost look like 'c's. It's not from the ribbon but from the key itself. That tells me every letter was probably typed on the same machine. It also might mean that this particular machine gets a lot of use and hasn't been repaired recently. Again, it doesn't help us find the killer, but it could come in handy if I can narrow down the suspects."

"It would be nice to have a list of suspects to narrow down," Carmichael said. "Did you find anything in Spann's notes that mentioned anyone? A name? He only told us information he felt was solid and never wanted to guess. I was hoping he had some ideas he was holding back from us until he was sure."

I may not have found any names in Spann's notes yet, but Carmichael's question brought one name to mind. "Mr. Weidermeyer."

"Weidermeyer?" Ross slapped his leg in glee. "I knew Spann had to have been on to someone. He was too good a detective not to have a suspect." He turned to face me fully. "Who is he? Where is he? I can have one of my boys pick him up right now."

I could tell by the look on Carmichael's face that he

recognized the name. "Mr. Weidermeyer? The fish monger?"

Ross hadn't picked up on it yet. "Sounds promising. Fishmongers are familiar with knives. Guts and blood don't bother them. Neither does the smell, if we're being blunt here."

I decided to let Ross in on it before he made more of a fool of himself. "Mr. Weidermeyer was the fishmonger in the neighborhood where the chief and I grew up."

Ross sank back in his chair, deflated. "Oh."

But the chief was intrigued. "What about him?"

"I remember he had a thick German accent but worked hard to hide it. Always used big words in the wrong places. Mixed up Americanisms a lot but couldn't pull it off."

Carmichael sat back in his chair, too. Only he was far from deflated. "Keep going."

"The way the killer writes reminds me of Mr. Weidermeyer," I explained. "The words he uses don't run together well. It reads like a guy who isn't smart but is trying to sound like he is. There's the misspellings, too. The words are in the right place, but they're spelled wrong. It's almost as if he's imitating someone smart. Maybe someone he sees and hears every day."

Now that I'd said it out loud, I felt like a dope. "I don't know. It's probably nothing."

"No." Carmichael held up a finger. "Don't do that, Charlie. Don't doubt yourself. Not now. Something always bothered me about those letters. Spann, too, but we couldn't figure out what it was. I think you just did."

He smiled at Ross. "Our boy's a pretender, Stuart. He's not the evil genius we've been thinking he is."

"Maybe not," Ross agreed, "but he's still a sick son of a bitch. And even if he's trying to sound fancier than he is, that doesn't help us find him. This city's lousy with phonies."

"He's not a dope," I went on. "He's smart in his own way, but not in the way he wants us to think. He's never left any clues or bodies for us to find. That takes smarts. He also took the time and effort to cut out the return addresses on the envelopes, but he was careful not to leave fingerprints on the paste when he covered over the holes. He knows how to taunt the families of his victims, but that last letter to the Washingtons is different."

"How different?" Carmichael asked.

"He brags more in that one," I said. "He's proud of what he's done. There's a real nasty streak in it. He knows his letters will upset the families, but in Lester Washington's letter, he seems cocky, and I don't know why."

"Probably because he's been getting away with it for ten years," Ross said.

I ignored him and kept my train of thought. The more I talked, the more things came to me. "The stationery is smaller than a regular sheet of paper. I think that's because he cuts off the letterhead, but he doesn't let the extra paper go to waste. He uses the blank spaces to cover up the return addresses on the envelope. Front and inside. Always neat cuts, too. Never crooked."

Carmichael was hooked. He moved to the edge of his chair. "Keep going, kid. What're you thinking?"

I didn't know what I was thinking, but I couldn't stop talking. I felt my face grow hot, like I had a fever. "Why go through the extra effort of reusing the pieces of the letterhead after he's cut it off? It's almost like he doesn't want to waste it."

No, that didn't sound right. I put a finer point on it. "Like he's not typing the letters out in a room somewhere. It's like he's afraid someone might see the cut off letterhead and ask questions."

"Great," Ross said. "So our boy works in an office. That narrows it down to a couple of million or so."

I saw Carmichael shoot him one of his classic withering looks. "You can consider yourself dismissed any time you want, Ross."

The deputy chief threw up his hands in surrender and lowered his head.

Carmichael looked at me. "What does all of this tell you about him, Charlie?"

I hadn't given any of this much thought. They'd just been random details I'd picked up while going through Spann's files. But I'd gotten this far running my mouth and decided to press my luck. "He knows how to type and doesn't make mistakes. He could've handwritten the letters but didn't. He has a typewriter, but he probably doesn't own one. If he had the money to buy it, he'd have the money to get it fixed. Maybe he's using the stationery of wherever he works. The same kind of stationery for the past ten years, given how far back the letters go."

I could feel a path open in my mind. "That means he's got a job. Maybe the same job for the past ten years. He's comfortable, but he's not a boss. He'd be able to have his own paper and typewriter if he was."

Carmichael looked like he was at the track, watching his horse break away from the rest. "Keep going."

"He's got a job, a routine. The kids have been taken at random times of day according to Spann's notes. Some on weekends, but during the week, too. He doesn't punch a clock, so he's got an open schedule, like a salesman or someone like that. He obviously knows how to talk to people, especially young people because none of the witnesses Spann scrounged up remembered any kind of scuffle or fight when they were taken. In fact, the witnesses only report seeing the kids were there one minute and gone the next. Like they'd wandered off somewhere. Whoever he is, he blends in."

"Except for the Spann boy," Carmichael added, "all of the victims we know about were black and lived in Harlem. You think he blends in because he's black, too?"

I hadn't thought that far ahead, but I went with it. "I walked a beat in Harlem when I first joined the force. Black men are wary of white men, especially those who make them promises. There's got to be something about him that puts them at ease. Maybe someone they know or have seen before."

Carmichael and Ross traded looks and I knew something in all my babbling had struck them.

"What?" I prodded. "What did I do."

Carmichael opened the top drawer of his desk and pulled out a thick file folder. It was one of those beige jobs with the red boarder around it. A thick red band went around the center of it.

It was the kind of folder the department used for its most sensitive files. Break the seal on one of those babies without written permission and it meant your job. Including me.

He handed the file across the desk to me. "These are the earliest notes of the Spann case."

He cut me off before I could ask him why I hadn't seen this until now. "Spann didn't have them because they have a full accounting of his wife's death and the investigation that followed. I kept it from him for his own good, though I'm sure he had copies. I didn't leave them in your office because they have very sensitive information. There's a lot in there, including the first letter from

The Wanderer. I want you to focus on the material at the top of the file for now. As you'll see, Spann may not have had a suspect, but we do. And I think you just described him right down to his socks."

I swallowed my questions because it sounded like I might already have the answers in my hand. I opened the file like a kid on Christmas morning.

It was bulging with typewritten reports of various sorts, but the top sheet was something I had seen many times.

A city personnel sheet, but not from the police department.

This was from the Department of Education.

It was the employment record of one Norman Honeywell. A math teacher born in Norway who taught at a public school in East Harlem. His age came out to about sixty, but judging by the picture stapled to the form, he was pushing a hundred.

He had watery eyes the form said were blue. He had sunken cheeks and his mouth hung open like he was having trouble breathing. His shirt was too big on him, and he'd made a half-assed effort in knotting his tie.

"Honeywell was Spann's chief suspect?"

Ross shifted in his chair. "Well, not exactly. I had some of my men do some digging on their own. They didn't know it was linked to The Wandering Man, of course. You could say this was more of a separate independent investigation."

"And this is the guy they came up with?" I held up the picture of the gaunt, ancient man for both chiefs to see. "The poor bastard looks like he could get knocked on his ass by a summer breeze. There's no way he could tackle and hold down a kid like Lester Washington the way he claims in the letter."

"Read the file," Ross encouraged me. "He taught at the same public school all of the victims attended at one point or another. He teaches math now. Before that, he taught biology. You'll see he was also a doctor in Canada some years back when he emigrated from Norway."

That bit caught my attention. "A doctor? Why'd he leave Canada?"

"We're trying to find out," Carmichael said, "but our neighbors to the north aren't being very cooperative. I'm pulling some strings to get around that, but I don't want to raise too much of a stink about it until we have more. Honeywell is the only link we've got between the victims, and he matches the exact same description you just spent the last half an hour talking about. His medical experience means he probably knows how to inflict the most damage with minimal effort, even on a young man more than half his age and twice his size."

Ross added, "He also happens to have the virtue of being the only lead we've got."

I put the sheet back in the file. The folder might have been thick, but the case against Honeywell was pretty thin. "That means every other teacher in that school has the same link to the boys as Honeywell. And I'd bet more than a few of them would be better candidates than this old scarecrow."

"They're all fine upstanding members of the community," Carmichael told me. "He's not. He's also a life-long bachelor. We even have reason to believe he's a swish."

I forgot myself for a minute and rolled my eyes. "For Christ's sake, Andy. Even if he's a little pink in the center, it doesn't make him a killer. Those guys don't tend to be violent, not like The Wanderer, anyway. And we'd better take a closer look at the other teachers in the school.

Don't forget Leopold and Loeb came from great homes, too."

I saw a hint of anger pass through Carmichael. "We've already checked out every other male teacher in the place from head to toe. They're clean, Charlie. Besides, Honeywell's the only one who has been at that school since the killings began. He's also very popular with his students. He could probably get any of them to follow him anywhere."

Ross chimed in. "He also matches the description of the man you shot fleeing the Spann shooting, doesn't he?"

He did, but I remembered something Carmichael told me in the cemetery the day before. I began rifling through the other file on my lap.

I could hear the annoyance in Carmichael's voice when he said, "What's wrong, Charlie?"

I didn't like to ignore him, but I was on to something and didn't want to be distracted. "Honeywell's not the only common link between the cases."

I kept digging through the papers until I found Spann's handwritten notes covering the timeline of when the families received letters from The Wandering Man. "The Jacobs family got their first letter in 1922. The Washington family was the last to report one last year in 1926."

"And?" Ross asked.

"And, when the families called in about the letters, their cases got mothballed. They were referred to the Harlem sector." I flicked the paper; glad my memory hadn't failed me. "Every call got referred to the same detective. Bob Keating."

I wasn't surprised when the chief's face soured.

"'Dead End' Keating," Carmichael spat. "One of the worst men I've ever known to put on the uniform."

Ross agreed. "His brother's a sachem down at the Hall, so we couldn't get rid of him no matter how hard we tried. We stuck him in one armpit of the department after another, but he wouldn't quit. I stuck him in the most dangerous precinct in Harlem. I'd hoped we'd get lucky, and someone would shoot the son of a bitch, but no dice. He finally retired earlier this year."

That explained why Spann had only recently gotten a bunch of old files. Keating had probably boxed them up before he left.

I focused on the notes in my hand. "Looks like Spann didn't get around to interviewing Keating, did he?"

"No," Carmichael told me. "I remember he'd called him several times, but never got an answer. He even wrote to him and had the letter slipped into his pension check. Keating cashed the check, but never replied to the letter."

"That sounds like Keating alright," Ross said. "Probably thought Spann was investigating him for something." He looked at Carmichael. "I think we ought to talk to Keating first before we risk bothering a civilian like Honeywell."

I was glad I'd been able to steer them away from Honeywell, at least for now.

The chief picked up the phone on his desk. "Rosie, get Bob Keating on the line. Retired detective. Lives in Jersey City somewhere, I think. Get his last known address, too. It's important."

He slammed down the phone in frustration. "Even after retirement, Keating remains a boil on my ass."

I tried to take some of the sting out of it for him.

"He might remember something worthwhile, Chief. A detail that might not be in Spann's files."

Carmichael shifted in his chair as he ran his index finger along his chin. He was thinking now, so I kept my trap shut and let his mind go to work.

"If Rosie can't reach him," Carmichael said, "I'll need you to drive out to his place and ask him about these missing young men directly. I want anything he can remember about the case that he didn't include in the files. Anything at all."

I sure hoped Rosie got him on the phone. I was already dead on my feet and I didn't particularly like Jersey. The place always made the roof of my mouth itch. "Whatever it takes, boss."

Carmichael acted as if he hadn't heard me. "Of course, you're not to mention anything about this having to do with Spann's death or The Wandering Man case to Keating. Don't forget his brother's a sachem at the Hall. One word to him and it'll be all over town by the time you get back to the city. Just tell him I'm looking to close some open cases as part of my Harlem policy. Given my recent efforts up there, he'll buy that and so will his brother."

Carmichael's desk phone rang, and he picked it up. I couldn't hear what Rosie had told him, but judging by his expression, I knew she hadn't been able to reach Keating. "Fine. What's his address?" He scribbled it down on a piece of paper and handed it to me as he kept talking to Rosie. "Jim Halloran's still in the building, isn't he? Have him meet Charlie down at Charlie's car in ten minutes."

Carmichael hung up the phone before I could stop the order from going out. Halloran was one of the chief's top enforcers. The kind of guy he sent to handle the rougher jobs that needed doing.

"I don't need Halloran or anyone else to come with me for an interview," I told him. "I can talk to Keating on my own."

"We'd feel better if Halloran's with you," Ross said. "Keating's always had a fondness for guns, and Big Jim's got a talent for keeping people in line."

I knew Big Jim also had a talent for putting people in the hospital. But the order had gone out and Carmichael wasn't in the mood for a debate.

I gathered up Spann's old files and got going. "I'll lock these up in my office before I head out. Halloran's not much of a reader, but there's no sense in tempting fate."

"Call me as soon as you're done with Keating," Carmichael called after me. "We'll want to know everything as soon as possible."

I told him I would as I quietly pulled the door shut behind me.

I just hoped I had something to tell him.

Chapter 11

WHEN I GOT DOWNSTAIRS, I found Halloran leaning against the front bumper of my Ford. He was called 'Big Jim' for a reason. He was well over six feet and wider than me but beginning to go soft in the middle. He had a lantern jaw and a naturally smug expression that begged to be punched. His size and his badge were usually enough to make people think twice before actually doing it. He moved through the world like he was doing it a favor just by breathing.

He thumbed his hat back on his head and popped a toothpick in his mouth when he saw me. "Well look who's here. Little Charlie Doherty. The chief's black hand. What've you been up to, Charlie?"

"Get in and find out." I climbed in behind the wheel. He got in the passenger's side.

I started up the engine and pulled away from the curb.

"Not that it's any of my business," Halloran asked, "but where are we going, anyway?"

Halloran might've been a fellow Tammany man, but

130

I still had to watch what I said around him. One slip up about The Wanderer and the whole thing was sunk. He had a habit of getting loaded after work and running his mouth when he did.

"We're heading over to Jersey City to see an old friend of yours," I told him. "Bob Keating."

"Dead End Bob's no friend of mine," Halloran grunted as he worked the toothpick from one side of his mouth to the other. "No wonder Carmichael sent me with you. Keating's always been an oddball. Quiet one minute and flying off the handle the next."

I felt him look at me as I drove west. "Say, what do you want to talk to him about anyway?"

I knew I had to tell him something. It couldn't be so far from the truth that I couldn't remember it. And it couldn't be the actual truth or Halloran would spill it all over town.

"You know how the chief is on this kick about calming things down up in Harlem."

Halloran watched me guardedly. "Yeah?"

"Well, there's a couple of missing person cases Keating signed off on that don't sit right with Carmichael," I explained. "One of the families got his ear about an unsolved case and the chief wants me to look into it for him. See if Keating remembers something."

Halloran studied me for a while before he went back to looking out the window. "That bit about bringing peace to Harlem is a lot of nonsense if you ask me. Carmichael kissing Queenie's ring like he did. It won't make a difference in the long run. Oh, sure, they'll be quiet for a month or so but, come the warmer months, when everyone's outside enjoying the nice weather, things will go to pot again. You just watch."

I didn't care about Halloran's opinion. He'd seemed to buy my excuse for the trip, which was fine by me. "Guys like you and me just do as we're told."

But I could tell Halloran was still stewing over it. "And why would he send you out on something like this? He trying to make an honest cop out of you?"

"What the hell is that supposed to mean?"

Halloran held up his thick hands in surrender. "No offense, Charlie. You know how much I like you and all, but you ain't exactly what anyone would call a real detective."

He might not have meant to offend me, but I was offended just the same. "And just who do you think you are? Philo Vance?"

Halloran grinned as he looked out the window, working the toothpick around his mouth. "Take it easy. I know what I am just like you know what you are is all. We serve a purpose, and that purpose is whatever the chief tells us to do at a particular moment. Any monkey could do it, but we do it right which is why they keep us around. We get killed or foul up? They get another couple of monkeys to do it. I ain't complaining, you understand, but I ain't in the habit of forgetting it, neither."

I guessed Halloran might've had a point after all. And if I stayed sore about it, it would only make him more likely to remember it later. I had to smooth things over before this became memorable. "Sorry for the short-temper. I've been catching hell from Carmichael all day for a whole bunch of things that weren't my fault. Guess I was just letting off some of the steam around my collar."

"Think nothing of it," Halloran said. "I've been on

the receiving end of that Irish temper of his more times than I can count. I know how it goes."

I knew he did. I'd witnessed most of Carmichael's tirades aimed at Halloran. They weren't pretty.

"How're we getting over to Jersey anyway?" he asked me when he saw we were heading west.

"The Holland Tunnel."

"But they're still building that thing," he reminded me. "It ain't even open yet."

I was happy to be able to surprise him. "Not to the public, but it is to us. The owner of the construction company has friends at the Hall. How do you think he got the gig?"

Halloran rolled down the window. "Serves me right for thinking like a civilian."

━━

THE PART of Jersey City that Keating called home was a pitiful, barren wasteland. I'd seen bombed out forests in France that had more life to them.

Faded old houses were just about the only thing that broke up the bleak landscape. Autumn had already taken firm hold of the area and a fair number of trees had shed their leaves, making Jersey look bleaker than normal for a city guy like me.

It was still morning, but the sunlight already had that crisp vividness to it that it gets as winter draws near.

Halloran wasn't impressed by Jersey, either. "Welcome to Jersey. The Garden State. The ass-end of nowhere is more like it."

I caught the Manhattan skyline in my mirrors. "It's got a nice view of the city."

"And that's about it."

The sun blinded me as I crested a curve at the top of a hill. I had to squint to see the sign for Keating's street.

I was making the turn when an old truck came barreling down the road toward us. I managed to swerve out of the way, but it still scraped me as it fishtailed onto the road.

Halloran shouted down my curses as he yelled, "That was Keating! The son of a bitch is making a run for it."

I had to take Halloran's word for it because I had only seen the silhouette of the truck, not the driver.

"You sure?" I barely missed hitting a mailbox as I turned the car around to chase the truck.

"Saw him plain as day," Halloran told me as he held on for dear life. "I'd know that old weasel anywhere."

I came out of the turn and floored it down the hill. There was no other traffic on the country road, so speed wasn't the problem. Distance was. Keating had put a good half a mile or so between us before I got back into the chase.

I watched him take a right at the next road, a main artery that I knew led through Jersey City proper.

Since we were already on a steep hill, I took my foot off the gas and coasted, tapping the brakes only when we hit the corner and skidded out onto the main road.

I kept the Ford under control and saw Keating's truck about three-quarters of a mile away. With nothing but air between us, I floored it again and quickly closed the distance.

Trash and other debris flew out from the flatbed as Keating hit the gas, too.

While I was doing my best to dodge the trash the truck was shedding, I saw Halloran had pulled his .45.

"What the hell are you doing?" I said as a small

wooden crate splintered on the road just in front of me. "Put that damned thing away."

Halloran already had the gun out the window. "Just slide to the left and hold her steady. This bastard's running days are over."

I ducked as a rotting head of lettuce bounced off the hood and missed the windshield. "Put it away. We need him alive."

Shooting Keating now wouldn't get us anywhere, but we had to stop him before he reached the city. He knew the area and we didn't. He'd have a better chance of losing us in town if he got that far.

As the amount of trash flying out from the back of Keating's truck began to ease up, I decided now was the time to make a move. I slid the car to the left and saw a milk truck was heading in our direction.

I could see Keating watching me in his sideview mirror as he moved the truck to the left to try to block me from passing him.

He was only looking at me. Not at the milk truck heading our way.

The other truck driver leaned on the horn, and I moved back behind Keating's flatbed.

Keating jerked the wheel to the right and almost drove into the tangle of wild bushes just off the road. The milk truck sped by us.

Without any other traffic coming our way, I floored it and brought my Ford around Keating's left side as he desperately tried to regain control of his truck.

He'd just about managed to get back on the road when I slammed into his right side, sending him crashing into the thick knot of bushes and branches growing on the side of the road.

I slammed on the brakes and skidded to a halt about

twenty yards away from the truck. I was out of the car and running back toward Keating before Halloran's feet had even touched the roadway. I had to get to him first before Halloran shot him.

The front of Keating's truck was deep in the bushes. A thin column of steam was beginning to escape from beneath the hood. I saw Keating frantically struggling to get his door open. He had a thick, bloody gash across his chin, probably caused by the steering wheel when he crashed.

He saw me running toward him and scrambled over to the passenger's side to escape. I watched him try to push the door open, but the thick branches kept slamming it shut. He was in the process of rolling the window down to climb out when I got close enough to yell, "Damn it, Keating. Stop! It's Doherty and Halloran. You remember us."

"Why do you think I took off?" Keating hollered back. "I know why you're here, too."

Bob Keating had never been a good-looking man, but now he had the wide, wild eyes of a cornered animal. He had always been thin, but as I saw him splayed in the cab of his truck, he looked like he'd lost ten pounds since his retirement.

Halloran had lumbered up beside me, and I kept talking so he wouldn't have the chance. "We only want to ask you some questions about some missing kids in Harlem. That's all."

I could see he had put all his weight against the passenger door while he talked, hoping I wouldn't notice. "If all you wanted to do was talk, why'd you chase me?"

I'll admit that the question stopped me cold.

Halloran answered for me. "Because you ran, you stupid bastard."

I watched Keating's heel slip on the bench as he failed to force the door open with his back. "And I only ran because you boys were chasing me."

I knew we'd get nowhere arguing about the reasons why everything had happened. "Sorry for the misunderstanding, but you're not in trouble. We just want to talk, I swear. No one wants to hurt you. So come on out and let us help you get your truck free of those branches."

Some of the fear had gone out of Keating's eyes, but not all of it. "If you mean no harm, why's that big ape got his gun out?"

I looked down and saw Halloran still had his .45 at his side. "I thought I told you to put that damned thing away."

"You're not my boss, shrimp. Only Carmichael tells me what to do." He pointed at Keating. "You'd better get out here before I lose my temper."

Halloran might've been a lot bigger than me, but I got between him and Keating. "If this goes sideways, I'll tell the chief it was all your fault. And who do you think he'll believe. His shadow or his thug?"

Halloran practically growled at me as he tucked the pistol back under his arm. I turned and faced Keating with my hands raised. "See? No guns. So, come out here and we can talk a bit."

Keating came to the driver's side door but stopped. "I'll talk to you and you alone, Charlie. That son of a bitch over there's had it in for me since—"

Halloran moved quicker than I'd expected. Keating tried to crawl away, but Halloran snatched him by the throat and pulled him out through the open driver's side window. He slammed him against the truck as if he was a sack of potatoes.

"You were always a miserable little drunk, you know

that?" Halloran seethed in Keating's face. "You damned near got us killed twice today. If I dusted you here and now, they'd give me a medal for it."

I grabbed hold of Halloran's fist and tried to pry Keating loose from his grip.

"Let him go," I ordered, "or I'll make sure you never work for the chief again."

Halloran released Keating with a shove. I took the retired cop by the arm to keep him from falling down and led him back to my car.

I told Halloran, "See if you can't work his truck free. We'll be back in a minute."

"Just don't light a match near him," Halloran yelled after us. "You'll blow yourselves to kingdom come."

I let go of Keating and gestured toward my Ford. Halloran was right about one thing. He reeked of booze. "Let's go over there and talk. We'll stay right out here in the open where God and everyone can see us."

"Just keep Halloran away from me," Keating said. "He knows I'm onto him and he'd just love to shut me up."

"You're only dealing with me, I promise."

Keating was in a sorry state. Besides smelling like stale beer, he had puffy bags beneath eyes that had seen too much. Too many late nights followed by early mornings. Too many cigarettes and not enough fresh air. Too many nightmares and not enough sleep. Too much life and not enough living.

"Why'd you run?" I asked him when we reached my car. "And I mean really. Not that guff you fed us back there."

"Because I ain't stupid, Charlie." Keating folded his arms across his skinny chest. "I know how it goes. You ever hear of a couple of guys from the job visiting a guy like me who weren't delivering a bullet from the Hall?"

I hadn't, but that was beside the point. "You're not everyone. Your brother's a sachem, remember?"

"He's the reason why I knew you two were coming," he said. "It took me the better part of an hour to get that damned engine to work. And when I finally did, I was almost too late." He looked up at me sheepishly. "You sure you ain't here to kill me, Charlie?"

"If we were, you'd be dead already," I assured him. "Besides, we really just want to ask you a few questions about some old cases you ran."

Keating shrugged. "I'll help you if I can, but I sure hope you're not expecting too much. Everything I know is in boxes I left behind when I retired. I never really ran cases as much as sat on them. They called me 'Dead End Keating' for a reason. Every case they wanted off their desks, they dumped on me."

"This one's different," I told him. "It's several cases, actually. About twenty or so young men going missing in Harlem over the past ten years."

If Keating knew anything about them, he was doing a good job of hiding it. "If you say so."

"You spent the last decade of your career up there and you're the last detective of record for each of them."

I could tell Keating was giving it some sincere thought. "I don't know, Charlie. Lots of kids go missing up there every week. You know that. Your first assignment out of the academy was a Harlem beat."

I was surprised he'd remembered. "Good memory."

He seemed to be pleased that I was impressed. "I used to be in Personnel before they put me out to pasture uptown. I had a pretty good head on my shoulders back then before, well, just before."

I hoped his head was good enough to help me. "They were all young black males over the age of eighteen. No criminal records, not even juvie beefs. Good kids who had jobs who just disappeared one day. Newsies and store clerks. Kids like that."

He was getting ready to tell me he didn't remember anything when something made him stop.

"Come to think of it, I do remember a bunch of cases like that." He bummed a cigarette from me. I even lit it for him. And contrary to Halloran's warning, we didn't get blown to Hell.

"I wondered why the cases kept getting kicked over to me when there was nothing in the file saying they'd investigated any of them. I usually only got the closed or dead-end stuff. They were all still open as far as I could see."

The tobacco seemed to have gotten his brain's juices flowing. I kept my mouth shut and got while the getting was good.

Keating kept talking. "You remember a guy by the name of Brunner from when you were up there?"

I let out a long whistle as I leaned on my car next to him. "I haven't thought about him in ages. Sure, I remember him. Nasty bastard."

"Crooked, too, and not like we were," Keating said. "He didn't care who knew it and couldn't understand why the Hall wouldn't touch him with a ten-foot pole. Anyway, he worked a bunch of those cases we're talking about, but not all of them. When I asked him why he'd referred them to me, he told me they were all dead-end numbers. Just another bunch of black kids who'd wandered off. 'Plenty more where they came from' he told me. When I pushed him on it, he flung his notebook at me and told me to work them myself."

I watched Keating's sad eyes grow sadder at the memory. "Did it in front of the whole squad, too. Got a pretty good laugh at my expense."

I might've found a way to feel bad for Keating if I'd had the time. I crossed my fingers and toes before I asked my next question. His answer could keep me from wasting a lot of time digging through boxes. "Did you ever look at those notebooks? Do you remember what he wrote?"

"Just a bunch of half-assed scrawl," Keating told me. "Nothing important. Though there was one thing that Brunner underlined that I never understood."

I tried hard to hide my excitement. "What was it?"

"A couple of the street vendors said they'd seen a black delivery truck in the areas where the kids were taken. At least for the cases Brunner worked, anyway."

"That so?" I played it off like I was mildly interested, but this was a major clue. "They say if they saw any writing on it?"

Keating's eyes squinted as he looked through his memory. "Nope. I remember they said it was just a plain steel delivery truck, like one of our paddy wagons, except it wasn't on account of all of our wagons being marked. This was all black. Those vendors see delivery trucks all the time, only this one was different. I remember that part clearly because I never had the chance to ask Brunner about it. He dropped dead of a heart attack that same weekend. Can't say as I shed any tears over him, the louse."

I was happy and annoyed at the same time. Happy I'd gotten Keating to talk, but annoyed that Brunner had thrown away such a promising lead. Our only lead.

But now I had something to look for. A black delivery

truck that looked like a paddy wagon. The Wanderer just got a bit easier to find.

We both looked up when we heard the honk of a horn. Halloran had managed to work Keating's truck clear of the bushes and was pulling it off the road in our direction. A thin trail of steam still spilled out from the engine, but not as much as before.

"Thanks," I called out to Halloran as he stepped out of the truck.

Halloran replied by flinging a cap at Keating, hitting him in the face before he caught it. "Found that on the floor in there. Guess it must've fallen off when you tried to kill us, you goddamned rummy."

I held out my hand to Keating, who took it. "Sorry about the mix up earlier, Bob. You sure you don't want me to bring you to a doctor? That chin's still bleeding pretty bad."

Keating dabbed at it with his hand like he'd just cut himself shaving. "I've survived worse. Besides, if I had enough dough for a doctor, I wouldn't be living out here. It was my uncle's place. Can't wait to sell it so I can use the money to move back to civilization. Know what I mean?"

If, by civilization, he meant Manhattan, I didn't know what he meant. But if he was thinking of somewhere warm, I understood him completely. "Best of luck to you," I said as I watched him get out of Halloran's way and scramble back to his truck.

Halloran seemed to enjoy watching the little man run. "That's right, weasel. Scurry back to your hole in the ground."

The gears of the truck creaked as Keating quickly put it into gear and made a quick U-turn back toward wherever he called home.

I looked at Halloran and didn't like what I saw. "Was that necessary?"

"What? Giving him the needle?" He'd fished a cigarette from a pack in his pocket and lit it. "He's lucky I didn't punch his face in for him. He could've killed us back there, or ain't your memory too good?"

I watched Keating drive away. A fog seemed to have settled in around his truck. I didn't know it was the steam from the engine or the cloud that seemed to hover over everything in his life. I wasn't sure it made a difference.

"My memory's just fine. And, lucky for us, so was Keating's."

"That juice belly?" Halloran let a long stream of smoke escape from the corner of his mouth. "Just about the only thing he can remember is the bottom of the last bottle he finished. The inside of his truck's full of empties. I'm lucky I didn't cut myself by climbing in there." He looked at me and grinned. "Maybe I ought to put in for hazard pay. Bet the chief would get a kick out of that."

I decided I'd had enough of Big Jim Halloran for one day and pushed myself off my car. "Get inside. We've got a long drive ahead of us back to the Castle."

But Halloran still had plenty to say. At least he'd kept his trap shut until I'd gotten back on the road to New York. "And another thing. The next time you threaten me with the chief, you and me are gonna trade more than words. I do the chief's dirty work same as you. Same coin, different sides. One's not better than the other and it spends the same no matter which side is up. Understand?"

I let Halloran babble and threaten me some more as we headed back toward the tunnel beneath the Hudson

River. My mind was busy with more important things. My mind was on The Wandering Man.

Is that you in the delivery truck? Where'd you get it? Will it help me find you, you son of a bitch?

I kept my eyes on the road as if the asphalt might give me an answer. But all it gave me was more questions.

Chapter 12

DESPITE THE CHIEF'S orders to call, I waited until we got back to the Castle to give him a full report. He'd been in the middle of a meeting but ended it as soon as Rosie told him I was back.

I stepped aside as a long blue line of department brass filed past me. They all gave me the high sign or patted me on the arm as they went by. Up here in Valhalla, it was safe to greet old Charlie. Out in the real world, it was a different story.

When I was finally able to go inside, I was glad it was just me and Carmichael. No sign of Fitzgerald or Ross.

The chief was already back behind his desk. "How'd it go?"

I took a seat and told him about Keating making a run for it and his news about the black delivery truck seen in the area around some of the disappearances.

"Sounds like it wasn't a wasted trip after all," Carmichael said. "A black truck that looks like a paddy wagon. You think that's real or just a product of Keating's rum-soaked brain?"

"It was real enough to him," I said. "He wasn't lying or making anything up. I think he was trying to be helpful."

"Maybe he was," Carmichael allowed. "At least it's something to go on. Black paddy wagons that aren't paddy wagons. What do you think they could be?"

"If the witnesses were just regular civilians, I'd ignore it. But those vendors are out there all day long. If they said something about the truck was different, I'd say there's something to it."

"Go through the files Spann pulled. See if Brunner's notebooks are in there. If not, I'll have Rosie call up records and see if they can't hunt them down." Carmichael drummed his fingers on the desk as he thought it over. "A delivery truck could mean a salesman, which fits nicely with your idea of the killer, Charlie. A convincing, friendly guy the kids saw before. Could fit like a glove."

"It's a lot better than bothering Honeywell," I said.

"I agree we can set him aside as a suspect for now," Carmichael said. "I'm not willing to forget about him entirely just yet, but something else has come up that requires more immediate attention."

He shoveled aside some papers on his desk and came up with a newspaper. "Saw an interesting article in the afternoon edition of today's *Mirror*."

I felt like a dope. All my talk about my memory and I'd forgotten to tell him about the shutterbug I'd found in the cemetery yesterday. "I'm sorry about that, boss. With everything going on, I forgot to tell you about the stringer for the *Mirror* who was following us during our walk. I got all the pictures he took of us, but to smooth it over, I gave him an interview with you. I didn't think you'd mind."

"I wouldn't have minded if he printed it." Carmichael tossed the paper on his desk facing me. "As you can see, he didn't print it. He wasn't a stringer, either."

The front page of the paper was filled with typical front-page stuff. The League of Nations had abolished something. Someone had started a revolution in China.

It was the last column on the right side that turned my stomach. The headline said it all:

MASSEY MAKES IT TO THE MIRROR
Acclaimed Crusader Vows to Take On Corruption

The picture beneath it looked like a cleaned-up, grown-up version of the young stringer I'd caught following me in the cemetery. He'd called himself Leon Street then.

But in the picture, Donald Massey's mess of dark hair had been tamed by a gallon of tonic and neatly combed. He wore round wire-rimmed spectacles that gave him a serious look. He sported a bow tie that hinted earnestness. The pipe tucked in the corner of his mouth alluded to thoughtful sophistication. He looked away from the camera to the left, like he was pondering the next great injustice he would tackle.

Or about the next dimwitted detective he'd sandbag.

I'd never heard of Leon Street, but I'd heard plenty about Donald Massey, the crusading journalist. He'd spent the past several years working for the *Chicago Tribune*. His syndicated column had run in the *Journal*.

He'd made a name for himself in Chicago for reporting on the deplorable conditions of the stockyards and tenements. He'd written about the corruption of

City Hall and the unions. He'd called on his readers to support better pay and shorter hours for workers. He promoted Red notions that stopped just shy of getting himself arrested for subversion. From each according to their abilities. To each according to their needs. Just don't lock me up for saying so. A real hero when it was convenient.

Just like Tammany.

Massey's rivals had dubbed him 'The Marx of the Midwest'. He'd never met an institution he didn't want to pull down in the name of what he called progress. Burn it all. We'll work out the details later. After a couple of million people starved to death, of course.

I picked up the paper and started reading Massey's article. It started out innocent enough, covering the Spann funeral. Sans pictures, of course. Guess he hadn't asked Krajnak for that favor after all.

He praised Spann's service to the city. How he had been a victim of crime ten years before when a stranger snapped up his young son, never to have been heard from again.

He wrote Spann was the one good apple in the bunch and that the city needed more like him. Nothing to squawk about there.

He only got nasty when he began to describe what he had seen at the cemetery.

'The leaders of the department flanked the widow Spann and her children; a blue line of gallantry too late to do anyone any good. The police were there in all their white-gloved, polished finery. Gold buttons and badges gleamed. Shoes, too.

They stood guard alongside their fallen comrade. Shoulders back and eyes front, offering crisp salutes on cue.

And of course, there were bagpipes. Nothing like a dash of the maudlin to bring a tear to the eye. Tears these men hope will blur your vision of reality that, with any luck, will keep you from seeing the grime beneath the gallantry. The erosion beneath the elegance.

Or the Tammany Tiger pacing restlessly back and forth among their ranks.'

I looked up at Carmichael, who hadn't taken his eyes off me while I read it. "I didn't tell him any of this."

"I know you didn't," he assured me. "Keep reading. It gets better."

I skimmed through the rest of the article. He spent a couple of paragraphs implying Carmichael was nothing but a tin soldier. It wasn't exactly original. His few critics often went after his dignified appearance first. Lazy writing found a home in New York papers.

But toward the end, he'd shifted his focus on a new target.

Me.

The article went on:

'As the service wound down, I found myself trailing a shadow. And not just any shadow. This was the chief's personal shadow. It even had a name. Charles Doherty.

He's a detective and attained that rank the old-fashioned way. Patronage. The unique relationship between chief and this particular shadow go back to their humble boyhood in Washington Heights and has stood the test of time ever since.

I followed Doherty to see where he might be going in the cemetery. What happens to a shadow when its master moves away?

I didn't have to wonder long, for it was only a few moments later when I saw Chief Carmichael's limousine circle around the drive. I stuck around to watch

Carmichael and Doherty take a leisurely stroll among the dead.

I may have been too far away to hear their conversation but given the various starts and stops of their journey, it was clear the topic was a clandestine one. And given Doherty's reactions to what Carmichael told him, it was no small matter.

Their talk was summed up by Carmichael passing a key to Doherty. One can only imagine the locks such a key can open. A room where all the nasty secrets of the NYPD are kept? A hidden dungeon beneath the headquarters Castle where confessions are rumored to be beaten out of suspects whether they are guilty or not?

It certainly wasn't the key to the city. Chief Carmichael already has that in his back pocket and guards it jealously.

When their conference ended and Carmichael was whisked away to his Castle, I caught up to Doherty and had the chance to talk to him. He has that Irish trait for being able to speak a lot without saying much at all.

I may be a newcomer to this town, but I could tell he's a man who stands much taller than he really is. The type whose shadow is long enough to block any warmth the sun can offer. Doherty has a reputation for being a man who makes things happen and makes problems go away. Sometimes he sweeps them under a rug or in darker, less admirable places.

I am sure you wonder what problems Carmichael and Doherty were discussing in the cemetery on a beautifully sad autumn morning. We will never know. If we did, men like Doherty wouldn't be doing their jobs.

But I have come to this fair city and the *Mirror* with a solemn vow that I'll continue to do what I've always done throughout my career.

Cast light into the shadows and see what's really there.

We, the people deserve nothing less.'

I folded the paper and tossed it back on Carmichael's desk.

"Shit."

"Yeah." The chief took the paper and dropped it in the garbage bin. "That was my first reaction, too."

Massey had fooled me twice. Once by trailing me without being spotted. The second was fooling me into thinking he was a rookie. "What do you want me to do about it?"

"You? Nothing. Massey's an Ahab who needs a whale to justify his paycheck from the *Mirror*. He's already flung his first spear at us. We can't afford to have him throw a second. Not now."

"And he didn't just happen to follow me through the cemetery," I told him. "That means he knew we'd be meeting. Someone must've tipped him off."

I knew if I came out and said what I was thinking, Carmichael would balk. I'd have to lead him there with facts. "I didn't tell him. You didn't tell him. Rosie didn't tell him."

"Dooley did."

I was glad he was able to see his driver was the only one who could've done it.

Carmichael picked up a pencil before casting it aside in anger. "I never confused his obedience for loyalty, but I counted on him to be smarter than this."

"What're you going to do, boss? You can't let Dooley go. He's connected to Andersson at the Hall. He'll kick hard if you cut him loose and he'll ask a lot of questions we don't want to answer."

Carmichael picked up the pencil again and began to

turn it from tip to eraser on his desk. "I won't fire Dooley. I'll use him instead. Don't ask me how, but I'll do it when the time comes."

He stopped turning his pencil long enough to look at me. "I know you're wrapped up in finding The Wanderer, but we can't let Massey shine a spotlight on us. Not with this Wanderer business lurking just below the surface."

I knew what he was thinking. A couple more articles like this and someone like Fitzgerald or Ross might break ranks. They might take some Tammany sachems into their confidence. To give them cover if the sky started falling.

Like I said, in the urban jungle, it's ultimately every man for himself.

"What do you want me to do, boss?"

"Find out everything you can about Donald Massey," Carmichael told me. "Something we can use as leverage. He didn't leave a cushy gig in Chicago without a damned good reason. Tell me what you find out and I'll have Halloran and some of the boys pick up this scribbler. Give him a personal tour of the dungeon."

I knew a bad idea when I heard it, and I'd just heard one now. "That's dangerous, Chief."

"Massey's playing a dangerous game," Carmichael said. "It's about time somebody taught him the rules."

"Somebody," I agreed, "but no one within the department. If Massey can trace it back to us, we'll be done for. A beating from us is just as liable to get his gander up. Might make him play the martyr bit to the hilt in his columns and that's bad for us, especially now."

Carmichael was getting frustrated. "So what should I do? Send a nasty letter to the editor?"

I had something better than that. "We have Doyle

invite him over to The Longford Lounge as his special guest. He's new in town and the Duke of New York would like to meet him. An aspiring boy like Massey won't be able to pass up an invitation to the swankiest place in town."

"And why would Doyle do that for us?"

"Not for us," I told him. "For himself. From what Massey wrote about Tammany, he's already got Doyle in his sights, and we all know how the Duke hates publicity. Let me have some of Doyle's boys work him over. That way, it doesn't lead back to you and, if Massey is suicidal enough to write about it in his column, it'll be Doyle's problem to handle, not yours."

I'd expected him to have half a dozen objections but was glad when he didn't. "It'll mean I'll owe Doyle a favor, but I can live with that. Just make sure he doesn't get too carried away. I want Massey hurt, not crippled. And I hear that new kid he's got working for him is a monster. Quinn, I think his name is. He was in line to fight Dempsey for the title."

But I didn't need the chief to tell me about Terry Quinn. I'd been there the night he'd refused to take a dive and killed his career, hence the reason why he was working for Archie Doyle now. "Don't worry. I'll be there in the shadows to make sure no one gets too carried away."

"Make sure those are some pretty deep shadows, Charlie. If we're not going to hurt Massey ourselves, then we can't be seen as having any part of this."

I might not have been much of a detective, but this was the part of the job I had down cold. "I'll be as quiet as a church mouse on Sunday."

He looked at the clock on his desk. It was just after two o'clock in the afternoon.

"I'll need you to put The Wanderer on hold for the rest of the day," Carmichael told me. "See if you can't get Doyle to take care of Massey PDQ. Tomorrow, it's back to The Wanderer for you. In the meantime, I'll have Ross get his men on the black truck lead. See if they come up with anything. If they do, Rosie will have it waiting for you in the morning."

I had my marching orders and I got up to leave. "I'll get right on it, Chief. Do you want me to tell you the details or do you just want to know when it's done?"

"When it's done." He waved a hand over the piles of paper on his desk. "I've got plenty to keep me busy until then. Let's talk tomorrow unless something serious pops up."

I hoped I wouldn't have to bother him. But things being as they were, I wasn't in the position to make any promises.

Chapter 13

I PARKED my Ford in front of The Longford Lounge on West Fifty-Fourth Street and Tenth Avenue. The fancy awning was hunter green with gold trim. It was going on four o'clock in the afternoon, so no one was watching the door yet.

The Lounge was legally billed as a supper club, which meant it technically couldn't open before five o'clock. But everyone knew the place never closed. Not for the right people, anyway.

Because the Lounge wasn't just any watering hole. It was where Aloysius 'Archie' Doyle called home. The seat of power from where The Duke of New York reigned supreme.

Every elected official in the city made the pilgrimage to the Lounge at one time or another. Every crook and mobster on the east coast too, if they knew what was good for them. They all needed Doyle's influence. He was the man who held the Tiger's leash. He wasn't the Grand Sachem of the place, but he was the one who kept the Tiger fed. He could make it purr or growl depending on his mood.

Doyle wasn't above making an honest buck, though. He had a couple of construction companies, one of which was building the tunnel I'd taken to Jersey. He also had some talented boxers under contract, a dozen or so thoroughbred horses, backed a couple of hit Broadway shows and, if the rumors were to be believed, was thinking about getting in the movie business one of these days.

If Doyle had been completely legitimate, my kids would probably be learning about him in school. He was a genuine New York success story. Doyle had climbed out of the gutter of Five Points with nothing but his fists, the clothes on his back and Fatty Corcoran at his side. Now he controlled the biggest criminal empire on the eastern seaboard. It was said that he had a piece of every crooked dollar spent from Maine to Miami. I saw no reason to doubt it was true.

I figured that was a big reason why the place always managed to avoid being raided.

I pulled the door open and walked inside. Despite all the booze and smoking that went on, the place never smelled like a saloon. I always caught the scent of cedar whenever I walked in, and it always put me at ease.

I spotted Francois Deveraux, the maître d', in his undershirt as he gabbed on the phone at the podium they had parked by the door. He was laying on the French act thick. His real name was Frank Deavers, an old safecracker out of New Orleans. The French bit was just a ruse for the suckers to give the place some class.

Deveraux hung up and was scribbling something in a ledger when he said in a convincing French accent, "Forgive me, monsieur, but we are closed at the moment."

"Knock it off, Frankie. I'm here to see Archie."

Deavers looked up at me and dropped the accent. "Hey, Charlie! Sorry, I was too busy writing something down." He stopped writing long enough to shake my hand before quickly finishing entering a reservation in his ledger. "What brings you around?" He checked the date in his ledger. "It's not Friday, is it?"

Friday was the day I picked up the special envelope for the chief and one for me along with any troubles he wanted us to solve. "No, it's not Friday. Like I said, I'm here to see Archie about something. He around?"

"Holding court in the back," Deavers told me. "Nothing big, just a card game that's been going on a while. Poke your head in and say hello. He could use the break. I hear Lady Luck is giving him the cold shoulder."

"Glad to see some things never change." I patted Frankie on the back as I passed by. "See you on the way out."

The Lounge had been an old warehouse Doyle had won in a card game a few years back. Now it was an Irishman's dream, two floors overdone with oak paneling, mirrors, chandeliers and gold trim wherever they could think to put it. It was just this side of gaudy, but that's the way Archie had wanted it. And The Duke always got what he wanted.

The bar was empty, but still glamorous. Dark wood and gentle lighting gave the place a dignified air. I guess that's why people lined up around the block each night to see the place. For the hint of romance. The warm elegance made the booze seem like it was more than just another way of getting high.

I crossed the dancefloor toward the private back room that was known as Doyle's Court. It was a heavily paneled affair with two French doors sporting stained glass in them.

And, as expected, Terry Quinn was sitting guard at a table right outside. He was reading the paper, smoking a cigarette and drinking some coffee. His tuxedo jacket hung on the back of his chair. His collar was open, and his black tie hadn't been knotted yet.

The .45 holstered under his left arm completed the look. I'd helped get him a permit for the gun, so he didn't get hassled every time he walked out the front door.

I'll admit I flinched when he looked up at me. I'd been in more than my fair share of scrapes and had come up against a lot of hard cases in my life. But there was always something about Quinn that just flat-out scared me. There'd never been so much as a cross look between us, much less words, but the kid had an element of death about him.

It wasn't just that he was ten years younger than me and big. At six-five and two-hundred-pounds of lean muscle, he was even bigger than Carmichael. And it wasn't just because he'd been a contender for the heavyweight title, either. I'd flattened plenty of ring rats in my day. Some of them heavyweights, too.

Maybe it was the way he moved. Like the difference between a plow horse and a thoroughbred. He just moved different than everyone else. His black hair was pasted to his head and his eyes were deep set and black as night.

Maybe it was the lantern jaw that did it. Or the nose that had broken more times than even he could count.

No, I never could quite put my finger on why the kid scared me, but he did. And I hoped I never had the chance to find out firsthand just how dangerous he could be. I'd seen him fight in the ring and knew one back hand from him would put me in traction for a year.

"Look who's here," Quinn grinned as he stood up to greet me. "Everyone's favorite cop." He held up the afternoon edition of the *Mirror*. "Can I get your autograph?"

I shook his hand and tried to keep the quiver out of my voice as I said, "Don't believe everything you read."

Quinn looked me over. "You on a bender, Charlie? You look like hell."

"Just burning the midnight oil," I told him. "Archie here? Frankie told me he's in a card game."

"His luck could use the break," Quinn said. "Wait here."

He went over to the French doors, knocked, then pulled them apart. He ducked his head inside and said, "You've got a visitor, boss."

"That so?" I heard Doyle's familiar growl from inside. "Friend or foe?"

"Neither one," Quinn said. "It's Charlie."

"You mean *the* Charlie Doherty?" Doyle boomed, then said, "Alright, you bums. The cards are running cold for everyone. Get out there and pour some coffee into you. But don't go anywhere. This game ain't over yet and I'll be damned if you're going home with all my money in your pockets."

Quinn pushed the doors all the way open, and I stood aside, averting my eyes as the men filed out of the card game. I saw an assemblyman from the Upper West Side, a state senator, an alderman and a ward heeler from the Bronx. I knew each of them and they all knew me. Each of them gave me a nod and I returned the courtesy.

When the room had cleared out, Doyle yelled. "Get

your skinny ass in here, Charlie. What're you waiting for? An invitation?"

Quinn waited until I was inside before he began to pull the doors closed behind me, but Doyle stopped him. "You too, Terry. Come on in and keep us company. Maybe a couple of fresh faces will turn my luck around."

I found Archie Doyle was sitting at the head of the round table covered with scattered playing cards and poker chips. I know a round table isn't supposed to have a head, but wherever Archie sat was always considered the head.

His thick shock of unruly gray hair and bushy gray eyebrows framed a deep-set gaze. Years spent working the docks and slaughterhouses of the Manhattan waterfront had left him broad shouldered and barrel-chested. His forearms were huge, almost deformed. I knew he was pushing fifty, but he looked stronger than a kid half his age.

"Well, if it ain't the *Mirror's* favorite cop," Doyle said as he poured himself a cup of coffee from a silver pot.

He looked like a man who'd just spent the entire night playing cards. His shirt was open, exposing a white T-shirt underneath. "What do you need, kid? An agent to go along with your newfound fame? Just say the word and I'll have you double-billed with Gloria Swanson. Have you play a cop. The pictures could stand the genuine article for a change."

"I was always more partial to Mary Pickford." I didn't mind the ribbing. It was Archie's way of showing affection.

"Got no pull with her," Doyle admitted, "but Gloria's a pip. The girl loves me."

After finishing pouring his cup, Doyle looked to the

man sitting at his right. "What about you, Fatty. Want a snort?"

"Please," the fat man said as he inched his cup closer so Archie could pour easier.

If Archie looked like he'd been playing cards all night, Fatty Corcoran looked like he'd just stepped out of haberdasher's front window. I'd never known his real first name and I'd never heard him called anything else besides Fatty. He lived up to the name. He was a round man who went at least three-hundred pounds, but he was no slob. Unlike Kronauer, Fatty was fussy about his appearance and went for bowlers rather than fedoras. He was always clean shaven, and his bow ties always sported a perfect knot.

Like me and Carmichael, Doyle and Fatty had grown up together. They might call it the Doyle Mob in the papers, but it was as much Fatty's outfit as it was Archie's. Between Archie's brawn and Fatty's brains, they made one hell of a team.

"Grab a seat," Doyle told us. "Or are you too good to slum with us regular types now, what with your newfound fame and all?"

Quinn and I took our seats as Archie slurped his coffee. He was a wealthy man, not a graceful one. I guess when you had his kind of pull, you didn't need to be.

"That newfound fame is part of the reason why I'm here," I admitted.

Fatty smiled at me. "You look tired, Charles."

"You look like shit, kid," Archie said as he lit a cigar. "I've got bar rags that look better than you. You on a toot or need a little hair of the dog what bit you? We'll fix you right up if you want."

"I'm as sober as a judge," I said. "And not like any of the judges we know."

He nodded at the copy of the *Mirror* that Quinn had brought in with him. "I sure hope that article ain't bothering you. It's nothing. Just some scribbler trying to get his feet wet in a new pond."

"You read the article?" I asked him.

Doyle grinned at me through the cigar smoke. "You know I ain't much of a reader, kid. That's what I've got Fatty for. He does my reading for me, though I heard the article gave you and your boss a rough time."

"This time," I allowed. "But he'll get bored with us pretty soon and after that, who knows what trail he'll follow?"

"That so?" Doyle wasn't an educated man, but anyone who had ever taken him for a dope was either broke or dead.

He looked at Fatty. "Sounds like intrigue if you ask me. I hate intrigue. Too complicated. Makes my head hurt. What do you make of it, fat man?"

Corcoran set his cup on the saucer. "You think Massey will become a problem, don't you?"

"He already is," I said. "A problem that's only bound to get worse. Do you know anything about him?"

I wasn't surprised when Corcoran didn't miss a beat. "Mr. Massey had a bad run of luck back in Chicago. Significant gambling debts, from what I understand. Found himself on the wrong side of Mr. Capone, too, hence his recent arrival in our fair city."

"Capone," Archie spat. "You know, the day that crazy guinea bastard went west was one of the happiest days of my life."

Fatty looked at me. "He's got a bit of the crusader about him from what I understand."

I liked how Fatty always knew the score. "You read what he said about Tammany. We both know it won't end there. He'll get tired of batting around the chief and when he does, we think he'll turn his attention to greener pastures. He'll keep digging until he hits paydirt and by then, it'll be too late to stop him."

Archie sat forward. "So you want us to nip this guy in the butt before it gets that far."

"Bud," Fatty told him. "Nip it in the bud. It's a gardening expression."

"No kidding? Is that what it means?"

Fatty nodded.

Doyle popped the cigar back in his mouth. "I like 'butt' better. Got more poetry to it."

Fatty shook his head and got back to business. "Is the chief as concerned about this as you?"

"I wouldn't be here otherwise."

"And you'd like us to be concerned about it, too," Fatty went on. "Perhaps address the situation before it becomes a bigger problem?"

"Like I said, I wouldn't be here otherwise."

Fatty sat back in his chair. His part of the discussion was over. He made sure all the facts had been laid out for Archie to see. What happened next was up to him.

He looked philosophical as he watched his cigar smoke trail up to the tin ceiling. "Sounds like we oughta give Massey a proper welcome to The Big Apple." He cocked an eyebrow in my direction. "You say he's a sporting man?"

"That's what Fatty said."

"No better place for a gambler to visit than the Lounge, right?" He looked at Corcoran. "What do you think, fatso?"

"A wise suggestion as always, Archie." Fatty looked at me. "Perhaps we should invite him to take his hand at some games of chance? Give him a tour of the place, particularly our wine cellar."

I knew the Lounge had a cellar, but they didn't keep wine down there. They served a more bitter brew. "I think the chief would appreciate the hospitality."

"Tonight's no good," Doyle decided. "I've got dinner with Gloria. Her drip boyfriend's in town so the poor girl needs someone to show her a good time. We'll do it tomorrow, say around five. I like to get this kind of thing over with early in the evening so as to not ruin the rest of the night."

"That sounds fine," I told him. "The chief will be happy to hear it."

"Oh, I bet he will," Doyle laughed as he sat further back in his chair. "Will His Eminence be joining us or just you?" He even crossed himself for effect.

"Just me this time," I told them. "But the chief will be by in a week or so. He needs some time off."

"Good," Archie said. "Haven't seen him in a while. I was beginning to think he didn't love us anymore."

"He's always valued your friendship, Archie. As have I."

Doyle looked over at Quinn. "Do me a favor and tell Frankie to call Massey at his office. Tell him he's been invited to the lounge as my personal guest. Tell him we'll expect him here at five. And make sure Frankie lays on the French real thick. A rube like Massey should fall for that gag hook, line and sinker."

Quinn got up to leave. "I'll tell him to call right now."

But Doyle stopped him up by raising his hand. "Don't be so hasty, Terry. After all, we're in the presence of a celebrity now. His Lordship's very own handpicked boy." He grinned at me. "Will that be all for today,

Detective Doherty, or will the chief be needing any other favors? A peeled grape, perhaps?"

I knew I was about to push my luck, both with Carmichael and with Doyle. But things being how they were, I didn't have much of a choice. "Actually, there's one more thing we could use your help on."

Archie's mouth dropped open. "You've gotta be shitting me. What?"

There was no sense in drawing it out. "I need a contact in Harlem. Someone we can trust to handle the kind of problem that's police business but off the books. Someone who knows how to keep their mouth shut. I wouldn't ask, but it's important."

This time, Archie didn't have to look to Fatty for an answer. And I felt Quinn's eyes boring into me from across the table.

"Afraid I can't help you there, kid." Archie flicked his ash into an ashtray. "Boxing the scribbler's ears for him isn't a problem, but Harlem's out. Bumpy's been getting frisky after Carmichael kowtowed to the Queen and the old hag has been putting on airs with me ever since. I know Carmichael wants peace uptown, so I've been letting it slide, but the chief and I need to talk before I do him any favors uptown. You know I help where I can, but that's a dead end. Tell your boss I hope he understands."

Between Doyle's answer and Quinn's eyes on me, I felt the walls closing in fast. It was time to make my exit. "Don't give it another thought, Archie. Thanks for even considering it."

"Thanks for understanding." Doyle flicked his cigar ash in the ashtray. Any annoyance forgotten. "Be sure to swing by a little after five tomorrow if you want to join in on the welcome party we'll be throwing for Massey. But don't be too late. I don't think he'll stand up too well to our kind of fun. And speaking of fun, send them bums back in when you leave. I plan on getting some of my money back."

I thanked him and Fatty again and I tried not to knock anything over as I left.

I knew I'd been pushing my luck by asking for a contact in Harlem, but it was my job to anticipate problems for the chief before they became problems.

But as soon as I'd gotten through the French doors, I felt Quinn's big hand on my shoulder. "Wait a second."

He told the card players to head back inside, and we walked together toward the front door.

Quinn said, "What kind of trouble are you having up in Harlem?"

"Just a police thing," I told him. "I need to meet some people and ask some questions and I can't use the department to do it. I know that sounds cagey, but I can't say any more than that."

"You said you need someone you can trust," Quinn said. "Someone who'll help and keep their mouth shut."

Everyone wrote off Quinn as a thug because of his size. I'd never been that stupid. "That's about the crux of it. Secrecy is important. For all of us."

Quinn's eyes narrowed. "This something that could hurt Archie?"

"Maybe not right away, but it could if I let it linger." I had a spark of hope. "Why? Do you know someone?"

He looked back toward the private room, then at me. "I do, but I'm not going against Archie, understand? He said he couldn't help you and he wasn't lying. But he didn't tell me to stay out of it."

I knew that was an important dividing line with Quinn. He was loyal to Archie and would never cross him. I knew what it was like to be loyal to a difficult man. "Anything you do would stay between us."

"Give me your pad."

I handed it over to him along with my pen. He scribbled down a name and an address before handing it back to me.

I had to read it twice. Not because of his handwriting, but because of the name and place he had written. "Are you sure?"

"We go back," he told me. "Make sure you tell him I sent you or he won't help. He might not help anyway, but this is as close to a shot as you'll get uptown."

I put the pad and pen away and shook his hand. "This is more than I hoped for. Thanks, pal."

As I went on my way, Quinn called after me. "Don't forget. Five o'clock sharp. And don't wear anything fancy. It's liable to be a lively party."

I hit the door and got to my car. I didn't want to think about what he meant by that, but I'd be finding out for myself soon enough.

Chapter 14

I FOUND a parking spot on 110th and Lenox Avenue and grabbed it.

The thoughts that ran through my weary mind as I angled my Ford between two parked cars were the same that had bothered me the whole ride up here.

They weren't tom-tom beats yet, but they were constant concerns that kept tumbling over in my mind.

What the hell am I doing?

What if this is a big waste time?

I knew every second I spent away from my desk was a second in The Wanderer's favor. Talking to Doyle about handling Massey was a necessity. But this Harlem trip was my idea. I might be wasting time I didn't have.

And trusting a man I didn't know at all.

I knew the clue to finding The Wanderer was somewhere in those files back at my office. I needed to get back there to continue the search. I'd never thought I'd be anxious to rifle through paperwork, but this was different. Everything about The Wanderer was different.

But I couldn't blindly chase possible leads down dead

ends until I took care of brush fires like Massey and the Harlem families first. Because if those brush fires had enough fuel, they'd burn us all down.

Me and Carmichael losing our jobs would be bad. Winding up dead at the bottom of the Gowanus Canal would be even worse.

But we had chosen our lives. If it wound up getting us killed, we had it coming. The idea of The Wandering Man getting off the hook if something happened to us was the one thing I couldn't allow. The boys he'd killed would never be avenged. And the killings would keep going on until The Wanderer was either caught or dead.

That was why I needed this Harlem gamble to pay off. I needed to buy time today so I could spend tomorrow hunting him down.

Besides, my main job was to protect the chief and the department. In my own way, I was doing that now.

I ignored the looks I drew from residents as I walked along Lenox to the address Quinn had given me. They'd all pegged me for a cop, and I didn't mind. I was there for a reason, and it wasn't to make friends.

The place I was looking for didn't have a fancy awning or a sign like The Longford Lounge, but I knew it was a speakeasy. The two black men in suits lounging on either side of a stoop told me I was in the right place.

Both of them had that same ring rat look. Fit and mean. Middleweights. Their dark suits and fedoras made them look classy, but they reeked hired muscle like I reeked cop. The ring may have left them behind, but the street had beckoned. It offered promise.

The one on the left smiled at me as he spoke to his partner. "Well, would you look at this, Fred. A white cop all the way up here and all alone. In broad daylight, no less. When was the last time you seen that?"

"Can't say," Fred told him, "but it ain't a good sign, Joe. Kinda like seein' a raccoon in the mornin'. Ain't a good sign at all. He might be rabid. Maybe we ought to shoot him, just to be safe."

"Take it easy, fellas. I come in peace." I held out my hands up and parted my legs. It was an invitation for them to frisk me, which I knew they were going to do anyway. Joe did the honors.

I talked them through what they'd find so they didn't get antsy when they found it. "I've got a .38 holstered on my left hip, a sap in the back of my pants and a pair of handcuffs on my belt. I've also got a wallet in my suit pocket that'll tell you who I am."

Joe did a thorough job of patting me down. "And just who the hell are you, cop?"

"I work out of the Castle and I'm here to see your boss on official police business."

Fred spoke while Joe found my wallet and opened it. "Who's your boss?"

I kept my hands raised and my eyes on Fred. "The king of the Castle. Harlem's best friend with a badge."

Joe folded my wallet and jammed it back into the same pocket where he'd found it. "Why do you want to see the champ for?"

I shook my head. "That's between me and your boss."

Fred closed the few feet between us to only an inch or so. "Whether or not you get to see him is up to us, so you'd best be spillin' and right now."

"Like we said," Joe sneered, "cops coming up here alone and unannounced just ain't natural. Anything could happen to you. Anything at all and no one would ever know."

I kept my eyes on Fred. "I came here alone. I stood

for a frisk. I didn't badge you and I didn't pull my gun. I showed respect. Now it's time for a little to come back my way. And if I'm not back at my desk in an hour, you'll see so much blue, you'll think the sky is falling."

Fred didn't seem to like that idea and I kept pushing. "So, we can do this easy, or we can do this real easy. And real easy, in case you forgot, means you go inside, tell your boss who I am and that I need to see him."

Fred held his ground. "And what if he says no?"

"Then I get back in my car and drive away and some nice people in Harlem go on suffering."

I heard Joe take a step closer behind me, boxing me in between him and Fred. "That sounds like a threat to me. That sound like a threat to you, Fred?"

"Not a threat," I said. "A fact."

Fred remained in front of me and signaled for Joe to go inside. I knew the play. Fred had taken a stance against a white cop and wouldn't back down without a better reason than one I could give him.

After a long minute of the two of us staring at each other, Joe popped his head out of the door underneath the stoop. "Boss says to let him in."

Reluctantly, Fred stepped aside and let me pass. He was quickly on my heels as I walked through the door under the stoop stairs and into The Congo Club.

The club was beneath the stoop and overdone with walls covered in thatched straw and bamboo shoots. Wooden masks above crossed spears every few feet completed the look. Lamp shades of table lamps matched the décor. So did the bar at the back of the place.

I followed Fred around the bar to a narrow hallway to the side. It led into the rest of the club where the singers and dancers would be later on that night. A bathroom was on either side of the hall for men and women. The door at the back alley was already open and some light filtered in.

Joe stopped and pointed to an open door on his right.

I went in and found a large black man behind a small desk. He was bald and had the kind of eyes that looked straight through a man, just like Quinn's. That's because they had fought the same wars in the same places.

Both had been the best of their time. Both had defied the odds and winning had cost them the thing they loved the most.

The ring.

Quinn had defied the Boys when he'd refused to take a dive.

Jack Johnson's sin? Being the best heavyweight in the world and living life on his own terms.

I could feel Joe and Fred standing behind me. Johnson's hard, silent stare felt like a brick wall in front of me. I was caught between the three of them and didn't move a muscle. I was determined to wait it out, no matter how long it took. Not for my sake, but for the sake of the dead I was here to avenge. For the sake of the chief and the department I was here to protect.

There were no other chairs in the office except for the one occupied by Jack Johnson. I figured that was by design.

The former heavyweight champion of the world looked me up and down. He didn't seem impressed by what he saw. "I hear you're Charlie Doherty. Joe told me your name like it's supposed to mean something to me. It doesn't."

He was looking for weakness. I hadn't shown any out on the street and I sure as hell couldn't show it in here.

"Sure it does. You know who I work for, or I wouldn't be in here now."

Johnson's expression was impossible to read. "Guess that makes you one of those smart white boys I've been reading about. Harlem's full of black men you could talk to. What makes me so special?"

"Beats me," I said. "Terry Quinn told me I could trust you. If he was wrong, tell me now and I'll be on my way."

That seemed to buy me something with him. "Quinn sent you? Not Doyle?"

"Doyle wouldn't help. Quinn said you would."

He looked past me at the two in the hallway. "One of you get this man a chair, then go back to watching the front door. Looks like me and this cop have some business to discuss."

I didn't know if it was Fred or Joe, but one of them set down a chair down behind me. I didn't sit until I heard they'd already moved on down the hall.

"Dropping Quinn's name bought you five minutes of my time," Johnson said. "Best use it wisely. I hate being this close to a cop."

I didn't exactly feel at home, so got right to it. "I'm here to ask you for a favor. It's a big one that'll go a long way to helping the people of Harlem."

"That so?" He shook his bald head. "The biggest problem Harlem has ever faced is white people with good intentions. What makes you any different from them?"

"Because I'm talking about a specific problem," I told him. "One that you can help me handle if you want."

Johnson's eyes moved over me again. "You new to this town, boy?"

"Far from it. Lived here my whole life."

"Bet you're mighty proud of that."

"Not particularly," I shrugged. "It's not for everybody, but it's home to me."

"Well said," Johnson told me. "You follow my career? My life?"

"I read the papers."

"Then you ought to know just as many black folks around here hate me as white folks," he said. "My own kind hates me because they say I didn't do enough to help them. That I lived the way I wanted. They don't like me owning nightclubs and taking white women to my bed."

He grinned. "Trouble is white folks hate me for the same reasons. Seems I'm too damned black and too damned proud for my own good. I don't bow every time some white man tells me to, and I don't duck my head to anyone, except royalty. And I *have* met royalty."

He held his large hands open wide. "So what can an unpopular man like me possibly do for a white cop like you all the way up here?"

I liked the way he talked and used it to my advantage. "You're forgetting a third kind of person."

"And who might that be?"

"The kind of people who are proud of you. Who respect you and trust you because of exactly the kind of man you are. The same kind of people I need to help now."

I could tell Johnson was interested. "Let's say I can help you. What do I get in return?"

"You get me," I told him. "A direct line to the chief's office any time you need it. And the Queen herself never needs to know about it."

"She ain't no queen," Johnson said. "I've met royalty,

mister. Real royalty. She's just some old Haitian witch who fell into the numbers racket. She ain't even American. I've never called her 'Queen'."

"And with a friend like me, you'll never have to."

I could tell that hooked Johnson good. He didn't want to be hooked, but he was. An in with the chief of police was always a good chit to have in your back pocket. "Your boss know about this?"

"He knows," I lied, "but first I'll need your word that whatever I tell you stays between us. No one else can know. It's a matter of life and death. The lives and deaths of young black men from Harlem."

Johnson slowly sat back in his chair. His eyes never left me. "What kind of evil have you brought in here with you today, boy?"

"First I need your word that anything I tell you stays between us. Because if I tell you, you'll be the fifth person in the city who knows what's going on."

"Let's say I help you," Johnson said, "but you don't take my calls after. What would that leave me with?"

"You'd be free to tell everyone what I'm about to tell you. I'm giving you a loaded gun pointed right at my head because it's that important."

Johnson's eyes narrowed. "That's a hell of a lot of faith to put in a man you just met five minutes ago."

"I know you." I narrowed my eyes, too. "Just like you know me. We know exactly what the other man is, which means we know we can trust each other. Now, do I have your word about keeping this private?"

He thought it over. "You have my word." He leaned forward and folded his hands on his desk. "Now talk."

I'D JUST FINISHED TELLING him about the letters and The Wandering Man when we silently moved into the empty lounge.

Neither of us spoke a word. There wasn't much to say. The dark truth of what I had just told him bonded us now.

I snagged a table. He brought over a half-empty bottle of rye and two full glasses from the bar.

He drained his glass of rye and poured himself another. I hadn't touched mine. I was barely keeping my eyes open, and one sip might knock me for a loop. I'd worked too hard to earn Johnson's respect to lose it now.

Johnson raised his glass to his lips but set it back on the table. He was a tough man, but looked every bit as shaken as I'd felt when I'd read the file.

At least he hadn't read the letters. I think they might've broken him. Even a hard man like Jack Johnson had limits.

"And you think Massey's articles might get some Harlem families talking to the press?"

"If he keeps writing about Spann and mentions The Wandering Man case, yeah. I do."

"And you think you're close to catching this bastard?"

"Closer than we've ever been," I said. "I've only been on it a couple of days, but I'm already seeing progress. That progress will be erased if those families start talking to reporters. Every paper in town will spill everything the families tell them about their missing sons. They'll even pay for the story. If that happens, me and the chief are out, and this gets swept under the rug. The killer goes free. I don't want that, and I don't think you want it, either."

Johnson didn't look so sure. "Might get a lot more

cops looking for him instead of just one man who looks as flat as yesterday's beer."

"For a week or two, maybe," I said. "The pressure will be on to find a killer. Any old killer will do. And since most of these dead boys lived in Harlem, I'll give you three guesses to figure out which kind of man they'll pin it on. Here's a hint. He won't be white."

Johnson glared at me a long while. He wasn't just looking me over. He was trying to look into my soul. "And if you catch him?"

"I'll kill him."

He gestured toward my jacket. "You said you had a list of the families with you."

I gave him the list I'd drawn up and spoke while he looked it over. "These are the families who received letters from The Wanderer. There are probably more, but these are the only families we know about. Getting them to agree to just remain quiet no matter what will go a long way to helping me get them the justice they deserve."

Johnson looked over the list. "It'll also help you keep your job. Save your own ass from the fire."

I saw no reason to deny it. "That's part of it. But just think about what happens if the one cop who's working this case gets canned. It'll mean Carmichael gets canned, too and even you've seen how good he's been for Harlem. Not squad cars parked in front of your dives. No cops rousting young men for no reason. Not to mention what people up here will do if they read how the cops didn't do anything to find a bunch of missing black kids. Harlem will burn. That won't be good for you or your business."

Johnson grinned. "You sure know how to appeal to a man's better nature, don't you, white boy?"

I knew I'd never say the right thing, so I stayed focused on the list. "All I need for those families to do is nothing. Nothing at all. And if you think I'm lying, then I've given you enough to pick up the phone, call a reporter and burn the whole thing down. But I don't think you'll do that."

"And why not?"

"Because you've had enough white men lie to you to know the truth when you hear it."

I watched Johnson's eyes run over the list and the addresses one more time. "I know all of these people. I'll talk to each of them in turn and I won't tell them there are others. I'll be persuasive. None of them will talk to any cops or reporters. You've got my word on that."

I wasn't a single step closer to finding The Wanderer, but I felt like I'd just won the lottery. "Thank you."

"Don't go thanking me just yet," he told me. "This ain't a blank check. I'll promise to keep them quiet, but only for a week or two. If you don't catch this bastard by then, you're on your own. I won't be troubling these people a second time. You understand me, white boy?"

I hoped it would be enough time, but I was in no position to argue. I pulled out one of my cards and wrote down the number to the chief's office on the back.

"My number is on the front, but the one on the back is the number for the chief. If you can't reach me, his office can get in touch with me."

Johnson took the card, folded it with the list and tucked them in his shirt pocket. "I hope I won't have to call you. And you'd better hope you catch this man while you've still got time."

For the first time since this mess had been dumped in my lap, I felt something close to hope. I held out my hand to him. "Thanks for this, Mr. Johnson."

"You can call me Jack now." The champ shook my hand and didn't try to crush it. But he didn't let it go, either. "You *will* tell me when you kill this man, won't you."

"You can count on it."

I'd never meant anything more in my life.

Chapter 15

THE NEXT MORNING, my girls found me on the couch and woke me with kisses. They peppered me with questions about why I wasn't in bed where I belonged. They came up with answers on their own, asking me if they were right.

I barely remembered coming home the night before, much less anything that happened after that. I remembered sitting on the couch while Theresa peppered me with questions about Massey's *Mirror* article when I passed out.

I'd woken up feeling horrible and figured I looked even worse. I'd fallen asleep in the same clothes I'd worn the last two days. My mouth felt as grimy as a whorehouse floor. My stomach growled. My head and back killed me from sleeping at an odd angle. I guess the sofa wasn't as comfortable as I'd remembered.

Theresa was cooking breakfast and the mere smell of coffee made me feel better. I realized I hadn't eaten anything in over a day.

Anne and Mary ran into the kitchen to help their mother set the table.

I saw Theresa had taken my plate from the breakfast table, so I figured I was in the doghouse. I decided not to ask about why for the sake of the girls. I used the time to take a shower instead.

The hot water made a lot of my aches go away. A quick shave made me feel like a new man. Once I had some coffee and eggs in me, I'd be ready to dive back into The Wanderer files and find that son of a bitch once and for all. I'd spent a good part of the previous day buying time to continue the hunt. Now it was time to put that hunt to good use.

I went into the bedroom and found a new gray suit and fresh white shirt to put on. I wrapped a paisley tie into a full knot and even tucked a pocket square into my suit jacket for good measure. I don't know why I felt like spiffing up, but I did. My shoes could've used a good shine, but I'd worry about that later.

I checked myself in the full-length mirror at the back of the door and didn't mind what I saw. I'd never be confused for a Barrymore, but I didn't look like the bum I was supposed to be, either. My crop top was a little grayer than I'd like, but I'd earned those colors. I was also a little skinnier than I should've been, but on the whole, not bad.

I stepped into the hallway, hoping to see the girls before they left for school, but the place was deserted. Theresa always walked them to school every day. She might not have been much of a wife, but she was a great mother. She'd die before she let anything happen to them. I guess that counted for something.

I found the pot of coffee was still warm and she'd left some scrambled eggs for me in the pan. I grabbed a fork and wolfed them down quickly. They were almost cold, but better than nothing.

I had just poured myself some more coffee when I spotted the note she'd stuck next to the wall phone.

It was in Theresa's handwriting:

Andersson from the Hall called. Wants to see you this morning. Said not to tell Andy.

There was a phone number, too.

I shut my eyes and leaned against the doorframe. As if The Wanderer wasn't enough to worry about, one of the sachems from the Hall had just sent for me. And not just any sachem, either. One of the enterprising younger men who had sprouted up over the last couple of years. Brian Andersson.

Although Theresa's note had warned me against telling Andy, the first thing I did was call Andy from the wall phone in my kitchen. Given the hour, I figured I'd still get him at home.

He picked up on the first ring. When he heard it was me, he asked, "What's wrong?"

Knowing anyone could've been listening on the line, I kept it vague. "I just got a message. I've been sent for."

I heard the earpiece scrape against his shoulder as he looked around to see if Helen or the kids were listening.

"Damn," he whispered into the mouthpiece. "Who?"

"Andersson. Wants me to call him back right away."

"What number?"

I told him and heard him begin to breathe again on the other end. "That's his home. That's good. Means it's not official. Massey's article probably has him curious. He's probably looking for something he can bring back to the others if he's asked."

I didn't care about Andersson's reasons. I only cared about what Carmichael wanted me to do. "I'll ignore it if you want. Claim I didn't get the message. I'd be better off using the time at the office looking for our friend, anyway."

"No. Meeting Andersson is time well spent. Call him back, find out where and when he wants to meet you, then let Rosie know the details. Come to my office as soon as you're done. I'll want to know everything."

The line went dead, and I put the earpiece back in the cradle.

It looked like I'd have to put my hunt for The Wanderer on hold for a couple of hours. I had a Tiger to tame.

ANDERSSON TOLD me to meet him at ten-thirty at a Tammany joint called Rudolph's. It was a restaurant off East Fourteenth Street where the boys from the Hall liked to be seen having meetings in public. It was like The Longford Lounge in that way, sans the booze and the elegance.

If he'd wanted to meet at the Hall itself, I would've been worried. Choosing a semi-public place meant this was probably a friendly sit-down.

It was after the morning rush and traffic into Manhattan was lighter than normal. I guess that's why I found myself checking my mirrors more than I normally did. I usually did it without thinking, but on that day, I kept thinking about Spann and how The Wanderer had found him. Staking out stationery stores was just a theory. He could've just as easily been trailing him by car, waiting for his chance to pounce. I didn't see any black trucks following me, but he could've been in any of the cars I saw in my rearview. If he was there at all.

I also knew there was a fine line between being cautious and paranoid. Caution was good. Paranoid made you jumpy. I did my best to remain calm. I'd need all the calm I could muster going up against a Tammany hack like Andersson.

I found a spot up the block from Randolph's on Fourteenth Street around the corner from the Hall. It was a run of the mill eatery, which was just how the Tammany boys liked it.

I walked inside and found Brian Andersson waiting for me at a corner table in the back. He was one of the few Tammany men who didn't have a nickname. The boys preferred to use nicknames instead of real names as a sort of code. Unless you were in on the joke, you didn't know who we were talking about.

Pinky had gotten his nickname because he turned pink when he was flustered. Boo-Boo earned his nickname because he had a habit of accidentally telling the truth when ambushed by reporters. Lil' Jimsy was their term of affection for Mayor Walker.

Andersson had somehow managed to avoid acquiring a nickname and I never knew why. Carmichael referred to him as 'The Man for All Seasons' given his mixed heritage. There was hardly an ethnic holiday that Andersson didn't celebrate. He was Scottish and Irish, but don't dare call him Scotts-Irish. He claimed Scandinavian blood, so that covered Finland, Sweden and Norway along with a few others. His grandparents on his father's side had been from Wales and England at one point, which he conveniently forgot on St. Patrick's Day, but otherwise played up when it suited him.

He'd grown up in Greenwich Village a few years behind Mayor Jimmy Walker. He was said to be 'Jimsy's' eyes and ears in the Hall, not that it had done Walker any good. Like the rest of us, Walker did what the Hall told him to do. Refuse and hear that Tiger growl.

Andersson stood when he saw me come in. "How good of you to make time to see me, Charlie. Always an honor."

We shook hands and I took my seat.

Andersson enjoyed all the trappings of being a Tammany sachem. He was only about thirty, an infant among the gray beards of the Hall, but he'd managed to carve out a niche for himself. He liked to show his influence by making sure his black book of contacts was always visible. On that particular morning, he had it next to his right hand, like a bible.

He had curly reddish hair and a waxed walrus mustache that was so out of fashion that it was about to come back into style. His starched collar and ascot completed the look. A gold watch chain adorned his gray vest and added gravity to what he lacked in years. The monocle that dangled from the buttonhole on his lapel was a bit much, but 'a bit much' was Andersson's style. In clothing and in politics.

"Thanks for the invitation, Brian," I said as I settled into a chair across from him. "Can't remember the last time I was here."

"Then we'll have to make it a point of bringing you here more often." He signaled for a waiter who produced a cup of fresh coffee for me and left the pot on the table. When he left, Andersson patted his jacket pocket and the flask of whiskey I knew he carried. "Want to make it Irish?"

I covered the cup with my hand. "Thanks, but I've got a busy day ahead."

"So I hear," he said. "You know, you're quite a popular man at the Hall these days."

That wasn't good news. Popularity was a fickle business among the sachems. "That because of the Massey article?"

"Of course not, though the article has upset a fair number of my colleagues."

"Tell them they can quit being upset," I told him. "It's being handled."

Andersson looked neither pleased nor concerned. "I know I don't have to tell you that discretion is our greatest strength."

"None of us were exactly turning cartwheels at the Castle over it, Brian," I told him. "But like I said, it's being handled."

Andersson sipped his coffee. "I understand his reputation precedes him. I don't know anything about the man. Do you?"

I saw no reason to hold back what I knew, so I repeated what Fatty had told me about Massey.

When I was done, Andersson toasted me with his coffee. "My compliments to you and the chief on your usual thoroughness. Earlier, you mentioned that it's being handled. I'd like to know how."

"No, you wouldn't." Information was the coin of our realm, and it was never free. "It's for your own good."

"And yours." Andersson set his mug on the table. "I trust you won't handle Massey too roughly."

"Don't worry. We won't."

"But it's my job to worry, Charlie. More than you know. You only have the department to think about, I have to worry about the entire organization."

I almost laughed in his face. He sounded like he was running Tammany Hall instead of being a ward boss from the Upper East Side. "You get a promotion I didn't hear about, Brian?"

"Not in so many words," he allowed, "though my influence has been steadily growing since the summer. In fact, that's part of the reason why I wanted to meet with you today."

"And the reason why you wanted me to keep this meeting a secret from Carmichael?"

"No. I've heard from certain concerned sources that there's trouble brewing inside the Castle. I was hoping you could shed some light on it for me."

I played it safe. "Someone's nose is always out of joint in that place. You know that."

"This is different," Andersson went on. "I've heard talk of a criminal who has recently come to light. Someone along the lines of Jack the Ripper, you might say."

My mouth went dry and not from the coffee. Someone had told him about The Wandering Man. Someone was getting cold feet.

I fought the urge to drink the coffee and laughed it off. "Jack the Ripper? Queen Victoria making a come-back, too? Someone's pulling your leg."

"I've only heard rumblings," Andersson persisted, "but rumblings often have a hint of truth to them. Massey's mention of your private meeting with the chief after the funeral yesterday added some weight to what I've heard. Some of our mutual friends have begun making enquiries on the matter."

It was my turn to get some information from him. "Who's telling you all this?"

Andersson acted like he didn't hear me. "They believe this Ripper matter may have been why Carmichael insisted on having a private conversation with you after Spann's funeral. That part about a key only served to fire their imaginations, Charlie."

"Sounds like they've got too much free time on their hands," I said. "Tell them to get a hobby. Stamps or coins. Hell, they might even try getting a job."

But Andersson wouldn't be distracted. He was on the scent of something. "If your private conference had something to do with the regular course of police business, why the secret stroll? Massey may be troublesome, but he's an experienced journalist. If he thought it important enough to include in his column, some of us think there must be something there. The fact that he knew enough to follow you is troubling, too. He obviously knew where you were going, but how?"

I figured Andersson was the answer to many of the questions he'd just asked. Dooley, Carmichael's driver, had known about my meeting with the chief. He'd probably gotten word to Massey and Andersson. Dooley was Andersson's pal, just like Ron Adams. I bet he let Andersson leaf through his crime scene notes to his heart's content. This was all part of the growing influence Andersson had bragged about earlier.

I only hope he didn't have other friends in the department. Friends with last names like Fitzgerald and Ross.

Andersson probably didn't know everything, but he knew enough. If I told him about The Wanderer, I'd be cutting my throat and Carmichael's at the same time. But I had to feed him something close to the truth. Something he'd believe. Something juicy enough to explain our cemetery meeting.

I decided to feed him an open secret. Something he probably already knew and could check if he didn't.

But I made him work for it by playing bashful. "It's a pretty sensitive subject, Brian. Something personal. It's not my secret to tell."

"There are no secrets among friends," Andersson reminded me. "And I'd like to think we're friends, you and I."

I flashed him my best grin. "I didn't know you cared."

He patted the black book at his right hand. "I've got a lot of friends at the Castle, but there's always room in my book for one more. Providing you tell me what you two talked about after the funeral."

I took a swig of coffee as if I needed caffeine courage. I hoped Carmichael would understand what I was about to do. "The chief's got a girl squirreled away up in the Bronx. Pretty swanky apartment, too, right on the Concourse."

Andersson's eyebrows rose. "I see."

I kept talking to seal the deal. "The key he gave me was to her place. He wanted me to drop off some flowers. He wanted her to see them when she came home from work."

I watched Andersson chew it over. I just hoped it was enough to distract him from The Wanderer investigation.

I could see he was intrigued by the dirt, but he wasn't off the scent yet. "And what of these reports about a killer roaming the streets of our fair city?"

"First I heard about it was from you five minutes ago," I lied.

Andersson slowly turned his cup of coffee. "Want to know what I think?" He didn't wait for me to answer. "I think a couple of our people noted some irregularities at the Spann crime scene. I think Carmichael ordered the coroner to write up his death as a hit-and-run job. I think you're running errands for the chief, but it has nothing to do with his mistress. And yes, I already knew she lived on the Concourse."

I swallowed my growing nerves. Andersson might not be as powerful as he thought, but he still had plenty of friends. "You think a lot."

Andersson was getting pretty good at ignoring what I said. "I think this Massey business is only a very small part of a much larger problem. And I think that beneath that cool exterior, that you and Carmichael are scared out of your wits."

I set my mug aside and leaned forward in the booth. "Want to know what I think?"

Andersson smiled as he sat back in his chair. "Enlighten me."

"I smell fish and it's not coming from the kitchen. You're fishing, Brian. Your basket is empty, your stomach is growling and it's starting to get dark." I shook my head slowly. "There's no ripper, no lunatic on the loose, nothing lurking in the shadows except a nosey reporter who needs to get taught a lesson. That's all."

Andersson was uncharacteristically quiet. He hadn't believed a word of what I had told him so far. I had no choice but to sit there and bear the silence until he was ready to speak to me.

Because even though I reported directly to the chief of police, I was still a Tammany man. Protocols had to be observed, just like in the service.

"Earlier, I told you that you're well thought of at the Hall. That opinion is independent of your current position with Chief Carmichael. You earned it. No one gave it to you, not even the chief."

I figured he was working up to a threat, but that didn't mean I couldn't be polite. "That's nice to hear."

"Loyalty is an admirable trait," Andersson went on,

"but misplaced loyalty can be more damaging to a career than no loyalty at all. I know how close you are with Carmichael. I know he gave you your shield. But you're both part of a system that's bigger than any of us. Bigger than any one governor or mayor. Certainly, bigger than you or me."

I figured the kicker was coming and Andersson didn't disappoint.

"I'm giving you the next day or two to think over every single thing you've just told me. I know your first instinct is to always protect the chief and I won't hold it against you. But when next we speak, I'll expect the truth about this killer. Don't count on Carmichael's influence to save you, Charlie. He's part of the same system we're all bound to protect. Bound by blood and sweat and other things. He's chosen to keep a deadly secret that's not his to keep. I'd hate for you to suffer for his error in judgement."

I knew the spiel was meant to scare me, but it came up short. All it told me was that a lot of people were talking to the chief.

I decided to compromise. "I told you I don't know anything about any mad killer and that's the truth. But I'll dig around a little over the next day or two. Let me see what I can find out. When do you want me to call you?"

"I'll call you," he said as he dug his pocket watch out of his vest pocket. "Now, if you'll excuse me, I have another appointment coming."

I'd been hoping I'd be allowed to eat, but that didn't seem to be in the cards. I made sure I finished my coffee, though. It made me feel as if I'd accomplished something.

As I got up to leave, I couldn't help but ask, "We still friends, Brian?"

He gave me his best fake smile as he extended his hand to me. "For now, Charlie. For now."

The warm coffee in my belly did nothing to kill the cold feeling spreading in my gut as I walked out of Rudolph's.

Because I knew Andy and I were in serious trouble.

Chapter 16

My mind was crowded as I walked to my car.

Andersson knew more than he should about The Wandering Man. That meant others in Tammany knew it, too.

Someone had talked and it wasn't me. Carmichael hadn't told them. Dooley had told them about our walk, but he didn't know about The Wanderer.

Adams knew about Spann's murder being covered up, but not about The Wanderer. Jack Johnson knew about The Wanderer, but he and Tammany had never been on good terms.

That meant either Fitzgerald or Ross had talked. Maybe both.

That was worse than bad. Massey's column had already sent them scrambling for lifeboats. They were covering their bets and Andersson was more than happy to extend them Hall credit. Massey's next article might send them over the edge, depending on who he targeted.

I needed to get back to the Castle fast. This kind of news couldn't be trusted to a phone call. Besides,

Carmichael liked getting his bad news the old-fashioned way. In person and with as many details as possible.

The whole business made me want to put my fist through a wall. All of this political nonsense looming over me, and I still had a killer to hunt.

I'd just reached my car when I caught a sudden movement from across the street. It was out of the corner of my eye, but I knew it was off.

Something that was quicker than it should have been. Something that didn't belong. The kind of something New Yorkers sense in the background without realizing it. Something we see when we least expect it.

Someone had moved too quickly for it to be natural. Like they were ducking out of sight.

Manhattan was a busy place, and I knew whatever I'd seen might not have anything to do with me. But after watching Spann get gunned down in front of a stationery store, it paid to be careful.

I knew better than to turn around and look across the street directly. I checked the reflection of my car window instead.

I saw a man standing at the mouth of a narrow alley across the street. Normally, a guy standing in an alley wouldn't cause any news bulletins, except this particular guy was staring straight at me.

And he was wearing a gray hat and coat.

The Wandering Man. It had to be.

I went for the car door handle with my left hand while I reached for my .38 with my right. I eyed the man in the reflection and watched his right hand slowly come out of his pocket.

I pulled my .38 and ducked as I turned to aim at him. "Police! Don't move!"

My target cut loose with three shots from a .45.

Each shot was high enough to miss me but shattered my car window. Glass rained down on me as I returned fire.

My first shot hit the wall to his right. My second shot barely missed him to the left as he ducked down the alley and ran off.

Pedestrians screamed and dropped back as if they'd just walked into a glass wall.

I got to my feet and gave chase. This time, there were no cars or people blocking my way. I was right on his tail. I watched him zigzag through the alley, dodging stacked piles of garbage instead of wasting time tipping it over to block my way.

He cracked off another blind shot as he ran. The bullet sailed high over my head and I kept chasing him.

I saw the bullet hole in the right side of his coat as it billowed out behind him. I knew I had Spann's killer in my sights.

I skidded to a stop in the courtyard, aimed at the center of his back and fired. He must've heard me stop because he dropped to a crouch as he ran. The bullet slammed into a wall to his right. It kicked up dust in his eyes, but not enough to stop him. He pawed at his face as he ran.

I chased him as he reached the end of the alley, took a right onto Thirteenth Street and disappeared.

I ran after him, listening for screams and curses from frightened people as he ran through the street. But all I heard was the usual New York noise.

I took the corner at the end of the alley as wide and slow as I could. My gun led the way. The few passersby on the sidewalk didn't even notice me.

And the Wandering Man was nowhere in sight.

I looked in both directions on both sides of the street

for any sign of a fleeing man. But it looked like the city had swallowed him whole once again.

I lowered my pistol and kept searching the street. Running after him blindly would be a good way for me to stop a bullet. I still hadn't seen his face. He could've shucked the coat and hat and walked right past me and I'd never know it was him. That was his gift. He knew how to blend in.

That's why I knew he hadn't kept running. I'd seen the hole in the back of his coat. I'd nailed him in the kidney and my bullet was still in him. Removing it would've meant a doctor and an operation. He still would've been off his feet.

That meant he was tired, which meant he was resting up somewhere. He was close.

I'd gotten to the mouth of the alley fast and the foot traffic had been normal. No one had been knocked aside. No one was hurling curses after him for almost knocking them down. No horns had honked when someone popped out into traffic, either.

Both sides of the street were lined with shops and shoppers about their business. It was just another early fall afternoon in the city.

That meant The Wanderer was still here. Somewhere on this very street. Every instinct I had told me so.

Because The Wanderer was a smart boy. He'd learned. His letters to the parents proved it. He remembered the panic he had caused the last time he ran away from me. The hole I'd put in him served as a constant reminder.

He was hiding somewhere close until he got up enough strength to get away. Somewhere in plain sight. Like in one of the many stores that lined both sides of the street.

He'd turned right when he exited the alley, which put him east bound toward the river.

I began heading in that direction. I kept my .38 flat against my leg.

I found a butcher shop right off the alley and looked inside. No customers, just the men behind the counter hacking at meat.

A flower shop was next door and I looked through the window. Just a man and a woman arranging flowers at their own pace. No customers there, either.

A cigar store was next. A man wearing a loud red jacket stood out front with his arm draped around a wooden Indian. He was trying to drum up business.

"That's a nice suit," the huckster said to me. "How about a cigar to go with it?"

I wasn't in the mood for a cigar, but he'd probably been standing there for a while. I asked, "You see a guy in a gray hat and coat come running out of that alley just now?"

"Say," the salesman said, "you know what goes great with information? A good cigar. How about you come inside, and we talk it over while you look for a stogie?"

I flashed my badge. "How about you answer my question and don't spend the next week in jail?"

There was nothing like the sight of a badge to make the shmaltz dry up quick. The salesman frowned as he inclined his head eastward. "That way. Breathing heavy. I think he ducked into the barber shop, but I can't swear to it. Just don't come back here and belt me if I'm wrong."

I spotted the striped barber pole a couple of store-fronts down and moved in that direction. I kept my pistol flat against my leg as I closed in.

I stopped just before the barber shop window and

stole a quick look inside. The place had four chairs with four barbers cutting hair. Several men were reading newspapers while they waited for a trim and a shave.

Only one of the customers was standing. He was at the back of the place. His gray hat was pulled low on his head and the lapels of his gray coat were pulled up to hide his face.

I gripped my pistol tight. The goddamned Wanderer was only twenty feet away.

And he turned his head just enough to see me standing there.

I pushed in the front door as The Wanderer bolted through the back door of the place.

The barbers and customers looked up as I ran in shouting, "Police!"

I heard the lock of the backdoor slide home just as I slammed into it. I bounced off it and jumped to the side just as two holes appeared in the door. They missed me but shattered the barber's mirror. Customers and hair cutters made their escape.

With my back against the wall, I mule kicked the door with my left leg. The door creaked and cracked, but the damned lock held.

I heard breaking glass from the other side of the door and knew The Wanderer had found a way out. I slammed my shoulder into the door as hard as I could.

A second hit made the door finally give way. I even managed to keep my feet as I tumbled inside.

A large window above the toilet had been shattered outward. It had been more than large enough for a man to easily fit through.

I hopped on the toilet and looked outside. The window led out to the same enclosed courtyard from where I'd just shot at The Wanderer. We were running in circles.

I knew I'd gotten to the window in time to see him running down the alley, but he was nowhere in sight.

Where the hell was he?

Hiding was the only answer.

I backed away from the shattered window just as a brick came sailing through it. If I hadn't ducked, it would've caught me square in the face. It put a good-sized hole in the plaster wall behind me instead.

I stole a quick glance out the broken window and saw The Wanderer running down the same alley I'd just chased him. I brought up my pistol, aimed as quickly as I could and got off a shot.

I saw the bullet ricochet low off the brick wall and caught him in the right foot. He cried out as if he'd just stepped on a nail and fell to the alley floor.

His hat had somehow stayed on his head, so I still couldn't see his face. But I'd finally managed to put him down. He was on his side, grasping at his wounded right foot.

I leveled my sights on the middle of him and squeezed off another round. But the angle was wrong, and my bullet came up short.

The Wanderer might've been wounded, but he still had enough energy to get to his feet and hobble away.

I pulled myself up and through the window, dropped over the other side and ran back down the alley after him. He had a good head start on me, but I'd managed to hurt him. He'd be a lot slower now with a bullet in his back and a wounded right foot.

People had already begun to gather around my car across the street and on this side, too. They were gaping and trading guesses on what had happened. A few of them were talking about the man who had just run past them.

Those who were looking were looking east.

I pushed through the crowd, expecting to see The Wanderer right in front of me.

Every couple of feet, I spotted a bloody smear on the sidewalk and knew he had to be close.

I stopped when I reached the corner and looked around, but there was no one in sight. Two women were clutching their bags against a building, pointing down at a smear of blood on the pavement.

"Where did he go?" I asked them.

"He jumped into our cab," one of them told me. "Stole it right out from under us before we could get there."

"Damned near knocked us over while he did it, too," said the other. "I'm still shaking."

"Don't move," I told them. "I'm a cop. I'll be right back."

I ran north, hoping I'd catch sight of the cab, but when I reached the next corner, there was no sign of him or the cab.

The bastard had gotten away from me. Again.

I ran back to the corner where I'd left the two women. They must not have believed I was a cop because they were long gone. They might have seen The Wanderer's face. They might've been able to tell me something that would've led me to narrow the search.

But now I had nothing except more troubles than I'd had when I walked into Randolph's.

More questions, too.

Chapter 17

"DAMN IT!" the chief yelled as he brought his hand down on his desk in frustration.

The knickknacks on his desk jumped. The American and Irish flag holder pitched forward. A wooden donkey he'd gotten as a birthday present from Governor Smith keeled over. "How can this sick bastard still be on his feet? With two bullets in him, no less."

I wasn't as angry as I was disappointed. "That's twice I let him get away, Chief. I guess that's my fault."

Carmichael glared down at me. "Knock that shit off right now, Detective. You put a hole in him each time you came up against him. That's a hell of a lot more than anyone else has been able to do in the past ten years, myself included."

The next part was harder for me to say. "I think he followed me home last night and tailed me this morning. That's the only way he could've known where to find me. That means he knows where I live, Andy. He—"

Carmichael held up his hand. "The girls are fine. I've

got two cars parked outside Anne and Mary's school and another two outside your house. They'll be there for the duration. No one's going to be able to lay a finger on your family, Charlie. You've got my oath on that."

That made me feel a bit better, but not much. The thought of The Wanderer being out there all night while I slept was enough to boil my blood.

Had I been so tired that I'd missed the tail last night?

Had I been too preoccupied to spot it this morning?

"Quit kicking yourself in the ass," Carmichael said, trying to snap me out of it. "Theresa's a little shaken up but she's fine. I'm more concerned about how you're doing."

But I didn't care about me. I was still hung up on how The Wanderer had found me. "If he followed me there by car, he must've parked close by. And since he got away in a cab, his car must still be there." I looked at Carmichael. "He kept running east of Randolph's, so chances are he's got his car parked over there. Or there's something on the east side that's important to him."

"Good thinking." Carmichael picked up the phone and told Rosie to connect him with Fitzgerald. "I'll have some uniforms take a look at all the cars in a two-block area from Randolph's. See if anything stands out."

Fitzgerald came on the line, and he repeated his orders to him. "The bastard escaped in a cab. He's got a wounded right foot. Put out a call to all the cab companies. Have them tell their drivers to check their back seats for blood. Give them a description of The Wanderer and tell them we want to know where they dropped him off. Put the hospitals on notice, too. If anyone comes in with so much as a stubbed toe, I want to know about it PDQ."

He hung up the phone and put his hands on his hips. "You've got him on the run and bleeding. He's going to stick out for certain now. He's bound to make a mistake."

I wasn't so sure. "This guy still runs like he's Jim Thorpe. Either he can take hell of a lot of pain, or he knows how to get his hands on some pretty powerful medicine to dull it for him."

"A bullet in the side is one thing," Carmichael pointed out, "but someone will notice that limp you put on him. We're closer to catching him now than we've ever been, Charlie. We've got to be. That why I'm going to need you to get back down to your office and keep working those files. The answer's got to be somewhere in there. I can almost feel it."

His mention of the files made me remember my talk with Andersson. "Speaking of pain killers, I think you're going to need some in a minute."

I spent the next several minutes telling him about my conversation with Andersson in Randolph's.

I expected him to kick up a fuss over the part about his mistress, but he took it like a champ. He slowly ran his hand across his chin, frowning as his eyes went vacant. "Telling him about Rene was smart thinking, Charlie. I wished it had been enough to satisfy him. Too bad he already knew about her."

"He knew about the Spann cover-up," I reminded him. "And he probably knew more than he was letting on. That means someone talked."

"Someone always talks, Charlie," Carmichael reminded me. "I guess I was a fool to think I could keep it from them. I was expecting someone to break ranks if things got hot, but not yet. I'm not happy about it, but I expected it. I guess the old saying is true. 'Two people can keep a secret if one of them is dead'." He grinned at me. "Present company excluded, of course."

I wasn't in the mood for jokes. "Who do you think told him?"

"Andersson means it's Ross," Carmichael concluded. "Fitzgerald is too afraid of me to risk opening his mouth, but Ross has eyes on my chair. Always has. He thought he should've gotten the nod this time around instead of me. He's hoping Andersson will protect him if this case blows up."

He sat down in his chair as if he was ready to get back to work. "Forget about this Andersson nonsense. I know how to handle it."

"All due respect, boss, I can't just forget it. My neck's in the noose next to yours."

"That wasn't a request, Charlie," Carmichael said. "Leave this to me and I'll take care of it. You just need to hit those files harder than you've ever hit them before. In fact, there's another letter in there that you probably haven't seen yet. The first letter he ever sent."

I'd wasted the last day trying to put out any fires Massey's column could have caused. I should've been spending it on The Wanderer case. I'd been preoccupied with saving our lives. "Who was the letter sent to?"

"Spann's wife," Carmichael told me. "It's pretty raw. Raw enough to have caused her to take her own life."

I lowered my head and ran my hand over the stubble on my head. Just when I didn't think this case could get any worse, the floor dropped out of it. "I'll get right on it."

"Not yet." He opened a desk drawer and plopped a .45 in a shoulder holster on his desk. "You're trading in that old .38 of yours for something that's got more stopping power."

I didn't particularly like that idea. "Andy…"

"Don't 'Andy' me. That's an order, not a suggestion. I know you're partial to that wheel gun, but I insist. He won't be hobbling anywhere with one of those slugs in him. And don't tell me you don't know how to use one because I know you do."

I reluctantly took my .38 from my hip and placed it on his desk. "Automatics have a tendency to jam, you know."

"You're a marine," he reminded me. "I thought you guys knew how to maintain your weapons."

I took off my jacket and shrugged into the shoulder holster. "They still jam."

"Well if you don't like that," the chief said, "get ready for the next bit of good news. You've got a shadow of your own now. Halloran will be going everywhere you go until further notice. No exceptions."

That was a bit too much. "Come on, Andy. That thug is more trouble than he's worth. He would've killed Keating if I hadn't been there to stop him."

"And he wouldn't have been anywhere near Keating unless you'd been there. Again, it's not a request." Carmichael was firm. "I'll feel better knowing you've got Halloran following you around. He serves a purpose."

I thought of something that might get me out of it. "You remember I've got an appointment with Massey up at the Lounge tonight."

"And Halloran goes with you," Carmichael said. "He's not to know anything about The Wanderer, but I don't think he'll blush about anything Doyle's crew does to Massey. Hell, he might even learn a thing or two about pulling his punches."

I wasn't so sure. "He and Quinn don't exactly get along, Chief."

"I'm sure you'll find a way to keep them away from each other." He picked up a pen and took hold of a sheaf of papers on his desk. "Back to the file room with you. You're not the only cop around here who has work to do."

Chapter 18

AFTER CALLING Theresa to check on her and the girls, I headed back to the storage room. I wanted to take a closer look at that letter Carmichael had mentioned. The first letter The Wanderer had sent had been to Mrs. Spann.

I hoped it might contain something to explain what had started all of this. What, besides the grief over losing her son, had caused Mrs. Spann to take her own life.

It was the first letter the killer had sent. He'd learned his craft since, but everyone made mistakes in the beginning of whatever they did. I was hoping The Wanderer was no different.

I opened the file folder and found the letter and the envelope at the very back of the file. I held the envelope in my left hand and the letter in my right.

A quick scan of both the envelope and the letter told me it was identical in look and feel to all the others sent by The Wanderer. The line in the 'e' was only beginning to fade.

The envelope had been addressed to Mrs. Spann on

Staten Island. The return address had been cut out and pasted over with another piece of the stationery, just like the others.

I reluctantly set the envelope aside for a moment and read the letter.

Mrs. Spann (i):

I wanted to send you a letter wishing you a happy anniversary of sorts. Perhaps not a happy occasion for you, but a most joyous occasion for me. For you see, it was one year ago today that your Tommy helped me find my true calling in this life of ours. Long have I romed through the world without direction or purpose until the day fate took me by the hand and guided me to your home that fateful afternoon.

It may have happened a year ago, but I remember it as if it had occurred only this morning. A warm August afternoon. The water was smooth and the wind most calm. The kind of day that one dreams of when we think of summertime. I found myself on Staten Island without point or purpose when I came upon your humble home and the quaint scene of three young boys playing in your yard.

Forgive me, only two of them were playing. One had been cast aside. As he was the smaller of the three, I imagined he had been shunned by the older boys. I knew what it was like to be shunned. To be left out.

And when your boy looked at me as I approached, I knew he was special. We were kindled spirits, he and I. As young as he was, we had a bond that only the two of us could share. We knew each other though we had never met before.

I suppose that's why he came to me so easily when I beckoned him.

I know the papers made it sound like I swooped into your yard and carried him away like a bird of pray, but it was much more serene then that. The decision to accompany me was his and his alone. He came with me because he had no reason to stay with his friends. And by correlation, no reason to stay with you, either.

Why should he have stayed? You were busy elsewhere. His own mother had forgotten him. His friends had ignored him. It's terribly lonely for a boy that age to be deserted such as this. It's lonely at any age.

I took him by the hand, and we borded the ferry without a fuss. I promised him a day of adventure in the big city. He said he'd always wanted to go, but that you'd always said he was too small to take him. We spoke of a great many things on our journey.

He was particularly excited about the prospect of seeing his father at his work. I have since learned that he is a patrolman in Manhattan. I did not know that when I took him. That changed things. I like to think of it as fait.

As we sailed closer to Manhattan, I took him to the railing so he could see the big city grow even bigger as the ferry drew closer to the dock. He was still smiling when I picked him up and allowed him to stand on the railing for an unobstructed view.

No one else was around, so no one objected. Lonliness was the story of our shared experience both in life and in death.

That is why their was no one to see me let him go and fall into the water. He was gone in an instant, swept away beneath the powerful engines of the ferry. I don't think he suffered. He was smiling as he fell. He didn't even cry out.

That day was a happy one for me because it joined us together. You and me and Mister Spann and Tommy. We are a family of sorts, forever bonded by Tommy. The memory of his last smile warms me just as I am shore the absence of him has haunted you all these weeks and months.

I hope you'll forgive me for not writing to you sooner, but the time never felt just right. I was saving it for a special occasion. I was going to write at Christmastime but feared my letter would be lost in all of the yuletide spirit of the season. That's why I decided the anniversary of his disappearance would be best.

I often wonder if you blame yourself for your son's death. You should. I'd passed by several houses that day and almost all of them had a mother keeping watch over her bruds. Your yard was the only one unattended.

That's why you must not despair! You must realize that it happened because we were meant to be joined together. You, me and John and Tommy forever. A family you may not have wanted but it's the one you have. For if you hadn't been too busy to pay attention to your child, you would still have him, and I would be alone.

But I am not alone. I have his memory with me always. I have your grief and guilt to make me whole.

Do you ever hear the voices, Mrs. Spann? When you're awake or asleep or in those quietest of moments when no one is around? Is it Tommy's voice or your own that you hear? Voices that ask if this was your fault? Do you relive that day and wonder if you could've done more?

That voice, Mrs. Spann, is my voice. And the answer will always be yes.

You gave Tommy to me as if you had handed him over to me and whished us well on our journey.

We are still on that journey, Mrs. Spann. And we will continue on that journey together for as long as we both shall live.

I've enjoyed this letter to you. I would like very much to keep in touch.

Sincerely,
Your Wandering Man

By the time I reached the end of the letter, I had to squint at it as if I was looking into the sun.

I slumped back in my chair and wiped the tears from my eyes before they hit the paper.

This was the letter that had caused Mrs. Spann to kill herself. I found the police report of the scene at the end of the file. Spann had come home that evening and found his wife had hung herself in the kitchen. She'd found a sturdy beam above the table, threw a noose over it and jumped.

The rope had been long enough for her to have easily stepped back onto the table, but she hadn't even tried.

The last words that poor, haunted woman had read in this life was mockery from her son's killer. The Wanderer was just as responsible for her death as if he'd strangled her himself.

It made me hate him more.

I found myself writing notes about the letter before I realized I was doing it.

The language was even more awkward. Was it new to him then?

Numerous misspellings.

It had a forced sound to it the other letters didn't have. Is he foreign?

The (i) next to her name was the coldest part of it all. Given all I knew about the case now, I figured it was the Roman numeral for one. Thomas Spann had been The Wanderer's first victim. Even back then, he knew there would be others. The letter he had written to the Washington family had (xx) next to their name. The double 'x' must've meant Lester Washington was his twentieth victim.

I flipped through the files, looking for notes on The Wanderer's claim about the ferry. I found a report from Lt. Carmichael at the time that claimed the crews of the boats had been thoroughly questioned and none of them remembered a man with a child. They'd even dredged the harbor along the ferry route and never found a body.

The Wandering Man had lied about how he'd killed Tommy. Had he lied about Lester Washington and how he'd killed all the other boys as well?

That was a clue.

If he hadn't let the boy fall from the railing, then what had he done with him? If he hadn't killed Lester near a train station, what had he done with him?

The Spann letter put all the other Wanderer letters in a new light. We'd never found a single corpse we could tie to his victims.

What had he done with them all?

I looked for answers in the other clue I had. The letter itself. The paper felt like the same kind of stock as the rest of the letters. It had yellowed some with age but was identical in every other way, including having the missing letterhead. This monster was nothing if not consistent.

I took a closer look at the letters on the page, not the poison he had typed out. The line in the 'e's was only beginning to show wear, but it was definitely lighter than it should have been.

That told me it was probably the same machine he had used throughout his career. That meant he'd had the same job for at least the past ten years.

Yeah, you can blend in pretty well, can't you?

But well enough to hide a hole in your back? A bloody foot? A limp?

I pushed those questions out of my mind and focused on the facts of what I had right in front of me. I looked at the top of the Spann letter closely and saw something new. I held the letter up to the desk lamp and looked through the sheet.

At the very top of the cut, the bottom portion of raised lettering was still there, though barely visible.

I felt my heart begin to beat faster as I took an even closer look. I ran my thumb gently over the area. I felt the raised ridges of letters that had been cut off. The ink had long since faded, but the imprint of the letters was still there.

It was his only mistake. But of course, it was. It had been his first letter.

If he had been this careless with the note, what about the envelope?

I picked up the envelope and held it up to the light. It had been cut out and covered over just like all the others. But here I could see tiny cracks had formed on the paste beneath the paper.

The paste had begun to dry out.

I placed the envelope on the desk and began to flick the edge of the paper covering the cutout return address with a fingernail. A portion of it raised easily without tearing the paper or the envelope.

I'll admit I said a quick prayer before I followed my gut and pinched the pasted areas hard. I was rewarded by the sound of tiny snaps.

I let go and saw the slips of paper covering both sides of the envelope's return address stuck to my hand.

All that remained was the flaking paste that had been holding the slips of paper in place. The paste was as cracked as a desert floor.

All that was possibly between me and The Wanderer was a smear of old paste thinner than a human hair.

There might be nothing to find beneath it, but I had to find out.

Carefully.

I gently blew on the broken remnants of paste, clearing many of the flakes from the paper. Only a few tiny pieces were left, so I began to gently graze my fingernail over the remaining specks.

All of them came loose without tearing the paper beneath it.

My hands shook as I looked at the envelope and saw it was as clean as the day the killer had used it.

And what I saw made me stop breathing for a moment.

A line of raised lettering ran along the top of the cut at the return address line.

Not entire letters, just the tops of the capital letters at the top and at the bottom where the city would be. The paste had absorbed the ink, but I could still see their raised outlines.

I looked closely at the lower cut and saw the very bottoms of letters along with a comma and bottom tips of letters that could only be 'N.Y.'

I had an address.

I pounded the desk in delight. I'd caught the bastard's first mistake. The only mistake he'd made so far.

I rifled the file for the thinnest slip of paper I could find. I tore off a piece of it and laid it over the envelope. Then, I took a pencil and lightly ran the side of it over the paper, hoping it would reveal the raised lettering beneath it.

I refused to allow myself to look at what I was uncovering until I was done. When I was sure there were no other letters to raise, I set my pencil aside and examined the results.

I'd been right. I saw what looked to be the very tops

of capital letters at the top cut. At the bottom were the bottoms of letters.

I found the pad I'd been using for notes and copied what I thought the rubbings revealed:

Th_ H_____ h_ S_____ L

_____ _____, N.Y.

I'd never been good at puzzles or games, so I couldn't tell what it meant. The "L" could've been a capital "I" or "J". The "S" could've been a "C" or a "G".

The missing bottom letters were undoubtedly a location somewhere in the city but could've been anywhere.

I added it to my notes and wrote:

Place with black trucks? Wagons?

Seeing as how all of the letters had been mailed from Grand Central, I figured the place was probably in the city. But where?

I checked my watch and was surprised to see it was already a quarter past four. Doherty and his boys were throwing their party for Donald Massey up at The Longford Lounge at five o'clock and I couldn't afford to be late. Tamping down Massey's influence was just as important to finding The Wanderer as what I'd just uncovered.

Besides, I figured I could do with some time away from the envelope. A bit of distance might help me make sense of it all.

I folded the letter and my rubbing and put it in the inside pocket of my jacket as I headed out the door.

I was close to finding The Wanderer. I could feel it.

I only hoped he couldn't feel it, too.

Chapter 19

WITH MY FORD shot to hell, Halloran insisted on driving up to The Longford Lounge. I tried to talk him out of going with me, but no luck.

"Keep dreaming, little man," he told me as he started up the car. "It's just you and me from now on, forsaking all others for as long as the chief says so."

I hadn't expected him to be happy about going up to The Longford Lounge and he didn't disappoint. "What's going on up there tonight, anyway?"

"A private party," I told him. "Relax, you'll enjoy it."

It was just a bit after five when we parked in front of the place. A line was already forming on the street for well-dressed swells waiting to get inside.

Halloran and I jumped the line and walked inside. Frankie Deavers was already in a tuxedo and laying on the French act thick for the customers waiting for a table or a spot at the bar to free up.

Frankie seemed relieved to see me, but his smile faded when he saw Halloran looming behind me.

"Ah, Monsieur Doherty and Monsieur Halloran."

He beckoned us to come in. "Your party is already here and waiting. Come let me show you to your table."

Two guys in tuxes started to protest until Halloran pushed past them.

Frankie dropped the French act as soon as we got away from the crowd. "You're late, Charlie. The boys are already downstairs looking for you." He tossed a thumb back at Halloran. "And what's that big ape doing here?"

Halloran heard it. "Drop dead, Froggy."

"Chief's orders," I told him. "Is there a back way down there?"

He shook his head as we tried to clear a path through the place. They were already five-deep at the bar and almost every table in the joint was taken.

"There's only one way in and one way out down to the wine cellar and that's through Archie's private dining room."

I'd been afraid of that. It meant we'd have to walk through the entire joint in order to get down there. That was bad news. I knew almost everyone in the place. One of them was bound to remember seeing me. And if they missed me, they'd remember seeing Halloran.

That was bad. If things went well with Massey, it wouldn't be a problem. But if something went wrong, being remembered could be a problem. I hoped the booze and smoke would dull their memories. People had a habit of remembering the oddest things when they were sauced.

I wasn't in the place ten seconds before I started drawing waves from old friends. Gloria Swanson spotted me and blew a kiss my way. Her bug-eyed, bootlegging boyfriend from Boston didn't look pleased. Joe Kennedy had a way of frowning even when he was smiling. Bill Powell threw me a wink from the next table over as he entertained some girl who looked like a dancer.

I looked around when I heard my name called loud above the din of the Lounge. I forced a smile when I saw Georgie Ruth ensconced in a booth surrounded by a bevy of blondes. He was pushing the table aside so he could get at me. And judging by the way he took the stairs up to greet me, he'd gotten an early start on what promised to be a long night. His eyes were already blurry going on blood-shot.

"Charlie!" the Sultan of Swat boomed as he threw his arms around me. "How's every little thing, pal? How's my favorite cop these days?"

I felt like one of Anne's teddy bears as he wrapped me up in a hug. Halloran stood back and gawked, awed by greatness.

I spotted Gehrig at his table. He was sipping water and checking his watch. This wasn't his scene. I knew how he felt.

Conscious of the time, I managed to pry myself from the big lug's embrace. "Everything's aces, Babe." Despite everything else filling my head, I remembered the favor I owed Bixby. "Listen, while you're here, I need you to do something for me."

"Anything for you. Want an autograph? I'll give you a bible full. Want me to hit a homer for you tomorrow? Just say the word and it's done."

I figured he'd hit a homer anyway, so I didn't bother asking. "I ran into Bixby a couple of days ago. He's feeling a bit lonely these days."

Ruth waved me off. "Ah, nuts to that bum. His big mouth queered things between me and this fine little thing I was sweet on. Real quality girl, too. I'd spent a whole week chasing her around. Flowers, chocolates, the works. And one word from that boozer sent her scrambling for the door. She was a Follies girl, too. Real sporting type."

I wondered if Mrs. Ruth would agree, but I saw how anxious Frankie was to get me downstairs. I tried cutting it as short as I could without being obvious. The Babe was a sensitive boy and hated the brush off. Besides, I owed Bixby a favor.

I nodded toward the booth full of beauties he'd just left behind. "You seem to have recovered pretty well."

Babe looked at them as if he'd forgotten they were there. He probably had. "Aw, they're easy. This girl I'm talkin' about had real class, Charlie. Real class."

Frankie tapped his wrist, and I knew we had to get going. Halloran was in no hurry. This was the closest he'd been to the Babe since the bleachers.

I shined Ruth on. "You've always had a way with the ladies, Georgie. You'll get her back. Besides, the city's lousy with pretty girls, but there's only one Bixby. Have a heart and give him another chance, will you? For me."

As he was known to do, the slugger pouted like an overgrown kid. "Aw, Wendell ain't that bad, I guess. If it means so much to you, I'll give him a call tomorrow. Tell him it's all forgotten."

"That's the spirit. Maybe you can give him a call tonight. I know he'd sleep better if you did." I tapped him on the arm and got away from him before he could grab hold of me again. "See you on my way out and don't do anything I wouldn't do."

The Babe laughed too hard at my bad joke. I was a funny guy if you were half in the bag.

As Frankie led us to the back room, I heard Babe bellowing how swell I was as he went back to his party.

"Next time you ask him for a favor," Frankie said as

we hurried through the crowd, "tell him to drink somewhere else. That big dope is a pain in the ass."

Halloran tapped me on the shoulder as we cut through the crowd. "You think you could introduce me to him later?"

"We're working, not sightseeing," I told him. "Keep your mind on business first."

I said it more for my own benefit than Halloran's.

Chapter 20

I'D HAD a lot of time to kill back when I was waiting to go into action overseas. Believe it or not, I spent a fair chunk of it reading whatever I could get my hands on. I even got around to reading some of the classics and found a lot of it wasn't half bad once you got around the flowery language.

I remembered reading Dante's 'Inferno' at one point, which wound up becoming one of my favorites. I remembered it now because there was something about that book that had always reminded me of The Longford Lounge.

The main floor was for the commoners, where the great washed and unwashed came to see and be seen. There were plenty of other gin mills in town where you could see famous people or clink glasses with a ballplayer or two, but none of them had the panache the Lounge had.

The floor beneath it catered to a more restricted crowd. That's where Doyle really made his money – the casino. Every night, the upper crust of Manhattan society gambled away their family fortunes on games of chance. Blackjack, poker and the roulette wheel were the biggest draws. You could even play the ponies with one of the house bookies always on hand to take your money.

The two pool tables in the back were the best kept secret in the place. Enough money changed hands over the way the balls rolled each night to put a healthy dent in Germany's reparations bill. The private room in the back catered to the high rollers intent to piss away their kids' inheritance over higher-stakes games. And Archie Doyle got a piece of it all.

Both levels were hard to get into, which is what made them so appealing to those who knew about them.

But it was the Wine Cellar where Archie Doyle had really built his empire. It was here where he maintained it. Just like back at the Castle, no one ever wanted to find themselves down there, not even me.

I didn't know what level of Hell old Dante would've placed Doyle's Wine Cellar, but I figured he would've plunked it down pretty close to the fire.

The two levels above us always smelled like expensive cigars and hair tonic and every type of perfume on the market.

The Wine Cellar reeked of stale sweat and blood. I could tell Halloran felt right at home.

The two of us watched from the shadows as Terry Quinn introduced Donald Massey to the Big Apple. The reporter was tied to a heavy wooden chair bolted to the floor in the center of the basement. A dull yellow light shined down on him from above as Terry Quinn buried another hard right hand in his gut. I could feel the impact of the blow from where I stood, in the shadows on the other side of the room.

Massey's head bobbed. His mouth hung open on his chest. A thin trail of blood flowed from the corner of his mouth onto his white dress shirt. The growing stain on the concrete beneath his chair told me his bladder had gone at some point before I'd gotten there. There was no shame in that. I'd seen many a man soil himself in that very chair.

Halloran and I stayed in the shadows by the stairway as Archie Doyle and Fatty Corcoran watched the carnage from padded leather chairs at the edge of the yellow circle of light. A table stood between them. A bottle of whiskey and two glasses sat at their elbows. A cut crystal ashtray was half filled with dead cigarettes and ashes.

Fatty Corcoran looked like he was watching a game of pool upstairs. Archie puffed mindlessly away on a cigar while Quinn nailed the reporter with a hard left to the side. Other than a severe look of pain, Massey's face remained untouched. No visible bruises. Quinn was a pro.

Massey barely had enough strength to groan.

Archie threw me a wink when he noticed I was there and told Quinn, "That's enough for now, Terry. What do you say we give Fatty a crack at him?"

That's the way Doyle gave orders. It was never direct and always came in the form of a question. Like you were doing him a favor. I guess that's why so many people had remained loyal to him since his days as a Five Points hood.

Quinn stopped in mid-blow and moved off to the side next to me. He acknowledged me with a nod. He looked Halloran up and down and gave him his best sneer. The two big men had never liked each other, and Quinn seemed to enjoy getting under my partner's skin.

I could tell Halloran was about to say something. An elbow tap in the belly and a finger to my lips reminded him to stay quiet.

This wasn't about his rivalry with Quinn. It was about Massey. It was about protecting Tammany so I could find The Wanderer.

Fatty Corcoran took a sip of whiskey before slowly rising from his chair. He made a point of buttoning his blue suit coat over his belly before approaching Massey. He looked like a lawyer about to question a witness. If this basement was a courtroom, Doyle would've been the judge.

"Can you hear me, Mr. Massey," Corcoran asked as he approached, "or do you require some refreshment?"

The reporter grunted and his head lolled limply on his chest. Archie gave Quinn a nod. Quinn grabbed a bucket of ice water and dumped it over Massey's head. Chunks of ice pelted him like rocks, and he snapped awake with a gasp.

"There you are," Fatty smiled. "Wonderful. Now, I'm sure you have many questions as to why we have brought you down here and why you are being treated so harshly. All of this will become clear to you in a few moments. For now, I need your undivided attention."

The fat man somehow managed to clasp his hands behind him as he began to slowly circle Massey. "I know you are a newcomer to our fair city, which is why we have been so delicate with you this evening."

"Delicate," Massey panted. "You call this delicate?"

"We're doing it for your benefit, Mr. Massey," Fatty continued. "We see you as a chick who has tumbled out of his nest only to find there's a much larger world than you have ever seen before. A world far greater and more complex than you first believed. The purpose of this evening's festivities is to show you the dangers of that world before you get yourself hurt."

He stopped walking and looked down at Massey. "Before your actions make it necessary for us to continue your education in a much harsher manner."

Massey shivered from the cold water and the pain. "A-any harsher and I'll be dead."

Fatty bent at the waist and whispered directly into the reporter's ear. "Oh, Mr. Massey. You have no idea just how far away from death you are. Your article mentioned something about the traits of the Irish. Tonight, you are learning one of our more admirable traits is the desire for revenge. You have a far longer journey ahead of you should you decide to defy us. I only hope you never come to appreciate just how well you've been treated tonight."

A shiver went through Massey, only this time, I didn't think it was just from the ice water.

Corcoran stood up and resumed his slow stroll around the reporter. "We know all about the reputation you enjoyed in Chicago, just as we know the circumstances under which you were forced to leave the Windy City. We imagine you believed you could come to New York and continue your brand of journalism without fear of reprisal or correction. You see yourself as something of a doctor, don't you? A physician of sorts who specializes in curing what you believe to be the disease that ails our great country's large cities. You believe you have found a malignant tumor on that city's lungs. And, like any good physician, you believe it is your sacred duty to cut away that tumor once and for all. But, instead of a scalpel, you believe your column will help cure the patient of his affliction."

I saw Doyle brimming with pride as he raised his glass to toast his friend's eloquence.

Corcoran acknowledged Doyle with a nod before stopping behind Massey. "Do you agree with my assessment so far, sir?"

Massey struggled to lift his head. "I agree you're just another fat bastard full of hot air."

Quinn stepped forward and gave Massey a hard slap to the back of the head before coming back to stand next to me.

Massey blinked his eyes and shook his head, trying to recover from the blow.

Fatty remained still. "I ask you again, sir. Do you agree with my assessment? And do make your answers formal for the sake of clarity. We wouldn't want another misunderstanding, would we?"

"Yeah," he said before quickly adding, "I mean yes, I agree."

I watched Fatty grin. The reporter's resolve was beginning to break. He resumed his slow walk around the prisoner. "I'm happy to hear that. And while I admire your belief in your cause, your diagnosis in this case is flawed. For what you see as a tumor is actually an organ. A vital, healthy organ that is essential to the very life blood of this fair city. I implore you to think of it as an extra liver that serves to filter out some of the more undesirable aspects of this great metropolis we call home."

Massey began to speak but had to clear his throat by spitting out a gob of blood. "If I ask you to explain, is that gorilla going to hit me again?"

Fatty looked at Quinn and shook his head. "As long as our discussion remains civil, I see no reason for Mr. Quinn's participation."

I had to hand it to the fat man. He knew how to work a guy over with words.

"As for our role in protecting the city," Fatty continued, "we do so by maintaining a certain order in our own unique way. We manage the basest aspects of the human condition, such as greed and vice and drinking and gambling. We provide the services the common man and the privileged elite seek as a way to amuse themselves. We provide a necessary distraction from the drudgery of everyday city life."

Massey coughed. "You make it sound almost noble."

"Perhaps because it is," Corcoran continued. "We also understand elected officials will always be susceptible to corruption. That is why we ensure said corruption will be controlled and, whenever possible, serve the public good."

Massey surprised me by saying, "After you get your cut, of course."

"And why not?" Corcoran asked. "Management is never free. The institutions you seek to attack in your columns actually serve to keep the worst elements of criminal nature at bay. Chicago has open warfare on its streets. We do not. We also ensure the liquor we serve meets a certain standard, lest people get sick or go blind or die as so many had before we took control of the situation. We harness the ambition of corrupt politicians and see to it that they all pull in the same direction to protect our society wherever possible."

Massey was clearly beginning to feel stronger. "And the cops?"

"Indispensable partners in our undertaking," Corcoran said as he resumed his slow circuit around Massey. "They enforce law and order while the rest of us deal with the many varied concerns that make this city function properly. Their cooperation is vital to making sure everything operates as smoothly as humanly possible."

"Like a machine?" Massey said. "The Tammany machine."

Fatty bent over and whispered in his ear. "Precisely, sir. Like a human machine, hence the flaws inherent to its nature. Flaws we do our best to mitigate in our own imperfect way."

"Machines need oil," Massey said. "And the best oil I know for a political machine is graft."

Quinn took a step forward, but Fatty held him at bay with a shake of his head. "That's part of it, but a small part. Influence is far more vital to the proper working of the entire system than what you call graft. Influence held in our capable, sturdy hands."

"Influence like that is usually held by one man." Massey nodded weakly toward Doyle. "I'm betting that man holds the Tiger's leash."

Archie let a long plume of cigar smoke escape his nose.

"I see you're familiar with our colloquialisms, sir," Fatty went on. "Yes, I suppose one could say Mr. Doyle enjoys the privilege of significant influence. He is also a man who has a great many acquaintances, but very few friends. He has invited you here tonight in an attempt to ask you for your friendship."

Massey strained his neck to look up at Fatty, who by now, was just off to his left. "This is how he makes friends? I'd hate to see how he treats enemies."

Fatty smiled down at him. "Yes, Mr. Massey. You would."

I watched Massey struggle to swallow. "H-how can we be friends?"

"By simply continuing to do what you've always done," Fatty explained. "By writing columns that are in the best interest of the city. Interests that further our shared goals rather than hinder progress. By focusing your efforts on the plight of the poor and needy. For better schools. For better working and living conditions. Stories where your impressive gifts can make a difference instead of stirring up resentment against the people who risk their lives each day to make this city a fine place to live and work."

Massey flinched when Fatty laid a heavy hand on his shoulder. "No one wants to write your columns for you, Donald. We simply want you to help us help the city as we've always done."

The reporter somehow managed a smirk. "As long as I don't gum up the works and dam up the graft, you don't break my legs. Is that it?" He gave a sharp, short laugh. "Boy, I really must've hit a nerve with Carmichael for me to deserve this kind of treatment. I've got to thank you boys, though. I was wondering what I was going to write about in my next column. And after tonight, it looks like I've got my story. I've even got a catchy head-line for it. Archie Doyle. The Duke of New York."

I watched Quinn start to go for him but stopped as Archie got to his feet.

Doyle took a final drag on his cigar before he set it down in his ashtray.

Corcoran took his cue and slowly walked back over to his chair, unbuttoning his jacket before he sat down. The prosecution rests.

Archie took his time crossing the distance between him and the reporter. His black tie was undone. His French cuffs were open, and his sleeves rolled up, revealing the massive forearms that had been his trademark. He was built like a fireplug and just as solid. What he lacked in height, he made up for in width and muscle.

His arms hung naturally away from his sides as he approached Massey.

I watched the scribe try to bone up as Doyle came toward him. He was doing a lousy job of trying to look tough. I couldn't blame him. I'd had nightmares about winding up in that same chair with Doyle looming over me.

And I knew that if Massey kept digging around the chief, there was a good chance that nightmare would become a reality.

Massey looked up at Doyle when he stopped about two feet in front of him. Archie didn't say a word. He didn't crack his knuckles or ball his fists. He wasn't even frowning. He looked at Massey as if he was a roach that had just crawled out from under the icebox.

And just like a roach, Doyle had control over whether Massey lived or died.

The reporter began to tremble the longer Archie stood quietly in front of him until Doyle tossed a thick thumb over his shoulder. "That fat man sure is something, ain't he? Hearing him make with them fancy words is almost enough to make me forget we both come from the same hell hole. A place called Five Points. A place that ain't there anymore and you sure as hell won't find it on any maps of the city. That's the problem with this town. It's got no memory."

Doyle tapped his temple. "Me? I'm just the opposite. I don't forget nothing."

I watched Massey swallow hard. The poor bastard had only just realized he'd lost.

Doyle threw open his hands. "Some call this memory of mine a blessing. Some call it a curse. Me? I figure that's how the good Lord made me. Comes in handy, what with all the back slapping and glad-handing I've gotta do each day."

He squatted and looked directly into Massey's eyes. "Wanna know another gift I've got? This one'll knock your socks right off your feet."

Massey almost cried out when Doyle slapped his knee. "Knowing what someone needs before they know it themselves. Take a fella like yourself for instance. I knew what a bright boy like you needed the second I finished reading your article. You needed a friend. And that's what I'm gonna be to you, Donny Boy. A true friend. A real pal."

Massey began to shake worse now.

Doyle went on. "And with all the knocks against me, the one thing anyone'll tell you is that I like doing favors for my friends. Seeing as how I wanted to make a good impression and all, wanna know what I did for you?" He stood up right. All smiles. "I went and squared you with the Big Boy out in Chicago."

Massey's mouth trembled. "Y-y-you what?"

"Squared you with the boys in Chicago," Doyle repeated. "Paid off what you owed them. The whole ten grand. I figure that's probably more than what you owed, but given the nature of our business and all, I can't blame them for padding it a little." He gave Massey a tap to the shoulder. "Can't go expecting a crook to play it honest, now can we? Might ruin their reputation."

"Y-y- you didn't have to do that," Massey said. "I'll repay you, Mr. Doyle. I promise."

Doyle recoiled as if he'd been slapped. "Donny, Donny, Donny! You insult me with that kinda talk. We're friends, ain't we? And what's a lousy ten grand compared to the friendship we've got? Because I'll do anything to help my friends. That's just the kind of big-hearted sap I am."

Massey's throat caught again, only this time instead of spitting, he swallowed it. "M-Mr. Doyle. I appreciate it, but…"

Doyle waved him off. "No 'buts' between you and me, Donny Boy. Because that sounds like pride talking and there's no pride between pals. Might make you sound ungrateful, see? And we wouldn't want you to sound ungrateful so early in our friendship, now would we? Might put us off on the wrong foot. Make me think we ain't such good friends after all. That'd make you something different, Donny Boy."

Doyle reached behind him.

Massey whimpered.

Doyle pulled out a long-nosed .38 and held it at his side. "Because if you ain't my friend, that'd make you an enemy."

He opened the cylinder and slowly dumped out six rounds onto the basement floor. Massey jerked as each round hit the concrete.

When the gun was empty, Doyle told Quinn, "Pick me out a winner, kid."

Quinn picked up a single bullet and handed it to Archie. Doyle made like he slid it into the cylinder, but I saw him palm it. "And if you're saying we're enemies, then this conversation takes a real nasty turn."

Massey cringed and began to whimper as Doyle spun the cylinder and flicked it shut.

Massey cried out when Doyle placed the barrel against his forehead. "The choice is yours, Donny Boy? You wanna be my friend or my enemy?"

"F-f-friend!" Massey screamed. "I want to be your friend!"

The tears flowed freely now as Doyle took the gun away and tucked it in the back of his pants. He looked over at me and winked again.

Massey was broken. His work here was done.

"That's it, Donny Boy." Doyle patted Massey's face. "Let it all out. We're all friends here. I'm taking them tears as being tears of joy. You're glad you've got all these new friends now. Ain't that right?"

"Y-yes," Massey nodded quickly. "I-I've never been so happy."

"Good man," Doyle said as tucked a finger under Massey's chin. And held the bullet he'd palmed in front of him.

"This here?" Doyle turned the bullet in his fingers. "This is a token of our friendship. Whenever you begin to doubt it, whenever you might forget it, I want you to look at this and remember everything we talked about here tonight. I want you to keep it on you at all times, to remind you how close we are. Remind you of all the friends you've got right here in this very room."

He wagged a finger in Massey's face. "I'm gonna ask you to see it every once in a while, so don't forget it, understand?"

Massey's eyes crossed as he looked at the bullet. "I understand, Mr. Doyle."

Doyle smiled as he dropped the bullet in the pocket of Massey's dinner jacket. "I'm gonna put it right there so you don't forget. And my friends call me Archie. None of that Mr. Doyle business."

He thumped his ribs and looked around at the rest of us. "Now, I don't know about you boys, but I'm hungry enough to eat the hind leg off the Holy Ghost." He gestured to Quinn. "Do me a favor and let our new pal calm down a little. When he's ready, bring him up to my place and let him get cleaned up. Let him use my shower and borrow one of my shirts." He pointed at the blood stain on Massey's shirt. "He seems to have gotten this one dirty. Once he's as good as new, I'll take him around and introduce him to the boys. Maybe even the mayor if he's sober."

He thumped Massey on the back as he walked away. "No pipes calling for you tonight, Donny Boy. Just high times and hijinks for any friend of mine. Rest here a little. You're gonna need it."

Quinn stepped aside as Doyle walked over to me and Halloran. He gestured for us to be quiet as he led us through the shadows to the stairway.

Massey's sobs filled the cellar.

Archie patted Halloran on the back. "Didn't think I'd see you here tonight, Big Jim. You keeping Charlie here company?"

"Chief's orders," Halloran told him, "though it's always good to see you, Archie."

"Always good to be seen." Doyle looked at me. "I don't think you'll have to worry about any more columns from him."

Doyle amazed me sometimes. He'd just spent the better part of the last hour terrorizing a man only to shrug it off like he'd dialed the wrong number. "I appreciate it, Archie. And so does my boss."

Fatty joined us as we walked up the stairs. "Masterful, Archie. As usual."

"What? That back there?" Archie waved him off. "That was nothing. The kid was beat the second Terry laid hands on him."

Halloran snickered. "You call that laying hands? If I ever get Quinn in the Dungeon, I'll show him how it's done."

"My dance card's empty the rest of the night," Quinn shot back. "Why wait?"

Halloran turned in the narrow stairway. "Talk like that'll cost you teeth, gym rat."

"Not from a two-bit flatfoot like you."

Halloran went for him, but Doyle and I were enough to block his way.

"Take it easy, Jimmy," Doyle said. "Quit riding the kid. You know he never takes the stick from you."

"One day, dancing boy," Halloran said as we pushed him up the stairs. "One day you and me will settle up."

"You know where to find me," Quinn said.

Doyle laughed as he began to do up his tie as we climbed. "Guess all that action back there's got everyone's blood up. Thank God me and Charlie are around to keep the peace."

Doyle nudged me as he finished knotting his bow tie. "Say, Charlie. You really mean what you said about showing me gratitude just now."

Given the weight he'd just taken off my shoulders with Massey, I wouldn't refuse him anything. "Sure. Just name it."

"Go up there and tell the Babe to drink somewhere else. That big gom is a pain in my ass."

Chapter 21

A**S WE WALKED BACK** to the car, Halloran was still plenty hot over his run-in with Quinn. Not even the autograph I got the Babe to give him had calmed him down.

I wasn't happy, either. "What the hell is the matter with you? Everything was going great until you had to go cross swords with Quinn."

"That two-bit punch-drunk bum?" Halloran yelled. "I'd have wiped the floor with him."

I'd seen Quinn fight at the Garden about a dozen times. On his worst day, Quinn would've laid out Halloran with one punch. But there was no good in saying that now.

"Just take me back to the Castle," I told him. "I've got some work to finish up."

Halloran punched the hood of his car as he walked around to the driver's side. "I've never laid down for a lousy punk like that in my life and I'm not about to start now. And if you think I ever will, you're nuts. You'll wind up in the same loony bin your pal Keating is headed for. They ought to throw a butterfly net over the both of you.

Give you matching padded cells, so you never get lonely."

Halloran climbed in behind the wheel.

I steadied myself against the car instead.

The big dope hadn't realized it, but he was a genius.

When he saw I hadn't gotten in, he got out of the car. "You're not gonna stand there and sulk all night, are you?"

He must've seen the expression on my face. "Jesus, Charlie. What's wrong?"

My mind was filling too fast with images of the rubbings I'd gotten off the envelope. Letters and spaces I had written down began changing places, becoming other letters. Halloran's big mouth had caused a storm in my head that blew a lot of things into place.

I knew I was close, but I had to be sure. I need to take a look at an old map of the city, and I knew where I might be able to find one.

I pawed at the door handle like I'd never used it before. "Take me to the one-eight. Right now."

"The precinct?" Halloran asked. "Why?"

"Just do it, goddamn it!" I yelled as I got in. "The one-eight. Now!"

Halloran climbed behind the wheel and shut the door after him. "One minute he's a mute and now he's yelling at me." He started up the car and pulled out into traffic. "This is shaping up to be one hell of a night."

I knew that, if I was right, Halloran didn't know what he was in for.

Halloran had barely stopped in front of the precinct before I opened the door and made a mad dash for the building.

Captain Sean Lynch was on the street and had no welcome for me as he saw me running toward him. "Christ, Doherty. What now? I was just on my way home and—"

I ran past him and bolted between four cops who were on their way out.

The desk sergeant bid me a hello and I ran by him, too. I hit the stairs and took them two at a time. I didn't slow down until I reached the second floor where the captain's office was. I dodged a couple of uniforms milling around and barged into the captain's empty office.

A map of the Eighteenth Precinct dominated the wall behind the desk. That wasn't what I was looking for.

I needed the framed wall map on the wall behind a line of filing cabinets on the left side of the office. The northern part of the borough was clear to see, but the midtown section was blocked by a stack of dusty books on top of the cabinet.

I put my arm around them and shoved them off, not caring where they fell or about the racket it caused.

It revealed an old map of the city from 1920. The city had issued maps with newer names since, but I knew Lynch had never been one to update his office.

This was the map I was looking for.

I ignored Lynch and Halloran as they rushed into the office.

"What is this?" Lynch complained. "A raid? Make yourself at home why don't you?"

"Shut up," I whispered as I took in the clear view I had of Midtown Manhattan on the map.

"What the hell's gotten into you?" I heard Halloran ask, though I was too taken by what I was looking at to answer him.

My hands shook as I dug into my jacket pocket and pulled out the Spann letter and envelope. Everything was beginning to make sense.

The black wagon the vendors saw near some of the victims.

The remnants of an address I'd found on the envelope.

Dozens of fragmented details came rushing together because that map made it all make sense.

I pulled out the rubbing I had made from the envelope and slowly held it up to the map.

I gripped the paper tightly as I finally realized what had been on the return address before the ', N.Y.'

The old map proved that I had been right about the stationery coming from somewhere in the city. I'd been right about the stationery being old, too.

I held up the rubbing to the map and saw that the bottom of the letters on the return address made sense after all.

And even though they were written in capital letters on the map, I was able to make out what they would be on the envelope.

A long strip of land in the East River. The place had been re-named Welfare Island a few years back.

But before then it had been called Blackwell's Island, N.Y.

The bottom of the letters matched perfectly to the rubbing. Even the spacing fit.

I got as close to the old wall map as I could with the filing cabinets in the way. I saw some buildings had been marked on the old map, but I was only interested in one of them.

A stretch of large prison buildings dominated the west coast of the narrow island.

Only one of them caught my eye. I held up the rubbing again to the map and saw all the mistakes I had made in the translation from the envelope.

I knew I had gotten some of the capital letters wrong, but now it made sense. It read: 'The Hospital for the Criminally Insane'.

I backed up until I hit the chief's desk and sagged against it, sending a pile of papers tumbling to the floor.

Lynch was incensed. "Damn it, Charlie. Quit wrecking my office."

I checked and rechecked the map to make sure I hadn't made a mistake.

I knew I hadn't. It all made sense.

They'd had to change out the stationery back in '21 when they renamed 'Blackwell's Island' as 'Welfare Island'. They'd probably had plenty of the old letterhead on hand.

The Wanderer had been using it for his letters because he figured no one would miss it. He used every scrap of paper he could so no one would see the old stuff was still around.

That meant The Wanderer was still there. Right now. I could feel it.

I picked up the captain's phone and ordered Lynch and Halloran out. The two of them were too taken with the way I was acting to argue. Lynch even closed the door behind him.

I had the switchboard operator connect me to the chief's office and, when he did, I told Rosie it was an emergency. Carmichael came on the line a second later.

"Charlie, I've got news. Ross's men came up with a list of places that use black wagons. It matches the customers from the stationery store—"

I didn't care about that. "I found him, Andy. He's working out of the Hospital for the Criminally Insane on Blackwell's Island."

"That's it," Carmichael told me. "That's what we found, too. The city uses black wagons to transport prisoners from Bellevue to the Blackwell ferry among other places. A doctor who works out of the place ordered the stationery personally. A Dr. Henry Mayfair."

It was all flooding together now. The picture of The Wanderer was becoming clearer by the second. "We've got him, Andy. We've really got him."

"What do you need from me?"

"A boat to pick me up at Twenty-Sixth Street and get me out to the island," I told him. "I need two good men we can trust, and I need you to handle it personally. I don't want to risk this bastard getting tipped off and making another run for it."

"Get over to the dock as fast as you can," Carmichael told me. "A boat from the Harbor Unit will be waiting. And Charlie, be careful."

The blood was roaring my ears. "I'll call you when I can."

I threw open the door and pulled Halloran along as I ran down the stairs.

"Thanks for the mess, you little shit," Lynch yelled after me.

But I had bigger things on my mind.

The Wandering Man was about to get caught.

Chapter 22

IT WAS ALREADY dark by the time the police boat began heading north on the East River toward Blackwell's Island. We'd parked the car at the pier.

Next to three black transport wagons.

I looked at the distant island as it slowly grew larger. The lights in the windows of the severe buildings were the only signs of life on the desolate rock. The stench from Blood Alley – the slaughterhouses and cattle pens on the eastern side of Manhattan – wafted across the river.

Halloran smoked his cigarette and leaned on the railing beside me. "Ah, Charlie. I'm a lucky girl. You take me to the most romantic places."

I had no time for sarcasm. "I need you to be serious from here on in." The hum of the motor kept the pilot from hearing us.

Halloran remained leaning against the railing, but I felt a change go through him. "Ok. What's the play?"

I was taking a chance in telling him anything, but it was a chance I had to take. Besides, it was his crack about winding up in a nuthouse that had triggered my thinking. I supposed I owed him something.

"This isn't a pleasure boat ride. We're going out here to kill a man. You don't have to be part of it if you don't want to. But if you stick with me, you'll have to keep your mouth shut." I looked up at him. "I mean forever, Halloran. You can never tell a soul about this."

"Won't be the first time." Halloran shrugged it off. "This for you or for the chief?"

I'll admit the question threw me. "Does it make a difference?"

"If it's for you, you'll owe me for the rest of your life," he said. "If it's for the chief, it's part of the job. Just don't lie because I'll check later."

I looked back at the looming island. "It's for the chief. His orders."

Halloran took a final drag on his butt and flicked it over the side, letting the river wind carry it away. "Just tell me who to shoot and where to dump the body."

"That part will come," I said. "But we have to find the bastard first. And we will find him. My way. I'm going to need you to follow my lead once we get ashore."

"Whatever you need, just say the word."

Halloran wasn't good for much, but I knew he was good for this.

I used the rails to walk over and stick my head into the pilot house. One cop was at the helm, and another was standing by to help with the boat.

They were Tammany boys, too, though I couldn't remember their names. The harbor boys always stuck to themselves. "You two know we're out here on chief's orders."

The driver was tall and bone skinny. The other was a bit leaner. Both looked like they were about twenty or so.

"Uncle Andy already told us. Don't worry about us. We'll keep our mouths shut."

I was glad Carmichael had picked his nephews for this. "When we reach the island, I'm going to need you boys to keep any other boats from leaving. That includes staff boats or any other private boats that might try to leave. Open fire on them if you have to. I'll be responsible for anything that happens. Hopefully, it'll be nice and quiet, and we'll just need you boys to give us a ride back."

Both men nodded. I was glad brains ran in the Carmichael family.

HALLORAN and I hit the dock as soon as the harbor patrol boys tied up to it. I saw a smaller launch tied to the other side of the pier and wondered if it belonged to the warden. I'd have to remember to ask him once we got there.

The wind picked up something fierce as Halloran and I walked to the main prison building. The smell of blood and cow shit from Blood Alley almost made me sick to my stomach. We had to hold onto our hats to keep them from blowing away.

The guard at the main gate to the prison had been dozing when we rattled the bars. He snapped out of it quick and looked at us like we were a couple of mermaids until he noticed the badges we were holding up.

"What's the idea, you two?" he said as he stifled a yawn. "We don't have any visitors scheduled for tonight."

"Surprise visit," I said. "Open up."

"Not without the warden's say so." The guard picked up a phone and cranked the box. He kept his voice low until he got someone important on the line. He held the earpiece to his shoulder as he poked his head out of the guardhouse. "What are your names, anyhow?"

"Detectives Doherty and Halloran. We work out of the Castle."

He repeated it to whomever he was talking to, listened, then hung up the phone. "Warden Schmidt says you boys can come in."

He rattled a large key ring and opened the main gate. "Just head to that door straight ahead and one of the boys will let you in. You two fellas must rate. The warden's coming to get you personally."

"Lucky us," Halloran said as we passed through the gate.

Every step brought us that much closer to The Wandering Man.

The steel door at the end of the walk creaked open and another guard beckoned us in.

In all my years as a cop, I'd never gotten used to the sound of that jailhouse door slamming shut. Maybe it was because I was afraid that one day, I wouldn't be allowed out again. Maybe it was the kind of sound you were never supposed to get used to.

The guard led us behind another steel door where Warden Chauncey 'Chintzy' Schmidt was waiting for us. The round little man was still flattening down his hair with spit and a promise as we walked in.

He'd earned the nickname because his contributions to the Hall for his job were always a bit light. Hence the reason why he was stuck out in the middle of the East River playing wet nurse to a bunch of criminals.

"Charlie!" he said as he shook my hand with enthusiasm. His palm was damp with worry. "And Big Jim, too!" He shook his hand, too. "My, this is certainly a surprise, especially at this hour. I'm usually not still here this late, so you boys got lucky."

He did his best to put a smile in his voice, but he was understandably worried. Surprise visits from me were rarely good news and that night was no different. "Everything fine downtown?"

The guard who'd let us in had moved to the next door that led to the prison proper. "Take it easy, Chintzy. We're not here for you. We need to talk to whoever runs The Hospital for the Criminally Insane."

Chintzy looked like he might faint. "Thank goodness. I thought there was a problem."

"There won't be," Halloran said, "so long as you do what he told you."

"Of course," he said as he led us to the other door and motioned for the guard to open it. "Though I'm afraid we'll have to ask you boys to check your weapons here. We don't allow firearms in the prison."

Halloran gestured to the guard holding open the door. "He's got a pistol."

"That's different," Chintzy told us. "Captain Parker here is the head guard here."

"Then we'll keep our guns, too," I told him.

He looked like he was about to object, but one look at Halloran made him decide against it. "Yes, of course. We can make an exception just this once. All of the inmates are already in their cells anyway."

But I wasn't worried about the inmates. I was more concerned about the staff, particularly one Henry Mayfair.

"The ward is just through this door and down Broadway. That's what we call the main aisle of the prison. I'm afraid it's all the way over on the other side of the building, so we'll have to walk past the prisoners. But I'm sure that won't bother you boys. You're used to the crowd we have here."

"Might recognize a few of them, too." I said, reminding myself to breathe.

Getting closer.

Captain Parker locked the door behind us and marched ahead of us as we cleared another gate and strode through the cell block.

The yelling and cursing of the prisoners blended into the background like Manhattan traffic.

Chintzy rambled on nervously over the din of convicted men. "I hope you don't mind me pointing out to you that we don't call it 'The Hospital of the Criminally Insane' anymore, Charlie. It's just another ward of the prison where we keep the lunatics."

That further explained the change in stationery. My stomach growled and not from hunger. "Who runs it?"

"A Dr. Henry Mayfair," Chintzy told me. "A good and pious man. His work on reforming our more troubled prisoners is nothing short of astounding. We give him free run of his side of the place. He takes care of his charges as he sees fit." Schmidt caught himself. "I certainly hope he's not in any trouble."

"Time will tell," I said over the noise from the prisoners.

Halloran grinned at men behind the bars as we passed by. One inmate slammed his fists against the bars of the cell. Halloran gave him the finger. The inmate went mad. Others joined in. Halloran's smile held.

I remembered a question I'd filed away for later. "That your boat out on the pier, Chintzy?"

"It certainly is, though all of the head officials of the

prison use it. We usually have one of the trustees ferry us back and forth to Manhattan or Brooklyn or Queens when the need arises."

"Trustees?" I repeated. "Letting a convict take you across the river is pretty trusting."

"Oh, they're not those kinds of trustees," Chintzy assured me. "They're actually staff and only one man in particular. We have so many trustees around here that it's just easier to lump them in all together. You know how it goes."

That was interesting. "What's his name?"

"Ernie, though his last name escapes me at the moment, pardon the pun given our present location."

Schmidt waited for one of us to laugh. Neither of us did.

"He's been with us for years," Chintzy went on. "I honestly don't know what Dr. Mayfair would do without him. He's always ready to lend a hand whenever we need him, day or night. Nice, quiet chap."

I'd have to make it a point to meet him. "You think Dr. Mayfair is still here?"

"Probably," Schmidt said as we reached the end of the cell block. "Everyone in the ward works all sorts of hours. I don't think he's got much of a home life, though I can't imagine what you need to see him for. He's doing important work here. He's going to put this place on the map if you ask me."

I figured he would, though probably not in the way Chintzy expected.

Halloran and I traded glances as the guard opened the door. I hadn't told him anything about The Wanderer, but he knew I was there for someone. He probably figured Mayfair was of particular interest. Like I said, Halloran wasn't a total loss.

We left the cellblock and found ourselves in a bricked hallway painted white. It felt completely different from the little slice of Hell we'd just walked through.

"This is the main entrance to the asylum," Chintzy told us. "Your Hospital for the Criminally Insane. This part is used only by staff. There's no reason for inmates to come here. They have their own separate entrance at the front."

"Any back exits?" Halloran asked.

"None that aren't locked or guarded, especially in this wing. Having one of our regular inmates escape would be bad enough. But having one of these lunatics on the loose would be nothing short of a catastrophe. Dr. Mayfair does a wonderful job with keeping his patients nice and calm. His work here will make him famous one day, I have no doubt about that."

I wasn't interested in hearing about his methods. I was only interested in meeting the man himself.

I felt my pulse quicken and my chest tighten as Captain Parker unlocked the door at the end of the hallway. Schmidt paddled in without a care in the world, nattering on nervously about the place as he went.

Halloran followed and I hung back to bring up the rear. I wanted to talk to the guard in private.

I didn't know him, so I laid some Tammany-speak on him. "You in on The Joke?"

"Been laughing for more than fifteen years now," he said as we resumed walking.

Knowing he was one of us made me feel better. "You hear any of what we were talking about just now."

"I hear everything that goes on in this place. Why? What do you need?"

"You trust this Mayfair character as much as the warden?"

"As far as it goes," Parker told me. "But dealing with nuts all day has a habit of rubbing off. He's a bit of an odd-ball, but so's everyone on his staff. Why?"

I leveled with him. "I'll need you to keep your eyes open while we're here. If you see anything off, be sure to let me know, okay?"

"Consider it done."

Parker sped up to the front of the group and gave the guard watching the next door the high sign. He let us in.

Everything in the ward was painted white. The ceiling. The floors. Even the bars on the doors and the cells. What's more, it was all spotless.

The prisoners in the cells on both sides of the aisle were in straightjackets. Each of them rocked back and forth on their bunks muttering quietly to themselves. They had the shaved heads of the condemned. Their eyes had the hollow look of the haunted.

I heard Chintzy calling my name. "Charlie, it looks like you're in luck. Dr. Mayfair is still here."

I stopped in my tracks when I looked up and saw a tall man with gray hair and a neatly trimmed Van Dyke beard. A pair of spectacles were perched on the end of his long nose.

And he wore a thin gray coat.

Just like I'd seen The Wandering Man wearing both times I shot him.

The doctor smiled at me warmly as he extended his hand to me. "Pleasure to meet you, Detective Doherty. What can I do for you?"

I shook his hand as if I was in a trance. If he recognized me from the street, he was doing a hell of a job hiding it. "I was wondering if there was a place we could talk for a moment. It's a private matter."

"Certainly." He handed his clipboard to an orderly at

the desk, who I noticed was also wearing a gray coat. "Follow me."

The whole gang of us followed Mayfair down the hall where he led us into an office.

Sweat broke out across my back when I noticed he was limping. He was favoring his right leg.

I glanced at Parker as we passed by. He stood guard outside the office. "I'm here if you need me."

Dr. Mayfair led us through a small outer waiting area into a much larger office.

I stopped when I saw a typewriter on a small table next to his desk.

I forgot all about my manners and made a bee line for the typewriter.

Dr. Mayfair and Chintzy looked more puzzled than troubled.

"What's the matter, Detective?" Mayfair asked. "Certainly you haven't come all this way to borrow my typewriter."

I found a pile of paper next to the desk. The letterhead was different than the one The Wanderer used. It read 'Welfare Island Penitentiary Asylum' and listed Dr. Henry Mayfair as its head physician.

I tried to keep my hand from trembling as I took a sheet of paper and held it up for him to see. "Pretty fancy stationery for a jail, Doctor."

The doctor smiled at me. "Paid for out of my own pocket, too. The academic in me is too vain to use the prison's regular stationery. I prefer the better stock. I find it adds a bit of gravitas to the harsh work we do here."

I fed it into the typewriter and drew in a deep breath.

The moment of truth.

I struck the 'e' key.

It hit the page. Crystal clear.

No faded bar in the 'e'.

I hit it again and got the same result.

My third try came up with the same thing.

I stepped back from the machine. This wasn't supposed to happen.

"Are you quite alright, Detective?" Dr. Mayfair asked me. "You seem somewhat troubled."

I checked the cabinet behind his desk for the old stationery and all I found were files. I began to open his desk drawers when Mayfair protested.

"What's the meaning of all this?" He turned to Chintzy while I searched. "Warden Schmidt. I'm afraid I require an explanation."

But I wasn't ready to give him one. Each drawer I opened had more files. Pens and pencils. Nothing out of the ordinary until I got the bottom drawer.

It was locked.

I looked up and saw Chintzy and Dr. Mayfair looking at me like I belonged I one of the cells down the hall. Only Halloran looked normal.

"The bottom drawer's locked. Give me the key."

Dr. Mayfair held firm. "Not until I get some answers. Now, I have every intention of cooperating with you gentlemen, but not until I get to the bottom of this."

I looked at Halloran, who moved in. "Take it easy, Doc. Just give the man the key like he asked."

Mayfair dug into his coat pocket and pulled out a set of keys. "It's where I keep the most sensitive files. I certainly hope you don't expect to review them without some sort of explanation."

Halloran snatched the keys from him. "Which one opens the drawer?"

He told him which one it was. Halloran held it and handed it over to me.

"Check his right side and his right foot," I told him as I opened the drawer. "He was limping a bit when we walked in here."

Dr. Mayfair reluctantly held up his hands while Halloran began to pat him down. "I sprained my knee when I was a surgeon in the war. It acts up when the seasons change."

I got the drawer unlocked and pulled it open.

I'd been hoping to see a sheaf of old stationery glowing up at me like a bar of gold.

All I saw were more files, just like Mayfair said.

I dumped the keys on the desk and began rifling through the files. They were jammed in there pretty tight. No stationery to be found.

I looked up at Halloran, hoping he'd found something on Mayfair. "Nothing here, Charlie. He's clean."

I felt the hope that had filled me since Lynch's office begin to quickly disappear. *It couldn't be.*

"Turn him around. I want to see for myself."

"Charlie," the warden tried. "What's gotten into you?"

"Just do it, goddamn it!"

Halloran placed a hand on the doctor's shoulder and slowly turned him. He even lifted the back of his gray coat for me.

The right side of his shirt was normal. I could even see the outline of his back beneath it. No bandages. No blood stains, either.

Halloran let the coat drop and took his hand off the doctor. Now he was beginning to look as concerned as the others.

Dr. Mayfair pulled his coat around him and folded his arms. "Now, if you're quite done, I'll have that explanation, Detective."

I couldn't be this wrong about everything. I just couldn't.

I felt my mouth move, but no sound came out until I managed to say, "Gray coats. Why do you wear gray coats?"

"I had the ward painted white to make it appear different from the rest of the prison," Mayfair told me. "White is more clinical, more soothing for our patients. Some of them grew anxious when our orderlies were dressed in white as well, so I changed them to gray. The lab coat makes them feel like they're in a hospital environment. It allows them to see us as physicians instead of jailers. Now—"

Mayfair repeated his demands for an explanation, but I didn't hear them.

I heard him well enough, but something else had caught my attention.

When Halloran had stepped aside, it allowed me to see the outer office. The desk. And the typewriter on it.

"Detective Doherty," Dr. Mayfair said. "I don't know what's going on here, but I believe you're under a great deal of stress. I need you to take a moment to calm yourself. Breathe in and out slowly and I'm sure we can help you get what you came for."

I yanked the paper free from Mayfair's typewriter and pushed past them into the outer office.

I quickly fed the paper into the typewriter and hit the letter 'e'.

I did it once, then twice, then five times.

And each time it looked the same.

Like a 'c'.

Just like in The Wander's letters.

I talked over Mayfair's questions. "Do you use this typewriter?"

"Why would I? I use the one on my desk."

"Who uses this one?"

"My assistant uses it from time to time," Mayfair admitted, "but I do most of my own typing. He handles some filing for me and——"

God, I was close. "His name Ernie?"

"Yes. Ernst Fisher. He's our chief orderly here. An excellent employee. He was a doctor in Bavaria, but——"

I didn't care about that. "He wear one of those gray coats, too? Does his have a hole in it? Does he have a limp?"

"He wears the same thing we all do," Mayfair said, "and I wouldn't go so far as to say he has a limp. He hurt his foot transporting a prisoner from Bellevue the other day. It's just a sprain. He'll be fine in a couple of days."

The room began to spin, and I held onto the desk before I fell over.

Everything fit. Everything right down to the limp I'd given him. "Where is he? I need to see him right now."

Mayfair checked his wristwatch. "He's making rounds like he always does this time of night. Now, I'm afraid I really must insist on knowing what's going on here."

"Take us to him," I said. "Right now." I gestured to Halloran, who led the doctor out into the hall.

I ignored Chintzy's questions and made a beeline for Parker, who was still standing guard in the hall. "I need you and your people to find Ernie right now. I want every door in this place shut tight until we find him."

Parker went over to the orderly's desk and picked up the phone.

Halloran was hot on Mayfair's tail as he walked to the end of the hallway. The doctor fumbled with the keys to the door. "I can't imagine why you'd want to see Ernie. He's a docile soul. Very temperate."

"Just open the door and shut your mouth," Halloran said.

He got the door open, and we didn't bother shutting it behind us. I eyeballed all the cells on either side of the hallway. Each of them was occupied by a poor soul staring at the ground or pawing at the walls of their cell. A couple of them were in straightjackets chained to the wall.

It wasn't until we reached the end of the hall where an even worse stench than what I'd smelled on the river from Blood Alley made me gag. I felt as if I'd just walked into an open sewer.

It came from a large room on the left that was the size of about four or five cells put together.

My legs refused to move as I saw who was beyond the bars in the cell.

It was a room full of patients. None of them wore straightjackets. All of them were male. Some were sitting in chairs. Some on the floor.

All of them had the same vacant stare.

All of them were young black men of about the same age.

Except for one.

A pale young man of about twenty who looked like he had never spent a day of his life in the sun. A man who had the same blank expression as all the other men in the room.

Except this young man happened to be the spitting image of John Spann.

I reached out and gripped the bars.

"Halloran! Bring Mayfair back here."

I heard a scuffle of shoes behind me, but I couldn't take my eyes off the patients.

"Who are they?" My voice was hardly a whisper.

"Ah, those are our special patients," Mayfield said in a clinical tone. "Ernie tends to them personally. Calls them his Menagerie of Misfortunates. They've all been lobotomized."

I shook my head. The term meant nothing to me, but the horror of what I was looking at did.

"It's a new procedure Ernie and I have been working on," Mayfair explained. "It's painless and humane, Detective, I assure you. We usually keep the black inmates segregated, but Ernie suggested that we allow that young man to stay with the others as part of an experiment. Seems to be going quite well. Why do you ask?"

I pointed to the young white man alone in the corner. "What's his name?"

"They don't have names," Mayfair told me. "They're all orphans, likely left behind by parents who could no longer care for them, given their mental instabilities. But they're docile enough now, don't you think?"

I felt my hand slip from the bars as I heard myself say, "That's why we didn't find any bodies. They were here all along."

I grabbed hold of Mayfair's shirt and slammed him against the bars before Halloran could stop me. "Where's Ernie, goddamn you? Where is he?"

Something close to fear appeared in Mayfair's eyes. At another time, I might've been proud of myself. I'd just frightened the hell out of a psychiatrist. But now wasn't the time for pride.

"I told you he's on rounds." Mayfair managed to

hold up a single key. "Here, this should open all the doors you require."

Halloran took the key from him and tried to pull me off the doctor. "Charlie, we've got what we need. Let's go."

I shoved Mayfair aside and found we were standing in the middle of a hallway that went right and left. "Which way?"

Mayfair sank against the bars and gestured we should take a right. I followed Halloran down the hall.

Halloran was walking as fast as I was. "Sounds like Ernie's your man."

"Keep your eyes peeled," I told him. "This bastard's dangerous."

We stopped when we heard whistling echoing through the hallway just as the piercing sound of a siren cut through the prison.

Through the other side of a barred door, I saw an orderly holding a clipboard. He was about my size and wearing the same gray lab coat Dr. Mayfair wore.

He was bald, but his eyes were dark and quick as they looked around at the sound of the siren.

It wasn't until he looked at me and Halloran that I knew.

And so did he.

Ernie was The Wandering Man.

The orderly dropped the clipboard and ran in the opposite direction as fast as his bad foot would allow. Halloran had the door open a moment later and I raced past him.

"He's here!" I yelled, hoping my voice would carry back over the sound of the siren to Captain Parker at the orderly's desk. "He's right here!"

I saw him take a left at the next intersection and I

took the turn wide. The Wanderer already had his key in the door to the next hallway as I reached for my .38.

But I remembered my .38 wasn't on my hip. It was on Carmichael's desk.

By then, he had already made it through the door and relocked it from the other side. Halloran ran past me, and I was quick on his heels. He got that door open, too and again, I went in first.

The inmates weren't docile now and the hallway was filled with screams and shouts and sounds. Food and other things were thrown out into the hallway, making me almost lose my footing.

But The Wanderer was only halfway down the hall away from me and I ran flat out after him. He had just gotten his key in the next door when I barreled into him with all my might. I heard a bone give way and he screamed out as we bounced off the steel door. My arm was around his neck as we fell to the floor together.

He might've been my size, but he was much stronger than he looked. He began flailing hard, digging elbow after elbow deep into my stomach and sides as he struggled to break free. One good shot on my right side broke my grip and the bastard scrambled to his feet.

I reached for my .45 when I saw Halloran grab Ernst by the neck and throw him against the wall like a ragdoll.

The Wanderer lashed out at him with something that caught the light of the hallway. A scalpel.

Halloran dodged the first thrust, but the orderly buried the second in his right shoulder near the neck. The big man hit the deck hard.

I'd just grabbed hold of my pistol when the orderly slammed a knee into my face, knocking me off my feet.

By the time I got up, the door was already open, and The Wanderer was down the hall.

"Here!" Halloran said as he held out a key to me with his left hand. Blood was already sopping his right shoulder. "Kill that son of a bitch."

I grabbed the key ring and went after him.

I rounded the corner and slammed into an inmate. I kept my footing and looked around to see Ernst had opened several of the cells, letting the inmates loose as he had already made it to the next door leading deeper into the prison.

I kept my grip on the key, knowing I'd need it before I'd have a chance to use the .45 holstered under my arm. I dodged inmates. I slid under a haymaker heading for my head. I jumped over another one who dove for my legs.

The siren continued to wail as the door at the end of the hallway slammed shut. The Wanderer had succeeded in getting just a bit further away from me. I hoped one of the prison guards nabbed him.

A final inmate popped out of his cell to bar my way, screaming at me in toothless, wide-eyed madness. I kicked him in the balls and tossed back into the others that were hot on my tail. I got the key in the hole and opened it. I managed to shut the door behind me just as they threw themselves against the bars, clawing at me with outstretched hands.

A cold rush of air came at me from the right side. I saw a regular door, not a barred one like the rest on the ward. I pulled my .45 and kicked the door in.

It slammed open, revealing what looked like a maintenance corridor. Pipes and a concrete floor. A single white bulb swung from a fixture, revealing a gated door that led to the outside. The gate was open. The bright lights of Manhattan beckoned in the distance.

I dropped the keys, figuring they'd be no good to me now. I chambered a round and shot out the light.

I dragged my feet as I slowly crept toward the open door. I knew The Wanderer would be waiting for me just on the other side of the door. He could've run off in the darkness. There had to be a thousand places to hide in broad daylight on this island. I figured there were twice that many in the dark.

But I knew he wouldn't run this time. He'd run from me too many times before. He knew I'd just keep coming. I had found him here and I'd find him anywhere.

Besides, he had me cornered. He knew where I was and where I was going. He had an edge.

Or so he thought.

In the darkness, I felt the broken glass from the bulb with the front of my shoe and did my best to step over it. Any sound would tell him where I was.

I made it outside without a sound.

I held my .45 tight. The Wanderer probably felt pretty good about his chances. It was dark. Neither of us could see anything. I was on his territory now. His ground.

But I'd spent half my life facing men who wanted to kill me in the dark. Here in Manhattan. Over in France. The ground wasn't as even as he thought.

I moved quietly across the grass and listened. I moved my eyes slowly as I let them adjust to the darkness.

I heard a thud, then a whisper of clothing. A feint, nothing more. I kept moving sideways, crouched and quiet. And listening, always listening.

I heard another whisper of cloth, this time louder, but no thud. I couldn't see, but I knew he'd taken off his lab coat. I'd learned to not hear the siren blaring throughout the prison now. All I could hear was what the darkness told me.

The sound like a flag waving in the wind. I ducked and felt a piece of the coat across my back. The clean sound of a blade cutting nothing but air.

The grunt when my .45 slammed up into his stomach.

The muffled blasts as I pumped three rounds into his belly.

The outside lights came on from the prison rooftops, blinding me for a second, but not before I saw the outline of The Wanderer staggering backward.

He still had the scalpel in his hand while he pawed at the blood quickly spreading across the front of his shirt.

He looked up at me as he staggered back from the light. His eyes as wild and empty as I remembered them that first night on Fifth Avenue.

He raised the scalpel and looked like he was about to charge me, but the blood was flowing freely now. He sliced weakly at the air as he sank to his knees.

I dropped the .45 and lunged at him. I grabbed hold of his blade hand as I bent him backward to the grass. He shrieked as his legs were pinned under him.

I held his arm out away from him with my left hand. With my right, I grabbed him under the jaw and made him look at me.

I held him there, powerless, unable to move. I wanted him to feel as powerless as that room full of brain-dead young men back there. His handiwork. His damnable menagerie.

His eyes fluttered from the loss of blood, but enough hate remained for one last rally. One last attempt on my life.

I grabbed his jaw tight and made sure he could see me. Only me.

"I'm the one who caught you, you son of a bitch. I'm the one who killed you."

Those wild eyes flared with hate and rage one final time before the fire went out.

I only hoped an eternity of fire consumed him now.

I pulled the scalpel from his hand and threw it toward the river. Whether or not it made it, I had no idea.

I saw where the floodlights swept the ground and knew I'd have to hide the body. Carmichael wouldn't want him found. Chief's orders. I grabbed him by the collar and dragged him over toward the doorway. I could find him easily in the dark after the flood lights went out. With Halloran out of action, I could get one of the harbor boys to help me bring him back to the boat.

I decided not to take any chances. I flipped him over on his belly and cuffed his hands behind his back. He'd gotten away from me before. He wouldn't get away this time.

Captain Parker came out of the doorway and caught me with the flashlight.

I stood up slowly from The Wanderer's corpse. My hands were raised and empty.

He moved the light from me to the orderly's cuffed body on the ground, then back to me. This time, he kept it out of my face.

"What happens now?" he asked.

I lowered my hands. "Help me find my gun and I'll tell you."

Chapter 23

I'D CALLED Carmichael from the warden's office and told him to meet me at the 26th Street Pier. I didn't have to tell him it was important. He already knew that. I didn't tell him any details, either. Some things were best said in person rather than over a phone wire.

I stepped off the police boat and found Carmichael's Imperial waiting for me beneath a streetlamp at the curb. I was glad he was behind the wheel, not Dooley. It would save us a lot of unnecessary walking around like we'd done at the cemetery. I barely had enough energy to walk to the car, much less the streets of Manhattan while I told my tale.

I opened the passenger side door and climbed inside. At least the Imperial was one of those new numbers that had heat in them. Having spent the past several hours on Blackwell's Island and boat launches, I was bone cold.

"Is it done?" Carmichael asked me.

"Not as cleanly as we would've liked, but, yeah, it's done."

Carmichael let out a long breath as he gripped the

steering wheel tightly. "Good. Thank God. How messy did it get?"

I told him everything. How I discovered the killer was an orderly in the mental ward of the prison, not Dr. Mayfair. How he'd kept the boys as mindless inmates all these years, including poor Tommy Spann. How he'd escaped through the prison and had stabbed Halloran in the shoulder. How I'd killed The Wanderer on the grounds of the prison. How Captain Parker snagged a vehicle and quietly helped me load his body onto the police launch. How me and his nephews weighed down the body and dumped it in the East River.

"Damn." Carmichael pounded the steering wheel. "Sounds like a lot of loose ends we still have to tie off."

"It's already been handled," I told him as I lit a cigarette.

"Handled?" Carmichael looked at me. "How?"

I cracked the window so the smoke would have somewhere to go. "Only the guard and Halloran know I killed him. I told them both we were investigating Ernst on a drug selling beef. I told them he escaped in the darkness, and they bought it. Chintzy will keep his mouth shut because I told him to. He wants to keep on being warden of that dump. Dr. Mayfair will keep his mouth shut because he doesn't want a scandal ruining his promising career. If word got out that his chief assistant was peddling drugs stolen from the prison, he wouldn't be able to get a job emptying bed pans in a leper colony. He'll take this with him to the grave." I blew smoke from the corner of my mouth. "Ambition has its upside."

But I could tell Carmichael wasn't satisfied yet. Not by a long shot. "What about the alert that was sounded in the prison? The staff who knew the orderly? They know something happened. We can't just ignore that, Charlie. The press is bound to get hold of it."

"Captain Parker's the only one who knows the truth," I told him. "He wants a transfer to Bellevue. He wants to be captain of the guards there. I told him that won't be a problem. He's a Tammany man, so he knows the score."

Carmichael relaxed a bit. He was getting used to the idea that we'd won. "And you're sure you got the right man."

"I took a look at The Wanderer's body after I shot him. I was right. I'd hit him just beneath the right kidney. The slug nicked his pelvis and went out his belly. The wound was packed with gauze and crudely stitched together. I checked his foot, and it was mangled. He had it wrapped with wadding and bandages. He'd moved pretty good for a guy in that much pain, so I figured he had to be on something. Halloran had Dr. Mayfair check the ward's drug supplies. Stores were low. Mayfair found Ernst had gone through a lot of morphine and other pain killers over the past few days. Antibiotics, too. That only supported our drug bust fiction."

Carmichael closed his eyes. "Christ, I forgot about Halloran. Now he knows, too."

"All he knows is that we were sent there to take care of a problem," I told him. "Seems his time working Vice came in handy. He doesn't know anything about The Wandering Man, and he doesn't want to know. He just wants a couple of weeks off and he doesn't want to get dinged for it. I'd give it to him. The Wanderer cut him pretty deep, but Mayfair patched him up. I'll head out there tomorrow to get him and bring him home. A pat on the back from you would go a long way with him. Trust me, he earned it."

"I'll see to it he's well compensated, don't worry." Carmichael tapped his fingers on the steering wheel as he thought the whole thing over. "Ernst Fisher. The Wandering Man. Christ, sounds like he ought to be a butcher or a fish monger instead of a monster."

"He's fish food now," I told him. "Your nephews on the boat know how to weigh down a body. If I didn't know better, I'd say they had practice."

Carmichael grinned and I didn't like the way the shadows fell across his face. "They had a good teacher." But his grin faded as quickly as it came. "What are we going to do about all those boys Fisher ruined? I hate to be heartless about this, but they can ruin us, too, Charlie."

I was glad to be able to give him some peace of mind. "Mayfair told me Fisher was a doctor in Bavaria before the war. Came here as a refugee. He practically ran the place for Mayfair. He piloted the private boat for the guys who run the prison. I think that's how he got to Staten Island and grabbed Tommy ten years ago. It also explains why they never saw him on the ferry. He also used to order Mayfair's stationery for him. The doc preferred the expensive kind and paid for it personally. I think that's how he found out about Spann making calls about the stationery. A clerk must've mentioned it somehow, but that's just a guess."

Carmichael looked confused. "What does that have to do with the kids he grabbed?"

"Fisher was also in charge of admissions," I told him. "Since no one reports a struggle when they went missing, I think he drugged the boys, got them in the back of the wagon, lobotomized them and entered them into the prison records as a John Doe. As far as anyone's concerned, they're dead and have been for some time."

"A lobotomy?" Carmichael repeated. "He could do something like that in the back of a wagon?"

"Not much to it the way Mayfair described it," I said. "Fisher was a doctor before the war and taught Mayfair how they handled patients over there. All you need is an ice pick, a couple of hard taps to the corner of the eye and it makes even the most troublesome prisoner as quiet as a lamb. They need care for the rest of their lives, but the procedure makes them harmless." I looked at him. "And quiet."

Carmichael balled his fist at his mouth. "But all of those families, Charlie. They thought their sons are dead, but yet—"

"They're dead," I told him. "Finding out how they wound up won't help anyone. Nothing we do will make any difference now, so it's best to just leave them where they are. Anything else would only cause suspicion."

I wasn't surprised to see Carmichael was having trouble understanding all of this. I'd be the same way if I allowed it to reach me. But I wouldn't allow that. Not yet.

Carmichael surprised me by getting philosophical. "We know what and we know how, but we don't know why. I suppose we'll never know."

"We know he's dead. That's good enough for me."

I felt him looking at me in the darkness. "You ok, Charlie? You've been through the ringer on this one."

I shrugged and flicked my cigarette out the window. "I'll be fine, Andy. And so will you. It's over. We're safe. The department is safe, and the victims have been avenged. The Wandering Man is dead and that's all there is to it."

But Carmichael looked at me and a strange feeling spread through my belly. That old saying came up again. 'Two people can keep a secret if one of them was dead.'

I felt better when Carmichael said, "You did it, Charlie. You really did it. You didn't think you could, but you did."

I wished that made me feel better. "Just following orders, Chief."

"That's bullshit and you know it." He dug something out of his pocket and handed it to me. "I'm giving you a promotion. You're now Lieutenant Charles Doherty. Effective immediately."

I looked down at the heavy gold badge. Even beneath a streetlamp, it looked beautiful. It had the rays of the sun radiating from the center of the department emblem. The word 'Lieutenant' stamped beneath it.

I'll admit that I hadn't been expecting that. "Andy, you just made me a detective six months ago. This'll set a lot of tongues wagging just when we want to keep things quiet."

"It's also my privilege to promote whomever I damned well please," Carmichael told me. "Take it. You've earned it and you're going to go on earning it, too. You're now in charge of the Office of Special Investigations and will officially report directly to me. You'll go on doing what you've always done, only more so." He added, almost as an afterthought, "More pay and a bigger piece of the pie come with it, which should help smooth things over with Theresa. You'll have seven men under your command, including Halloran. Good Tammany boys, all of them."

I knew this was a big moment. Bigger than I had ever thought possible. I'd been content just being Andy's black hand. I'd never thought I'd be anything more than that.

I guess I was. I only wish it meant something to me, but just then, it didn't.

I took the shield and Carmichael held out his hand to me. "I'll never forget what you did, Charlie. What you did for me."

I forced a smile and shook his hand. "You can always count on me, boss."

He started up the engine and threw the Imperial into gear. "Where to? Home or do you want to celebrate first? Just name the place. It's on me, Lieutenant Doherty."

I could've counted the number of times I'd seen Andrew J. Carmichael shocked on one hand. But when I told him where I wanted to go was one of them. "Are you sure?"

"I'm sure," I told him. "Something I've got to do before it's too late."

And despite his misgivings, he took me there.

——

He left me on the street about a half a block from where I wanted to go. And as I walked alone along Lennox Avenue, the weight of all that had happened that night finally settled on me.

The mindless young men I'd seen. The madman I'd killed. The way I'd covered it all up as if I was telling the truth.

The problem that now resided at the bottom of the East River. Even if Fisher's body popped up tomorrow, it wouldn't lead back to us.

I'd done my job, yet it felt like I'd done nothing. Because nothing I could do could make up for all the pain and suffering Ernst Fisher had caused.

And I could never take away the pain of all the families he had destroyed. It wasn't because I'd never know why he'd done it. It was because there was nothing to be done. They were the living dead now and not even their parents' grief could make much of a difference. If anything, they'd only have to grieve all over again.

At least the man who had made them that way was dead. I told myself that was something, but I wasn't sure I believed it.

I found that I'd become a sort of wandering man myself as I approached The Congo Club. I ignored the bouncers at the door who threw insults at me as I walked past them. Fred and Joe mouthed at me but did not touch.

I ignored the dirty looks and curses hurled my way inside the packed little club. Their indignation only grew louder once the band stopped playing. I guess I ignored it because none of it mattered to me.

Just about the only thing that mattered was the look on Jack Johnson's face when he rose from a table to find out who was causing all the trouble. And when he saw it was me, he knew why I was there.

"Out!" I remember him yelling to everyone. "Everybody go home. Now!"

The patrons jostled me and called me names as they filed out past me. One or two of them might've even spat on me. I don't really remember that, either.

My clearest memory is standing in the middle of the deserted club alone, watching Johnson go behind the bar, grab a full bottle of whiskey and two glasses and bring them over to a table. The same table where we'd sat the day before to make our pact.

I heard him order the bouncers to leave and make sure no one else came in.

He stood next to the table, and it was just the two of

us. Any hint of the music or festivities that had happened only a few minutes before was already fading into distant memory.

Johnson raised his chin to me from across the room. "I lived up to my end of the bargain. Looks like you've lived up to yours."

I felt a single tear race down my cheek and didn't bother to wipe it away. "Yeah. I guess I did."

Johnson poured two drinks, then held one glass out to me. "You've got a drink coming. And I'd be mighty honored to share it with you."

I somehow found the energy to walk over to him even though he seemed to be standing a mile away.

I took the drink from him, and he picked up his glass.

"To doing what needs doing. No matter the cost."

We drank down our shots and he poured us another. I set my glass on the table before I spilled it. "I wish it made me feel better."

"Ain't nothing on earth that can do that," Johnson told me, "but sometimes it makes it a little easier to live with."

I hung my head and let the tears come fully. I couldn't stop them and didn't have the energy to try.

Johnson placed a hand on the back of my neck and guided me into my chair. I didn't feel ashamed to cry in front of this man and he didn't seem embarrassed by them.

We both understood blood. About what it cost.

"I know, Charlie," he told me. "I know."

I kept on crying because I knew he did.

Take a Look at The University
Book One:
SYMPATHY FOR THE DEVIL

A FAST-PACED CONTEMPORARY THRILLER.

Old war. New enemies. The devil has arrived.

The University has been a clandestine organization since the days of the OSS. The University and its agents have always lived in the shadows; using its vast intelligence resources to help defeat the Nazis, end the Cold War and strike back at terrorists all over the globe. They have been at the forefront of global espionage for decades. Entrusted with running The University, James Hicks is one of the most powerful—and secretive—men alive.

But when Hick's brilliant protege is turned by a terrorist group that has alarmingly already begun operating on U.S. soil, Hicks finds himself in a race against time to find out just how the agent has been turned and why. He must use The University's covert global network to uncover a deadly biological plot that threatens to unleash a new era of chaos and anarchy not only on the United States, but on the entire western world.

"Hard to put down…the story line succeeds in large part because of the gritty and stylish narrative, the virtually nonstop action…those looking for some top-shelf adrenaline-fueled escapism will be rewarded." —
Publishers Weekly

AVAILABLE NOW!

About the Author

Terrence McCauley is an award-winning writer of Thrillers, Crime Fiction and Westerns. A proud native of The Bronx, NY, he currently lives in Dutchess County, NY where he is writing his next work of fiction.